THE
DEATH OF
AN ARDENT
BIBLIOPHILE

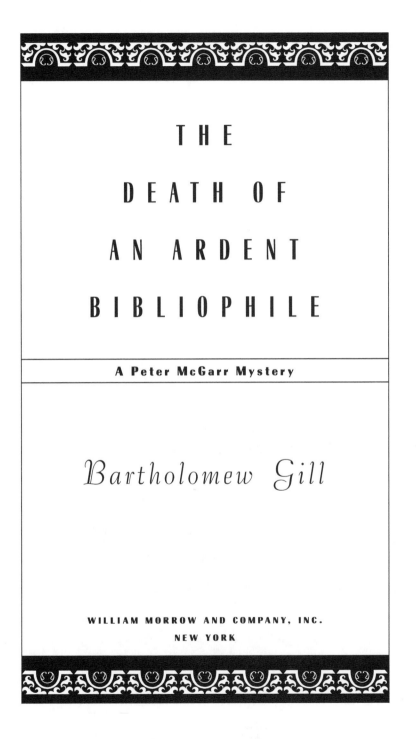

THE DEATH OF AN ARDENT BIBLIOPHILE

A Peter McGarr Mystery

Bartholomew Gill

WILLIAM MORROW AND COMPANY, INC.
NEW YORK

It is the policy of William Morrow and Company, Inc., and its imprints and affiliates, recognizing the importance of preserving what has been written, to print the books we publish on acid-free paper, and we exert our best efforts to that end.

Gill, Bartholomew, 1943–
The death of an ardent bibliophile: a Peter McGarr mystery /
Bartholomew Gill.
p.   cm.
ISBN 0-688-12909-9
1. McGarr, Peter (Fictitious character)—Fiction. I. Title.
PS3563.A296D433 1995
823'.914—dc20   94-26524
CIP

Printed in the United States of America

2 3 4 5 6 7 8 9 10

BOOK DESIGN BY BRIAN MULLIGAN

*Human brutes, like other beasts, find snares
and poison in the provision of life, and are allured
by their appetites to their destruction.*

—JONATHAN SWIFT

THE
DEATH OF
AN ARDENT
BIBLIOPHILE

$\mathcal{P}art\ I$

DESTRUCTION

I

Peter McGarr

PETER MCGARR pulled up in front of the large house on the Shrewsbury Road. Driving his forest-green Mini-Cooper right onto the wide footpath, he switched off the engine and lowered the visor that declared the car OFFICIAL. It was not a night to be mucking about.

A bitter mist, dense as a ball of steel wool, had descended on the city. It stung the face, obscured lights, and dampened any sound. Climbing out of the Cooper, McGarr watched as cars shot by him, like quarks, their red rear lights vanishing into the murk.

Somewhere off on the Merrion Road, the brakes of a double-deck bus screeched then thumped, stopping to pick up fares. As McGarr closed and locked the car door, the bus lurched by in a whoosh, like a pitching, lighted ship at sea—a face in every window, other forms packing the aisles. Homeward-bound on a foul winter evening.

Dubh Linn. In Irish it meant Black Pool. The surrounding mountains and hills formed a bowl around the city, and once in a great while—in summer when it was very hot, or, like now—a sudden, chill west wind off the Irish sea established an atmospheric inversion. Combined with urban air pollution and the smoke from the hearth fires that Irish people still preferred, its effect was stunning and foul.

Even the ornate lamp above the front door of the large Edwardian house was ringed by a bluish halo, yellowing at the fringe. McGarr's eyes swept the brass nameplate as he reached for the bell. *B.H.P. Herrick, D.Litt.* He glanced down at the large granite Janus figure that had once probably graced the lintel of some Roman archway and had evidently been placed there as a decoration. What did he know about B.H.P. Herrick?

Little more than having seen him several times at the cultural events that McGarr's wife, Noreen, sometimes dragged McGarr to. And that Herrick was considered to be a Dublin "character," albeit prominent and well connected.

Tall and balding, Herrick had kept his hair in long, steely ringlets—"In the manner of the portraits of Swift," Noreen had informed McGarr. With a round face and a heavy beard that made his shaved cheeks look blue, the man had appeared comically feminine, like a kind of inexpert cross-dresser, until he opened his mouth.

His voice was decidedly masculine, deep and orotund, and he said little that was not emphatically to the point. At an opening in Noreen's picture gallery in Dawson Street, Herrick had waited until everybody else had ooh-ed and aah-ed at a series of pretty pictures that a celebrated artist/actor/poet had painted of rural scenes. Most were twilight vistas of distant islands, or sheep in gorsy barrens, or boats on misty lakes.

Only when prodded had Herrick said, "A painter either paints hard enough to break her head on it, or she doesn't paint at all. *Wanting to* won't do it."

"But don't you think these scenes are beautifully rendered?" one sycophant of the artist *manqué* asked, astounded that Herrick would destroy what up until then had been a brilliant affair with more than a few of the works sold and the art critics of the major papers obviously taken in by the woman's charm.

Said Herrick, "I stand with the Bauhaus, but tonight, unfortunately, not in it: The pretty is never the beautiful. Anything more than the truth is too much and sappy."

"Is he drunk?" somebody had asked.

Turning to McGarr, Herrick had muttered, "Not half enough to wink at that."

Better still, in McGarr's opinion, was the column—"The Cybernetic Operations of the Spirit, An Essay,"—that appeared every once in a while in the *Irish Times*. Noreen said it was "... a play on Swift's satiric essay 'The Mechanical Operations of the Spirit.' But an update. It's supposed to be humorous"—and was, but the humor was dark and bitter.

One article in particular, McGarr had cut out of the paper and pinned to his office bulletin board. Widely condemned by political and church leaders, it said that the Irish government, "acting freely under no external pressure other than the greed of the few and the gullibility of the many," had discovered and was "systematically employing" a "scheme of human management" that was an improvement upon Swift's suggested course of action in "A Modest Proposal."

Rather than feeding the children of the poor to the rich, in order to relieve the urchins quickly of their viciousness and misery, the Irish government had revived a more "cosmetically humane policy" that had been employed by the "host of oppressors who had beset the country before independence. Their reasons, however, had been political."

After father and mother had "raised up" a child—"fed,

clothed, schooled, and nurtured him or her for seventeen or twenty-one years, depending upon the child's schooling"—it then became compulsory to "ship them out to some foreign part" where they either became "illegal aliens" or were treated as such.

"But their fate, be it good but more likely ill," Herrick wrote, was then "determined out of sight, if not mind." And all the "drug addiction, petty thievery, prostitution, alcoholism, and thuggery" that afflicted the "unemployed and recalcitrant wastrels, who through some lapse in official enforcement" remained in the country and had no known means of support other than the dole, occurred someplace else.

"Thus the cost of their apprehension, trial, punishment, and detention (or hospitalization and burial)" was borne by some other nation. Parents were also spared "the immediate knowledge of their offsprings' fate, with all that can bring by way of recrimination and sorrow. And this is no proposal; it is our reality. Just think, we rid ourselves of some thirty thousand such problematical lives in a good year! What other forward-looking nation but Ireland could apprise such progress with equanimity?"

As chief superintendent of the Serious Crimes Unit of the Garda Soichana (the Irish police), McGarr knew whereof Herrick had written. There was scarcely a week that went by that a murder was not committed in a country that, three decades earlier, had seen as few as two murders in a year. Two had already occurred this week, and it was only Friday.

Now "The Dean"—as he had been called, not without some characteristic Dublin derision—was dead, so a caller to McGarr's office had reported. McGarr was about to reach for the bell again, when the gleaming panels of the oak door opened, and a tall, pretty, older woman appeared there. She touched the back of her ash-blond hair. "Yes?"

"I'm Peter McGarr," said McGarr, showing her the photo I.D. in his billfold.

"Oh—really?" The woman seemed surprised. "I didn't realize that they'd send—I mean, it didn't occur to me that you'd come yourself. I thought perhaps"—her hazel eyes glanced over McGarr's shoulder, as though she expected others behind him—"your staff."

"And you are?"

"Oh, sorry—I'm Charlotte Bing. Actually, I think we met once—at your wife's gallery. I didn't recognize you without my glasses." From between ample breasts that were crossed by the lapels of a heather-colored tweed suit, she lifted a pair of gold-frame eyeglasses that she fitted on. Her hazel eyes moved from McGarr to the I.D. and back.

Charlotte Bing saw a short, well-built man of fifty-five with an aquiline nose that had been broken more than once and was now set off to one side. The hair that could be seen beneath a waterproof fedora was red and curled at the back of his neck. Otherwise, he was bald.

McGarr's eyes were clear and light gray in color. Wearing a dark herringbone overcoat and a pearl-gray tie, he looked like a stockbroker or banker from one of the financial institutions that were headquartered in nearby Ballsbridge.

Charlotte Bing stepped back to let him in. "I was Brian's—I mean, I'm deputy keeper at Marsh's Library, and I was his—"

McGarr did not catch what she said next, but he thought she might have said "friend." She had turned into the house, which was lighted throughout its impressive length. Windows were open, perhaps to diminish the smell that now assaulted McGarr's nostrils and that he recognized. In reflex, he reached into his suit coat for a cigarette.

"He told me a full week ago that he had some private work to do and that he'd be at home if anything . . . if something at the library—Marsh's—required his attention." A tall woman, she had long legs, and McGarr admired the svelte shape of her ankles as she moved down a long, central hall.

Now looking this way and that, McGarr could not help but notice the stunning period details of the sumptuously appointed house. The small entry hall was patterned with *coquillage.* On the rosewood grand staircase, there was a graceful newel-post light fixture showing brass birds in flight. Several art-glass windows gleamed in the higher reaches. If McGarr was not mistaken, the interior of the back parlor was by Eastlake with a jib-door window, which was open. There, a lace curtain was billowing into the room.

Lined along one wall of the kitchen, like twin battleships, were two lime-green and massive, claw-footed Agas. On the top of one, a ring of blue flame drummed on the bottom of a kettle. No poor scholar Herrick—he had lived in high style; McGarr wondered at the source of his income. Keeper of Marsh's Library could not pay much.

On a counter, the red light of a telephone/answering machine was blinking insistently.

Charlotte Bing stopped and cast a long, slender hand toward the kettle. "Would you care for a cup? I debated touching anything, but I'm afraid I would have expired myself had I not had something." She frowned and glanced at a wide, pocket door at the bottom of four tiled stairs. "Now that was an unfortunate turn of phrase, was it not?" She was plainly nervous or distraught.

McGarr struck a match to the end of a Sweet Afton—the unfiltered cigarettes that he had been smoking of late—and inhaled the strong blue smoke. Having limited himself to six a day, which he had already smoked, he could not keep himself from thinking how even the most morbid situation had its bright side. At least from the perspective of a thoroughly jaded senior officer of the "Murder Squad," as the Serious Crimes Unit was known in Dublin parlance. "You were saying."

The kettle had begun its whistle, and she moved toward it.

McGarr noticed two empty liter bottles of Glenfinnan, a rare and exorbitantly expensive single-malt Scots whiskey, on the sideboard. Near them was a carton labeled with a Customs declaration from Dublin Airport. A complimentary card was still inside. With the tip of a fingernail, McGarr opened it.

Brian

Consider this a pleasant reminder. You're late again. Save the best for last.

Jan

"Who's Jan?" McGarr asked.

"It's pronounced 'Yahn,'" said Charlotte Bing. "Jan deKuyper is his full name. He's the conservator at the Delmas Conservation Bindery, which is a part of Marsh's."

"What would Herrick have been late about again?"

"I'm sure I have no idea."

"Rather a handsome reminder, wouldn't you say?" McGarr tried to compute what something like two liter bottles of Glenfinnan would cost, even if purchased at its point of origin, which was somewhere around Inverness. Easily the better part of a hundred quid.

One deep well of an array of four set-tubs held a small number of dirty dishes in the bottom. McGarr wondered if the man had employed a housekeeper? Surely, he hadn't kept the house of—how many? At least a dozen, perhaps fifteen—large rooms himself.

Pouring the boiling water into a teapot, Charlotte Bing continued. "Well—on the third day I grew a bit worried. Even on his holidays, Brian was in the habit of phoning in. Also, the other employees of the library had not heard from him, in particular a . . . novice conservator whom he'd been seeing quite a lot of recently, I understand." Over the tops of the eyeglasses, her hazel eyes met McGarr's.

"So I began trying to reach him by phone. I only got the answering device."

Bing added milk and sugar, then stirred the tea and raised the cup. With closed eyes, she took a long drink, as though in need of its comfort, and then regarded McGarr once more.

"That evening I drove by, hoping to see a light or some sign that he was in the house. But there was none. I considered ringing the bell or, failing to rouse him, even coming in. Brian once gave me his keys, you see." A kind of blush came to her pale cheeks, and she gestured with the cup toward a ring with three keys that was on the cutting block in the center of the kitchen. "But that was years ago.

"So, I hesitated, not wishing to invade his privacy, about which—may I say?—he was most particular. Even a direct personal question he considered an affront. Also, Brian was an avid book collector, as you'll see, and I assumed he had left town on a buying jaunt. Only this evening did I decide that, his wrath aside, I'd look in on him myself. If you care to step this way—he's in the conservatory." As though burying her long, thin nose in the cup once more, Charlotte Bing pulled on the tea before moving toward the stairs.

"I found the door—this door—open, but not quite as much as it is now. I'm rather a large person, and I had to slide it open farther, say, six inches. Or eight."

McGarr glanced at the lovely coffered panels of yellow larch checkered with inlaid purple rowan, and he wondered why she was telling him that. Hung above the doors was a ship's name board with gold-leafed, intaglio letters glowing in the thin light through the kitchen windows:

"Antelope"
May 4, 1669

"The date on which Lemuel Gulliver set fictional sail from Bristol on his first voyage," Bing explained. "Brian simply doted on Swift, as you doubtless know. This way, please."

McGarr then followed her into one of the strangest rooms he had ever seen.

First was its size. Like a kind of ballroom but narrow, it extended for perhaps the eighty or ninety feet that had once been the back garden. There was a door at its farther end.

"Where does that go?"

"The door? Why, into a back alley. Brian had it put in when he built the library."

"With what does it communicate?"

"The alley leads into the Merrion Road."

McGarr wondered why Herrick had thought he needed another entrance, and what the construction project had entailed with permissions and costs. Granted, the property was on a corner, but it still seemed strange.

More surprising, however, was the look of the room. Apart from the large pots of plants that lined both walls, the room resembled a library; in fact, Marsh's Library. There were two rows of tall oak bookcases set in the middle of the floor, with a center aisle running between them.

"Of course, you recognize these." Charlotte Bing's long fingers brushed over the dark oak of the cases they were passing.

Each had a carved and lettered gable, topped by a mitre, and canted reading shelves at waist level. Most of the shelves were well filled out with books. McGarr counted thirteen cases to a side, with a long library reading table at the end where he could see the naked body of a large man slumped over an edge. The corpse was the source of the odor in the room; McGarr pulled on his cigarette.

"Brian had the bookcases made up from the original plans of the cases in Marsh's, oh—twenty or so years ago, when he decided he would begin collecting rare books. He told me he considered the cases in Marsh's Library to be the most elegant in the world. It was the reason he was first attracted to the library and why he set his sights on becoming its keeper. As you may already have deduced, Brian was acquisitive and a materialist, in spite of what he might have seemed like in his newspaper column."

"Which was what?"

"A man who was above . . . petty passions." She flashed McGarr a brittle smile. "Of course, he had the means to acquire all these things," she went on, continuing into the room. "His father was a distinguished botanist, who made his fortune in pharmaceuticals, deriving cures and things from exotic plants." She pointed to the potted flora along the walls. "When his father's estate was settled, Brian kept a few of the more exotic species for himself, as a kind of memorial."

In contrast to her conventional appearance—the low heels, the tweed suit, the high pile of ashen hair, and wire-frame eyeglasses—Charlotte Bing had a low, dulcet, and contained voice that McGarr found rather pleasing. He imagined that with another costume and a (what was the current term?) makeover, she might appear quite attractive.

"But, alas—there he is." Raising the dishcloth to her nose, she turned and swept the other arm toward the table.

McGarr stepped forward.

2

Herrick Mortuus

HERRICK WAS SIX DAYS DEAD, McGarr estimated. At least. McGarr had never viewed a pretty corpse, but few were perfectly naked, and none—in his recent experience—had looked as swollen or foul.

It was no longer the Brian Herrick whom McGarr had known. His head and torso were sprawled across the long table, his once well-muscled arms dangling over the edge. Blood, having pooled in his suspended hands, had made his fingers black. Like macabre sausages, they were swollen, and several had actually popped at the nails. From both thumbs, a dark, viscous fluid was drooling onto the Persian carpet.

McGarr stepped around the corpse, the better to see the face.

Swollen in morbid rictus, Herrick's tongue was lolling from his mouth. His cheeks were puffy and his eyes opaque, the outer lenses having decomposed to the aspect of phlegm. Like the skin of a rotting pear, his balding scalp had split to expose a blue film of membrane below. And yet the entire effect of the death mask was both comical and fearsome—like the leer of a totemic figure from some exotic fertility cult.

All that was missing was the outsized erection. Also filled with old, dead blood, Herrick's scrotum and penis were dangling from the edge of the chair, the penis black and plumulous with its fringe of hair and foreskin sheath.

Perhaps because of the potted plants along the walls, the conservatory was warm. Glancing up, McGarr imagined that the sun, which had been out several days earlier, had poured through the two rows of glass panels at the peak of the roof and fallen directly on the corpse, accelerating decomposition.

Also, there was a wide smear of what looked like dried feces—something like diarrhea—or vomit or both to one side of the chair, under the table, and on the seat and frame of the tall, padded chair. The same sort of . . . meringue was stuck to the skin of the corpse's knees and shins, forearms and elbows, and palms, as though Herrick had been down on his hands and knees and had crawled through his own wretchedness.

Had he been ill before he died? There was the evidence of alcohol—the two empty liter bottles of Glenfinnan in the kitchen, and here a crystal decanter that was filled to only an inch or so. Could Herrick have been an alcoholic and binged on the whiskey, vomited, and then died of alcohol poisoning? Or of a heart attack, or a hemorrhage? Might he have choked?

McGarr hunkered down to get a better view of the chest and stomach, which was swollen with gas. There seemed to be no visible wounds anywhere on the body; the split of the skin on his bald pate seemed to be another effect of postmortem decomposition, though McGarr could be wrong.

He straightened up and studied the objects on the table:

the decanter and two cocktail glasses, one of which had spilled, leaving a fan-shaped stain. There were also two old leather-bound volumes within easy reach of the chair.

Directly in front of the corpse was a third book that was open. Herrick's face was lying on one page. In the margins, it appeared, Herrick had been writing notes. A variety of pencils was lying nearby, and the handwriting was both archaic and eccentric.

Finally, there was a photocopy of the same page that was open in the book, including the marginalia. In all, it seemed like Herrick had been taken by some fatal attack while sitting in the chair, working on the book. But what sort of work?

"What was he doing here—copying the writing on this page into this book?"

"It would appear so."

"Why?"

Charlotte Bing shrugged. "The book is a copy of Clarendon's *History of the Rebellion.* Our copy in Marsh's was owned by Swift and contains annotations by him condemning the Scots for the treacherous role they played in helping the British subdue Ireland."

"You mean this page." McGarr pointed to the photocopy. "This page is from that book in Marsh's."

"That's Swift's handwriting. There's only one book like it."

"And Herrick wanted a copy—for this library?" McGarr was thinking aloud; he glanced over at the bookcases that had been reproduced from the plans of those at Marsh's. "What was Herrick's . . . intent in doing all of this?" McGarr's hand swept from the table to the bookcases and back. "A book, like that, a . . . *copy* wouldn't be worth anything, would it? Could his wish have been to *re-create* Marsh's Library here in this room?"

Charlotte Bing's eyes rolled, as though to suggest that Herrick's wants had been beyond her knowing. "I'm afraid we weren't that close in recent years. But I could speculate?"

McGarr nodded.

"It's not charitable to demean the dead, I know. But I should say this about Brian, and I hope you won't take it amiss."

Again McGarr tilted his head.

"Brian was two people. He was the person who was the keeper of Marsh's Library and the owner of this exquisite house. There's no other word for it. But Brian also had a second side, a fantasy side. He was the Brian of the *Times* column that you've probably read—"

McGarr pulled on his cigarette.

"—with the rapierlike mind and wit, à la Swift, whom he revered and emulated as much as was possible. In that way, Brian was really like a child. Or, rather, like some research students who get swept up and carried away with the subject of their study.

"Brian had been a brilliant research student, you see. His thesis on the Swift opus, its publication and history, sailed through Oxford. First reading. His dons didn't change a comma, and he finished the doctorate in two years! But, alas, Brian never made a break with his subject.

"I think"—Charlotte Bing folded her arms across her substantial breasts and sighed—"Swift provided Brian with a persona, a sense of self that he was lacking. He *became* Swift, at least in his own mind, and he thereby inherited—gladly, I think—the burden of Swift's foibles."

Which were? McGarr might have been moved to ask, did he not think they were getting rather far afield from the *substantiality* of the reeking corpse, which suggested a death by some natural cause, at least until a pathologist told him otherwise. "Why was he naked?"

"Brian was always naked in this room. He said it was too hot for clothes, but that wasn't the reason."

McGarr watched as Charlotte Bing's eyes moved toward a video camera near the small stage; it was displaying a small red light, as though it was either still filming or had run to the end of its reel but had not been switched off. "What was that for? The camera, the stage."

"Frolic."

"Sorry?" McGarr asked, not understanding.

"Listed under 'F' for frolic." She pointed toward the bookshelves at the beginning of the room. "Spelled with two 'L's and a 'K' on the end. The 'F' is capitalized. You'll find several dozen videotapes that will show you what he meant by the word, what he used the stage for."

"Which was . . . ?"

She turned her head away. "I'd prefer not to discuss it. You'll understand why when you view them yourself."

McGarr did not know whether he would. Or should, unless and until he had to. "Let me ask you something else, then?"

With the cloth back over her nose and mouth, Charlotte Bing nodded. It made her look like a concubine in a seraglio, eyeing him over the top of a *yashmak*.

"Why did you phone the police?"

She pulled it down. "Well—I didn't phone the police per se, I phoned your office. The Serious Crimes Unit."

"Why?"

"Because I thought you might handle the death of a man so prominent and . . . conspicuous, as was Brian, with some dignity. I hope I was not mistaken in that."

Which was soft soap. McGarr waited for her to tell him the real reason.

Her eyes left his and glanced at the table. "And because of those two books." She pointed to the volumes that appeared to have been arranged on the table within easy reach of Herrick.

Still McGarr waited; she had more to tell him.

"After getting over the shock and . . . revulsion of discovering Brian, I noticed what he had been about before he died."

"Copying the Swift marginal notes into the Clarendon book?"

She nodded. "It's one thing to want to possess antique or rare books, manuscripts, *objets d'art.*" She pointed to some of the accoutrements of the room. "And Brian, as you can see from the house, was a collector. It also could be innocently eccentric to wish to *be* Swift, or at least to *characterize* him, for want of a better term."

Which was caricature, McGarr supposed.

"Even if you possessed sufficient wit, which Brian obviously did. But"—she shook her head—"it's quite another impetus altogether, I should imagine, to wish to possess and mock up, as he was doing here, a *fraudulent* copy of a unique object, of which there can be no other. I had to ask myself why, which caused me to examine those two books." Bing meant the other two books that were close by the corpse.

"The one on top is a fifteenth-century edition of Cicero's *Letters to His Friends.* The other volume is *Le Rommant Galliot de la Rose,* printed in Paris by Galliot du Pré. They're the originals from Marsh's Library. Having conserved them myself some years ago, I'd know them anywhere. When I recognized the volumes, it occurred to me what Brian was about here, when he died. He was mocking up a Clarendon in the manner of Swift so that he could"—she looked away and shook her head—"substitute it for the original, I can only assume."

Somewhere off in the house a clock was chiming the hour—nine. After it stopped, McGarr said, "What you're saying, then, is that Herrick took those two books from Marsh's Library."

She nodded. "It would appear so."

"But you presently *have* two books, like those, in the library?"

Again.

"Then the Cicero and the *Rommant de la Rose* that you have in Marsh's are . . . ?"

"Forgeries. I won't know for certain until I examine them. But I should imagine they're *period* forgeries, since only four days ago we had a scholar come in to Marsh's to admire our Cicero, and neither he nor I noticed anything 'wrong' with it. On cursory perusal, of course. I had no reason to suspect it. Then."

"*Period* forgeries?" McGarr asked. The cigarette was now burning his fingers.

"Do you know anything about book publishing from the fifteenth to the eighteenth centuries?"

McGarr suppressed the urge to chuckle, if only for comic relief. He knew little or nothing about book publishing in the twentieth century. But his eyes fell on the corpse. In the achromatic wash from the stage light, Herrick looked rather green and like nothing more than a stuffed bullfrog—the thin legs, the distended belly, the whitish eyes and mouth popped open. The tongue sticking out.

Death was never dignified, at least the sort that McGarr

usually viewed. And Herrick's rather less than most, given who he had been—a man who had "kept" a notable library, who had owned one of the finest homes in Dublin, and who had presumed to *be* Jonathan Swift in various ways. Rather more or rather less, according to opinion.

"I wonder—could we speak about this in the morning?" Charlotte Bing asked. "I'm afraid all of this has been rather much for me. I'm subject to migraine headaches. They give me some warning, you see, and I can feel one coming on." Her complexion had suddenly gone pale, and there was a bead of sweat on her well-formed forehead.

McGarr looked away. He would prefer to get her statement tonight, while the details of her entering the house and discovering the body were still fresh in her mind. But, he supposed, a migraine headache would make that impossible anyhow, and by morning he could arrange to have somebody present who knew something about rare books. And Swift. Namely: his wife, Noreen.

Outside at Bing's car, he asked, "Are you sure you can drive? I could take you home, and you could fetch your car in the morning."

"I can manage, thanks. I only live in Sandymount," which was less than a mile or so away.

"Do you have a card or something? I'm afraid I need your address."

"I'm in the book." She closed the door and drove off into the heavy mist.

Back in the large, well-appointed house, McGarr first rang up the pathologist and then the Technical Squad, in case the death should prove suspicious.

He hoped not. With the poor economy and what he thought of as a climate of lawlessness that Herrick himself had written about in his column, his small staff was already burdened to the max.

McGarr considered phoning in a subordinate, so he could take himself home to his wife and child. But he recalled Charlotte Bing's stated reason for contacting the police. And he was intrigued by what Herrick might have shelved under "F" for "Frollick."

Also, there was the still-activated video camera and the answering machine, which had been backed up for nearly a week, if McGarr was any judge of death.

3

Hangover

MCGARR DID NOT GET HOME until first light, the hour of the day that he usually arose. Knowing he would not sleep even if he tried, he merely eased off his shoes in the front hall of his Georgian House in Belgrave Square—a somewhat tatty, middle-class neighborhood of Rathmines, a suburb of Dublin—and padded into the kitchen. There his own Aga was gently heating the flagstones underfoot, and the warmth and the peaceful quiet of the kitchen soothed him, after the long, curious night.

Even the ritual of tending to the Aga was welcome this morning. Opening the ash door so that the unburned briquettes of EU-acceptable composite fuel (which produced little smoke) would flare up, he reached for the coffeepot. He would wait until the fire was burning strong before shaking out the ashes and adding more fuel.

Filling a six-cup "Vesuvius" coffeemaker with fresh water, he then packed the steam bin with a plenum of pulverized dark-roast coffee. He screwed down the top and set it where the freshening fire. would make the water boil quickly. A pot of milk was placed off to a side to warm.

Turning, McGarr eased his back into the hot enamel surface of the stove and glanced through tall, arched Georgian windows into his back garden, which he tended three seasons a year with great care. Now his twenty "Chinese raised beds," as he called them, were heaped with aged seaweed, dung, and compost in preparation for spring planting, which was three months away. Bright plumes of vaporing rot were seeping up into the dun, early-morning light.

Both wider and longer than traditional Irish "lazy beds," they now looked for all the world like the burial ground of a race of giants. What had Swift called his giants in *Gulliver?* Something strange that McGarr's mind was too tired to recall. And then, of course, he had only read as much of Swift in school as he had to—to get by. McGarr's focus had always been on the world, not on books.

Behind him, the coffeepot now roared, jetting its steam through the finely ground dark beans. It popped and hissed. A bubble of dark fluid broke from the lid and sizzled down the silver side to evaporate on the now-torrid surface of the stove. The aroma it gave off—of burned dark-roast coffee— was perhaps more welcome to McGarr than even the smell of a single-malt-pot-stilled whiskey, like Glenfinnan, at least at this time of the morning.

McGarr had tasted several Glenfinnans, courtesy of Brian Herrick, before leaving the dead man's home. And welcome they were, while McGarr viewed the videotape that he had discovered in the camera that had been pointed at the chair where Herrick had been sitting. He had also watched some of the other tapes filed under "F" for "Frollick."

That people—Herrick, who had obviously orchestrated the sexual charades—were moved to . . . debase their humanity (consciously, actively, enthusiastically, Herrick roaring his delight to the tall ceiling of the conservatory) had filled McGarr with a kind of loathing that he had not felt in years. For the human animal.

It also amazed him that Herrick could have maintained the facade of moral rectitude in his daily life, even to addressing the nation via his "Essay" in the *Times,* while secretly engaging in lurid carnal escapades that would make a sybarite blush. How had he squared the two . . . in his own mind and heart? McGarr shook his head and looked down at his stockinged feet.

And finally, how often was a murder captured on videotape? Or at least the filming of an ugly death. The spectacle had required no little . . . amelioration, and McGarr had not spared himself the liquor.

The other tapes of "Frollick" were no better, a record of Herrick's previous sexual capers with mainly two of the three persons who had been present on the night of his death, and usually some young woman. The latter seemed to have been recruited from foreign sources—England, the Continent, Japan, Thailand, the Philippines. "I know how yiz love a little sum'tin' different, darlin'," the hag was wont to say, introducing the younger woman. "Look at her now. Hain't she the livin' end!"

Whereupon Herrick had roared his approval of the phrase and taken the "living end" upon his lap while the hag plied him as well. Could some of the "women" have been children, made up to look older? It was difficult to tell, the way they were costumed. McGarr hoped not.

Yet the man's taste for small women—*tiny,* actually—was definite, at least in regard to the women who played the part of the . . . ingenue. Thus, McGarr had left the Shrewsbury Road residence feeling rather heartsick—as though his own urges had been tainted by the defilement that he had witnessed. And, again, by the fact that Herrick had so skillfully concealed his dark side.

Now the diurnal details of McGarr's life seemed filled with special meaning and made him feel as though he were different from the . . . enormity that he had viewed the night long. Or, at least, that he *could* be different, if he concentrated on the normal, usual, staid, humdrum, commonplace things in life. Like the coffee.

Spooning two sugars into the oily fluid, McGarr added a dollop of hot milk from the pot and stirred the cup. He would need the jolt that the concoction would give him. By evening the papers would have the story that Brian Herrick was dead and that the police had sequestered both the house and Marsh's Library. McGarr sipped from the scalding coffee and tended to the Aga.

The chore done, he glanced at the clock and saw that it was time for Maddie and Noreen to begin getting up—for work and school. Well, perhaps a different kind of work for Noreen this morning, since McGarr would need her help. Fixing her coffee and fetching some juice for Maddie, he tried to turn his mind to the hard facts of what he had learned the night long.

First was Charlotte Bing's opinion that Brian Herrick had been acquiring "period forgeries," which phrase was still to be explained, and substituting them for books already in Marsh's Library.

Later there came the pathologist's opinion that Herrick had been poisoned, " 'Though I can't be sure until the postmortem tests come back from the lab. But it's my guess, just looking at him, that it was something quick and nasty enough to cause this." With a shoe, he had pointed toward the smears of dried putrescence on the carpet and on the shins and forearms of the corpse.

"He voided and vomited *before* he died. He only managed to crawl up here before a violent convulsion took him." The pathologist had indicated the table, which had been knocked off center, and the spilled glass.

McGarr had then ordered the Tech Squad to examine all food, drink, and comestibles of any kind, as well as glasses and vessels. "Don't bother with that decanter." McGarr had already taken a drink of that and was still standing.

Next, having found Charlotte Bing's name in the Dublin phone book, he dispatched a Murder Squad staffer to the address and was relieved to learn that her car was parked outside. He then turned his attention to the answering machine, the video camera that seemed to corroborate the pathologist's opinion of murder by poison, and the other videotapes. McGarr was unable to get them out of his mind.

Now stopping in the hallway to set down the tray of coffee and juice before proceeding upstairs, he opened the front door and retrieved the three morning newspapers, each of which had been rolled and flung up onto the tall landing of the Georgian house by special arrangement with the son of a local newsagent.

Opening the first, McGarr shook his head, marveling, as he always did, at the speed and ubiquity of that capacious instrument, Dublin gossip. He wondered if there was anything anywhere in the city that could occur in absolute privacy, free from public comment.

DEAN DEAD

MURDER SUSPECTED

The article went on to describe how McGarr was observed entering the dead man's Shrewsbury Road house in the early evening, following which an ambulance and more police vehicles arrived. A litter covered by a sheet was brought out, "and the police have established a guard on the premises as well as on Marsh's Library, where Dr. Herrick was Keeper."

A biddy across the street, McGarr imagined, although it could as easily have been some one of Herrick's peers. Dublin was a great place for dark rooms and open curtains with people watching what others were about. People prowled the streets and public places all day everyday with no greater purpose in mind.

Even a pint of Guinness was now called a "scoop" in modern Dublin parlance. And, sure, it was never too late at night to relate a choice morsel of hitherto-unknown information about somebody as prominent and—what was the word that Charlotte Bing had used?—*conspicuous* as Herrick had been. To the press.

Stepping back into the house, McGarr glanced up. There above him at some incredible distance, a patch of the purest cerulean-blue sky now appeared. The foul weather would soon clear, he knew; the leaden storm sky was marching smartly to the east.

Closing the door, McGarr scanned the other two papers. While no less well connected to the "jungle telegraph," as it were, they were more reticent about running gossip on their front pages. But similar stories, also absent of significant detail, appeared within.

In the master bedroom, McGarr discovered Noreen and Maddie in the "big bed," as Maddie put it, still fast asleep.

Children's books were scattered all over the coverlet, Noreen evidently having read the five-year-old to sleep.

McGarr drew back the curtains and set the tray on the nightstand.

Opening her eyes, Noreen said, "And where the divil have you been the night long?"

Exactly, McGarr thought—divil it was. "How do you know I was out the night long?"

"Why"—her turquoise-colored eyes snapped to the bedside clock—"you're only home now a half hour? And the stink off you. Jasus—what *is* that?"

She had been listening for the door; it was nice to know he had been missed, even if her concern was couched in terms of obloquy.

"At least you might have rung us up?"

"It was too late, and I kept thinking I was coming home."

"Ach, now I've heard everything." Noreen pushed herself up against the headboard, a trim, small woman who was an even dozen years younger than McGarr. With both hands, she forked back her copper-colored curls. "The perfect pubsman's argument. 'Yeh know,' " she made her voice low, gravelly, and pure Dublin. " 'Oi wanted teh phone yiz, sure I did. But it was too late. Und 'dere for the longest time, I kept t'inking Oi was comin' home directly.' "

Her long, thin nose, which was ruler straight, twitched. "So far, I've got on you cigarettes (a whole packet of them and whatever others you filched from your mates), whiskey (and plenty of that), and some sort of . . . corruption."

Right again. McGarr snapped on the light beside the bed and handed her the *Press* with its banner headline about Brian Herrick. He pivoted and made for the shower. "I was thinking you might give me an hour or two of your time this morning. I need an opinion on a couple of matters. Charlotte Bing is to tell me what she means by 'period forgeries.' You know her?"

"Of course." Noreen reached for her reading glasses. "A tall, elegant woman. Her mother died a year or two ago and left her an interesting old house on Sandymount Green. She also attended the Courtald, although some years before me. I went to a fund-raiser she threw . . . oh, I don't know. In the spring." Noreen meant the Courtald Institute in London, where she had studied the history of art before taking over her father's picture gallery in Dawson Street.

"Openings, museum shows, that class of thing. I run into her every few months." Noreen had fitted on her glasses and now glanced down. "Oh, my God—do they mean *the* Brian Herrick, 'The Dean'? Is that where you were last night?" She looked up at McGarr, who was standing in the door of the bathroom. *"Murdered?"*

"I hope not. But it seems Herrick was even more than what met the eye," which with the long ringlets of "Swiftian" hair had been enough. "Charlotte Bing seems to think he might also have been a thief, a forger, and"—McGarr's tired mind searched for an adequate descriptive phrase to explain what else he had viewed the night long—"an *ardent* bibliophile, to say the least."

"And you need help with the 'period forgeries'?"

McGarr could see from the color that had risen to his wife's fair cheeks that she was game. While in no way a malicious person, Noreen was nonetheless a Dubliner born and bred, and she could not resist the least bit of . . . "insider information" about one of McGarr's cases, especially when it involved somebody as notable as Herrick had been. Not infrequently McGarr wondered how much she had married him—the *real* McGarr, the one apart from his occupation—as she had the McGarr of the "Murder Squad," the one who was written about in the pages of the press.

In such a way, McGarr's professional involvements had become a kind of leitmotif in their marriage. He imagined that Noreen would get great mileage out of whatever she discovered this morning, when importuned, as she would be, by the other shopkeepers and business owners in the select environs of Dawson Street.

Even in the best Dublin circles, that fiercest of cultural strains of the city—the yen for repeatable dirt—remained intact. Especially when it came from the horse's mouth, which was McGarr himself. Twisting on the hot water, he whinnied and yet again thought of Swift. What had Swift called his race of superior horses in *Gulliver?* He could not recall that, either, and would have to look it up, too. Or ask Noreen.

It also now occurred to McGarr that Herrick had traveled with the crowd who patronized Noreen's picture gallery and were involved in the arts. Had he not seen Herrick there himself? Noreen might be able to trade information, *quid pro quo.*

By the time McGarr was out of the shower and dressed, Noreen was up and had Maddie ready for school. A full Irish breakfast—rashers, eggs, sausage, black pudding, grilled tomatoes, and toast— was on the table.

"Daddy—where *were* you last night?" his daughter scolded, as he kissed her good morning and took a seat at the table. "Mammy said it was something important that kept you away, but I don't believe her." Yet another redhead (how could she help but be?), she fixed her starburst blue eyes on him, as though he would fill her in.

"You should always believe your mammy," he said, wondering if the need for stories—good, bad, or even apocryphal— was something inhaled in the air or inbibed in the water. Or could it be racial and genetic?

4

The Perquisites of
a Profession

IT WAS QUARTER TO TEN by the time the McGarrs got to Brian Herrick's large Edwardian house on the Shrewsbury Road. The weather had indeed changed. Overhead the sun, though pale, was nearly too brilliant to look at directly and imparted a hard edge to every shape and line. Winter had indeed arrived. A chill north wind plucked at McGarr's trilby as he stepped out of the car, and Noreen had to turn her back to the blast. Fallen leaves swirled in devil's cones along the footpath.

Charlotte Bing was waiting inside the spiked iron fence. Three uniformed gardai were present to watch over the property and to keep the curious away. McGarr had also posted a guard at the rear of the house where, during the night, he had opened the door near the small stage in the conservatory and found himself suddenly in an alley. The third key on Charlotte Bing's key ring fit that heavy lock.

As the McGarrs approached the house, a lone reporter with her photographer in tow broke from a car at the curb, only to be cut off by the largest of the guards. Arms spread wide, he asked, "Can yous name this gesture?"

Surprised by the remark, the young woman stopped. She brushed wispy brown hair from before a pretty, oval face. "Yeh're tryin' to floy," she said in the pancake accent that marked her as a Dubliner born and bred. "But yeh left yehr wings back at the barracks."

McGarr opened the gate and gave Noreen a gentle push toward Charlotte Bing.

"Nothing of the sort—guess again."

She stepped one way and then the other, but the guard, who was a sergeant, blocked her every move. "Your old woman starched the shite out of your uniform, and you can't lower your arms. Fair play to her."

"Nah, Jasus—you'll never make a go of this business. Don't you know who John Paul is?"

"The other half of Ringo and George. Hey, McGarr," she shouted through the fence. "Who's the woman?"

"Only the wife."

"What d'you mean, *only*?" Noreen asked. She was dressed in a new cashmere suit that fit her diminutive but angular frame like demurely suggestive second skin. It was just the turquoise color of her eyes. In the bright sunlight, her copper-colored curls looked almost blond.

Knowing she was being sent up, the reporter bawled like a fishwife, "Do yeh always drag the wife along with yeh on a moorder investigation?"

"Only when I can't find another interested party."

"What about my readers? *They're* interested parties. Can't you give us a statement?"

Pronounced the sergeant, "Your readers are a pack of nosy, jaded, sadistic mutts, and the less they know, the better off we'll all be."

"Like your ignorant self, you mean."

"Exactly. Which is bliss. Now, be off wid yiz, or I'll run yeh in. Nappies"—he pointed to her—"snappies," he pointed to the photographer—"and all." He meant the car, which was illegally parked.

McGarr heard a camera shutter clash and imagined that the exchange and a picture of his back would be enough for front-page coverage.

Charlotte Bing was dressed in a black satin suit that was patterned with silver sheen whenever she moved in the full sunlight. With a pillbox hat and black veil, she looked down-right attractive and more as if she were about to attend a race meeting than she was in mourning. She offered her hand. "Ah, Noreen—I was hoping your husband would think to bring you along. I'm afraid all this has been rather much for me."

"Really, Charlotte? Then appearances are deceiving. You look in great form altogether." Noreen took the taller woman's arm as they approached the stairs.

"It's the stress," Bing went on. "What a disaster! Brian was still very youthful and had such a full life."

As we'll soon see, thought McGarr, thinking of the videotapes.

"And then there's Marsh's—did your husband tell you about the books?"

"Only what you and he discussed, which has piqued his interest, I must say. It was the reason he asked me along. To . . . interpret."

"Well, then, I'm glad you came. I'm afraid I had one of my headaches last night, and I don't know how long I'll be able to carry on." Beneath the veil, her long face did, in fact, look rather wan, yet the complex weave of her ash-blond hair had been arranged with perfect care.

McGarr offered her his other arm, and they led Bing up the tall flight of marble stairs to the main door, which opened before McGarr could ring.

In it stood a short, squat middle-aged man with a thick shock of blond hair and dark, bright eyes. Dressed in shirtsleeves and tie, he placed his hands on his wide hips and regarded them. His face was cherubic, his smile conspiratorial.

"Who're ... ?" Charlotte Bing began to ask.

"Me? Why, I'm Bernie, goat boy. I thought everybody knew that. And who might you be?" He offered his hand, which Charlotte Bing did not take. "So much for ceremony."

Detective Superintendent Bernie McKeon, McGarr's chief of staff, stepped aside. "*Entrez, si* boob play. Won't you beautiful people continue on to the conservatory. As for you, Chief Super or Super Chief—octane rating unknown—I'd like a word with you in private." McKeon waved McGarr into the sitting room off the main entrance hall, where, it appeared, he had established a kind of command post.

A desk that McGarr recognized from their Dublin Castle office had been placed in the middle of the room. A brace of telephones, two radios, and a fax were plugged into a portable jack with a thick length of electrical cable running out the window, which was open a crack. "As per your orders," McKeon explained. "Now, then, coffee?"

McGarr shook his head. "Had some."

McKeon regarded him. "With or without octane?"

"Well ... without. Why, is that an offer?" McGarr pulled out a cigarette and lit it up.

"The gall of the man, when he knows there's not a drop in the house."

"First come, first served."

"Which is a difficult point to swallow at nine in the morning."

"Sure, I was only thinking of your work*day*."

"You call this work?" McKeon pointed to the desk; as an inside man, he frequently complained that he never got out of the office to enjoy the "perquisites of my profession," was his phrase. And here he was *out* but *inside* and *without* the most preferred emolument of said phrase.

McGarr raised a finger and made a circle with it, signaling McKeon to speed things up.

"All business today, I see." *After having drunk the pleasure,* went unsaid. With unfeigned disgust, McKeon picked a sheaf of papers off the desk. "First the pathologist's report, hot off the fax." McKeon glanced down. "He worked all night, so he did. Staff and all. Let's see.

"You were right about Herrick's condition, which was foul. He had vomited. The other substance on the carpet, on his elbows and shanks, was shit, no other word for it. Diarrhea. The doc writes, 'Herrick was riven by convulsions.' "

"Cause of death?" McGarr asked.

"Respiratory failure."

"But what *caused* the respiratory failure?"

"Dunno. Final word—'findings of autopsy inclusive.' In other words, the poor bugger pooped, puked, and then punched out." With the flat of his hand, McKeon smacked his chest. "End of nudey show. Stop action. Video coverage over. Apart from bank heists, how often have we ever been treated to a murder on film? Tell you this much—I've seen some . . . high jinks in me time, but that film takes the biscuit, so it does.

"Would you say that blue movies get the name from the

blue lights? You know, even the black hair of the little one, the *tiny* one, looks blue—the black merry widow, the black tights. What you see in the *absence* of tights. Her . . . *patch.*" McKeon smiled.

Thought McGarr: Bernie McKeon, father of thirteen and a man's man by Irish standards, had passed his days almost exclusively in the company of men—as a child in Ireland's gender-segregated schools, at work, in the pub, at sporting events, at home, where he probably devoted most of his time to his wee lads. Not being a man who attended the cinema that McGarr knew of, McKeon had probably never actually seen another visual display that could pass as a blue movie.

"Anything else?" McGarr asked, heading for the door. Like a bird released from his cage, McKeon would warble all morning, if allowed.

"Two things. I believe I've discovered Herrick's financial records in that desk over there." He pointed to the ornate desk by the window. "From the checkbook, I should be able to put together an idea of how he was set and also the names of any medical treatment he might have had. Second, the lab is still trying to 'Name That Poison,' " he said, as if announcing a game show on the teley.

"The problem is the absence of much of anything in his stomach or intestines. Blood? They're still working on that. The computer analysis could not name the foreign substance, which, it says here, matches up 'with no commonly known toxin.' They're still working on a sample, and they've sent specimens off to Porton Down."

It was the location of the British center that analyzed infectious diseases and toxins. Results, McGarr knew from experience, would not be back for at least a week.

"The Tech Squad report about the house itself won't be ready until noon."

"Where's Hughie and Ruth?" Detective Superintendent Hugh Ward and Detective Inspector Ruth Bresnahan were key members of his staff, and McGarr had asked them to be present.

"The lovebirds? They're around somewheres, maybe upstairs. It seems the house and furnishings has struck their fancy, them being in the 'nesting' mode, don't you know. 'Oh, isn't this handsome?' says she. 'Oh, beautiful,' says he. Dazed, like, you know. His eyes *not* on the furniture."

After nearly a year leave of absence, Bresnahan had only recently returned to the squad and had renewed what McGarr imagined—but did not want to be told—was a torrid relationship with Ward. Did he know in fact, he would have to recommend that one of them be transferred, which was a situation he wished to avoid. Both were excellent investigators.

Leaving the room, McGarr remarked, "I assume you've gone over the entire premises."

"With a fine-toothed t'irst."

"And you tried the Holy Bible on the nightstand in the master bedroom?"

"What *is* this, a trick question? The *Bible?*"

"Did y'not think it a bit odd that a man like Herrick would keep something like that beside him while he slept?"

"I did indeed. Says I to meself, he was asking for a thunderbolt, and his request was granted." Dawn then broke on McKeon. "You mean to say it's hollow?"

McGarr walked out into the hall. "I don't mean to say anything, apart from now you know why you're an *inside* man."

"But—I had *things* to do. This desk, the fax. If I had begun opening books in this place, why, Christ, I'd still be at it—"

"Priorities, Bernie. Or should I say *perquisites.*" Moving toward the kitchen and the conservatory beyond, McGarr soon heard McKeon's heavy step on the staircase. "And send down the lovebirds."

"You mean they might learn a thing or two from the videotape. When's the next showing?"

"In due time." McGarr would deal with the books first, while Noreen was present—what Charlotte Bing had called "period forgeries." And viewing Herrick's videotapes, especially that of his murder, was not for everybody. Noreen in particular.

"Make sure to call me."

"Another 'perquisite of your profession'?"

"There you have it," McKeon said gleefully. "Me very words." He hustled up the stairs.

5

Period Forgeries

WHEN MCGARR REACHED THE CONSERVATORY he found Noreen examining one of the books that Brian Herrick had on the table beside him when he died, and that Charlotte Bing said belonged in Marsh's Library. It was Cicero's *Letters to His Friends.*

Turning the volume over to examine the spine with its tooled-leather ridges, Noreen remarked, "Isn't it a handsome thing?" She opened to a neatly printed page. "I only wish my Latin were better."

Said Charlotte Bing, "And an important book in the history of literature. It was printed in Milan in 1472, and some two hundred years later, several literary critics, using what were then considered 'modern' methods of philology, declared that it could not possibly have been written by Cicero. The style, the sentiments, even the subjects of some of the letters, were not 'Ciceronian.'"

"Which gave rise to the 'Ancients' versus 'Moderns' controversy."

Bing nodded. "Swift's contribution, in defense of his mentor—Sir William Temple, who was an 'Ancient'—was his squib *The Battle of the Books.* The controversy as to whether Cicero actually wrote the volume has still not been put to rest entirely, but a genuine first edition is a prize that the director of even the most exalted library would be eager to possess."

To say nothing of a private collector and practicing antiquarian, as Herrick had been, thought McGarr, lighting up another cigarette. The reek of death would linger in the room for quite some time, to say nothing of the foul carpet that Herrick's heirs would have to clean. McGarr made a mental note to discover who stood to inherit the handsome period dwelling with its carefully chosen furnishings. And whatever else Herrick's estate contained.

"Last night you mentioned the possibility that Dr. Herrick might have substituted 'period forgeries' for some of the books in Marsh's Library and brought the originals here."

With care Charlotte Bing raised the black veil from before her face and then removed her hat, spilling the aroma of some expensive scent into the room. "I rather overdid the perfume this morning, as a precaution." Touching the back of her precisely coiffured ash-blond hair in a self-conscious manner, she went on, "Yes, those two books, for instance. As for any others, I'll have to see. By that, I mean I will have to conduct a complete, investigative inventory of the Marsh's collection, and I should like to perform the same on these books." She pointed to the bookcases at the other end of the conservatory. "With your permission, of course."

McGarr nodded, although he would provide her with some help, since she was not a disinterested party. Not only had she disapproved of Herrick, who was her former lover, she also might gain from his death. He wondered if she would now be named keeper of Marsh's Library, and how that decision would

be made. It was something else he would have to find out.
" 'Period' forgeries," he again suggested.

"Yes, well—by that I mean forgeries from the period in
which a document was first published, and not a book that
has been mocked up in recent years to 'look' old. These are
the hardest forgeries to discover and . . . pin down."

The McGarrs waited while Charlotte Bing seemed to
gather her thoughts. "It's rather well known to experts in the
field of printed documents that, from the fifteenth through
the eighteenth centuries, an untold number of reprints exist
that are in fact complete resettings from standing type. In
other words, the work may pass every test—scientific and
literary—as to age and seeming authenticity, but it may not
in fact have been printed by, printed for, or sold by those
whose names it bears—author and publisher or printer. That's
called binary forgery—a forgery of a known and genuine
original."

"As opposed to . . . ?" McGarr asked.

"A 'creative' forgery," said Noreen. "You know, 'discovering'
a heretofore unknown manuscript by some literary notable."

"Exactly," Charlotte Bing agreed. "A manuscript that adds
to the canon of known documents. Forgery, you see, was much
easier and more prevalent in earlier centuries because of either
the absence of copyright laws or lack of enforcement. Swift,
for instance, published most of his work anonymously, and it
was easy at the time for an unscrupulous printer to obtain a
copy of the genuine book and to reproduce it almost exactly.
Or exactly, if he were clever enough to obtain the same type,
same paper, and binding materials. Then he could sell it as
the original."

"Without paying Swift."

"That, too. Even the original printer might whip up another edition but date it as the original, saying that 'a little remainder' turned up in the back of the shop. *Gulliver,* for instance, went through dozens of printings in Swift's lifetime, not even half of which were agreed to by him."

"Sounds like it was not the time to be a writer," said McGarr, if only to keep the woman speaking. She had something to tell them.

Charlotte Bing nodded. "The vast majority of imprints that appear on Swift's list of published works are at worst fake and at best misleading."

"So, what makes a book genuine?" he asked.

"Its provenance."

Now that was something McGarr knew about, courtesy of Noreen. "Just as for an important painting."

"That's right. The record, the documentation of the book complete with names and dates of owners, perhaps written right into the cover or front matter of the book, or supplied with verification by the known buyer, who is then the seller, of the book. Or from one respected and honest dealer or collector to another, as the treasured book is passed from hand to hand down through the centuries."

Noreen spoke up. "But certainly there are genuine books that have lain ignored in somebody's attic or in the library of a vicarage out in the country. Suddenly, they are discovered and appear *without* a proper provenance."

Charlotte Bing nodded. "It happens now and then, although less so as the years go by. But such finds require the imprimatur of a known expert—better, several experts—before their value is established. And, as I said, bookselling in the centuries before copyright laws was at its best. I should imagine that even the collection of somebody like Brian, who was a good judge of genuine documents and a punctilious archivist, contains more than a few 'period' forgeries. Unless, of course—" Her hazel eyes tumbled down on the book that Herrick seemed to have been writing in before he died: Clarendon's *History of the Rebellion* with marginalia by "Swift."

"Unless Herrick had been systematically substituting 'period' forgeries for the books he brought home here from Marsh's," Noreen concluded.

Charlotte Bing's nostrils flared. She had twined her hands beneath her arms in a way that flared the black satin sheen of her broad chest. In such a way, her pose seemed almost militant. "I doubt that. I would have noticed any wholesale substitutions long before now. But it's my reason for wishing to conduct a complete inventory."

"Perhaps he was only . . . completing his fantasy of being . . . of *becoming* the Swift of our era," Noreen ventured. "His eccentricity. The costumes he got himself up in, the way he wore his hair in those ringlets, and in the column. All the—"

"Foolishness and knavery," Bing supplied.

"—of his witty thoughts and observations."

On the pinion of a high heel, Bing had raised one foot, which she looked down at. "Perhaps. But with a collection such as Marsh's, one can't be too careful."

And perhaps something else, thought McGarr; it was what Charlotte Bing had to tell them. He asked, "Say, if Herrick had accomplished what you say he wished—to re-create the important holdings of Marsh's Library here in this room—what would he have done with those books?"

"Or, worse—managed to purloin the important holdings of Marsh's Library without anybody suspecting," said Noreen, warming to the possibility.

Now Bing's ears had pulled back, and her eyes flashed from

the books on the table to the ornate oak shelves of the bookcases at the front of the room. "Brian, as I said, *was* without doubt an expert. Also, he had the time and inclination, I believe, to pursue such a . . . project. Some other collectors have neither, but they possess far more money. And a complete, unimpeachable collection of fifteenth-through-eighteenth-century original editions might command a veritable fortune. No two ways about it.

"Do you recall what happened to the treasures that were pilfered from the Russian National Library in St. Petersburg?"

"I believe I read something about that," said Noreen.

McGarr looked impassive; he had never heard of the library, much less the theft. He pulled on his cigarette.

"Over a period of years, the cream of their medieval Jewish manuscripts were stolen. Thirty-eight texts in all were taken—Torah scrolls, Talmudic commentaries, marriage contracts, and books of psalms and prayers dating to the thirteenth century. The only hint that the librarians had that their collection might have been purloined was when texts, the like of which the librarians believed they had in their collection, began showing up on the international market with asking prices in the millions of dollars.

"The loss was only discovered when an Israeli diplomat and Hebrew scholar asked to view a few of the over seventeen thousand items. It seems a former library employee, who had since escaped to the West, had substituted other, less valuable documents for the thirty-eight documents he took with him. He had shuffled hundreds of items in an attempt to cover up the crime.

"Most of the valuable documents had been woven through a number of dealers and sold to private collectors and were lost. The asking price for one manuscript was ten million dollars. When the prospective buyer called back with a counter-offer, he was told that it had already been sold. For close to the asking price!

"I'll let you decide what the 'cream' of Marsh's Library might have been worth, had . . . nature not intervened and Brian had gone through with his scheme."

Conclusion? From Charlotte Bing's point of view, Brian Herrick's death had been fortuitous, *if* he had intended what she supposed and *if* whatever other books he had removed from Marsh's Library had not already been sold. "Then you believe Herrick's intent was to pilfer and sell the cream of Marsh's Library?"

"Again—I won't know until I conduct an inventory, but how else could you explain that?" She pointed to the stained page where Herrick's head had been resting and that was still opened on the table. "His copying Swift's marginalia into a volume of the *History of the Rebellion?*"

Something on the stained page caught Bing's eye, and she reached into her purse for her eyeglasses.

Meanwhile, Noreen said, "Perhaps it was just more of his *playing* at being like Swift?"

"Not likely," Bing snapped dismissively. She pointed to the two other books. "Cicero is not Swift. *Le Rommant Galliot de la Rose* is not Swift. I also happen to know that Brian's finances were not what they would seem." By the house, she meant. "He was spoiled and profligate. Nothing but the best would do him. In everything! He squandered his father's generous bequest, and for the last few years he had been living off his siblings' generosity."

"How do you know all this?"

"Brian, being a genius, was beyond all the humdrum details of life." There was definite sarcasm in that. "Unlike

Swift himself, he couldn't even manage his own correspondence, which he left to me via Dictaphone. As *deputy* keeper."
Fitting on her glasses, she craned her head and looked down at the page of Clarendon's *History of the Rebellion* that Herrick had evidently been copying into when he died.

McGarr explained, "That last bit—the date—only became visible when the pathologist moved his head."

The inscription was written in a hand different from the carefully formed, Swift-like letters above. Dashed off *in extremis* while Herrrick was dying, it was only, "9-5-'11." The videotape showed him writing it.

"Mean anything to you?" he asked.

"I don't think it does. That's over eighty years ago."

"Can you think of any reason that he would write something like that as his last . . ."

"Words?" Bing straightened up and removed her glasses. "I have no idea, but Brian was himself, wasn't he? Or, rather, Swift. To the end."

Nevertheless, Herrick had to have known he was dying; the videotape revealed as much.

What else? McGarr looked around him. "Who cleaned the house?"

"He rang up a cleaning service whenever the four bins in the kitchen were crammed with dishes or the dust balls became too much for him. Or before . . . company."

Which cleaning must have occurred just before Herrick died, McGarr concluded, the dishes filling only one set-tub and the house being quite clean. It would make any fingerprint identifications that the Tech Squad discovered that much more pertinent. "Was Herrick an alcoholic?"

Charlotte Bing cocked her head, considering. "Certainly he wouldn't have admitted to it. But, did he drink to excess?

Whenever he drank, which was irregularly—when out with friends, at race meetings, which he was fond of, whenever he would stage"—she shook her head—"a 'Frollick.' At those times, he would go to an off-license and purchase whatever amount he planned to drink." Bing looked away suddenly and blushed, having revealed her knowledge of the details of a "Frollick."

"But he knew that about himself," she hurried on, "and kept no stocks of alcohol in the house. In some ways, Brian had great discipline."

"Two liter bottles of Glenfinnan being great discipline?" McGarr asked.

"That wasn't like Brian. One, perhaps, but not two. And I never knew him to plump for anything but a bottle of Paddy. 'It's only firewater for cowboys and Injuns,' he would say, when on a toot. In fact, I wouldn't know where he'd even purchase Glenfinnan in Dublin."

McGarr had an idea from the tax stamps on the bottle and a message left on the answering machine, but that would come later.

He waited, but she had no more to say. "When do you plan to begin your inventory?"

"This morning, as soon as I can."

"Well"—McGarr glanced at Ruth Bresnahan and Hugh Ward, who were now entering the conservatory, turning this way and that to admire the handsome bookshelves, the plants along both walls, the table, the stage—"I'd appreciate your remaining here a bit longer. There're some identifications I'd like you to help me with." He pointed to the stage where McKeon had earlier set up a television and a VCR. "I also thought you might recognize some of the voices on the telephone answering machine."

"As you wish," Bing replied distantly. "But only because you've asked. I don't view such things willingly."

Turning to Noreen, McGarr said, "Shall I see you at home? Or will I phone you later?"—for your opinion, he meant.

Noreen was confused. "I don't understand."

McGarr tried out his "innocent" smile. "Why, I've taken up too much of your time already. I hope I haven't kept you away from the shop too long."

"Not by half. If you think I'm leaving this room after all I've heard, you're daft. Flick on the frolic." She pointed to the television.

McGarr hunched his shoulders, knowing it was pointless to argue with her. "You'll wish you had. Where's Bernie?" he asked Bresnahan and Ward.

"Last time I saw him, he was in the master bedroom," said Ward.

"Reading, no doubt."

"Now that you mention it, Chief—he had a book in his hands." Bresnahan pulled a chair away from the library table and sat, crossing her long, shapely legs before her. She was a tall woman who was richly curved, and both her stylish clothes and long, haughty face belied her origins in rural Kerry.

Small, square, dark, and natty, Ward leaned against an edge of the table where he could both see the television and admire her without having to stare.

Said McGarr, "We'll just have to start without him."

"Sure and he's seen it before," said Ward. "By now he's got it down by heart."

Which was not quite the operative organ, McGarr thought.

6

Supporting Cast

MCGARR AIMED THE REMOTE-CONTROL DEVICE at the television and VCR, then settled himself on the edge of the table near Ward.

At first they heard only a concertina playing a sprightly jig, but as the television brightened, they saw:

PRESENTING: A Frollick
(Inspired by Swift)

The screen went black again, and a man's deep voice was heard to intone, *"Pars minima est ipsa Puella sui."*

"Is that Herrick?" McGarr asked.

Charlotte Bing nodded. "Drunk, by the sound of him."

"Quoting from Ovid, I believe," said Noreen, rising to the challenge of Herrick's pedantry. "It translates, 'A woman is the least part of herself,' you know—when stripped of . . . artificial aids. Swift employed the quote as a subtitle to his poem 'A Beautiful Young Nymph Going to Bed' in the edition that was published by Roberts in 1734. Ovid being as . . . *sublime* a misogynist as his admirer Swift."

"How do you know all of that?" McGarr asked Noreen.

Feigning nonchalance, she replied. "Why—I read Swift as an undergraduate in Trinity. And wrote a long paper on his poetry, which at the time was being ignored, largely because few seemed to know what to make of it."

McGarr paused the video and waited. He had not had the opportunity to go to university, but he was an inveterate reader who remembered nothing with the specificity of his wife. Her ready command of culture never ceased to amaze him.

"Swift, like Herrick—or, rather, Herrick, like Swift—was an enigmatic character perhaps by his own design. There was the public Swift, who, as a moralist, questioned authority on many of the important issues of his day. Then there was the other Swift, who in his private writings seemed only able to love women from afar—"

"Virgins," Charlotte Bing supplied.

"Or, at least, virgins to him, some think. There were 'Stella,' 'Varina,' and 'Vanessa,' he dubbed them: three women with whom he maintained a voluminous and intimate correspondence but, some have theorized, nothing more. On the other hand, there were the women of his poems, who were—"

"Whores." Again it was Bing.

"—well, let's say women . . . espied unromantically. Also slatterns and tarts. Remember, it was the beginning of the lusty and antiromantic Augustan age, and, even though Dean of Saint Patrick's, Swift was not beyond taking the odd cup and—again some believe—the odd—"

"Wench."

"Although there's little proof of that, since he was obsessively secretive. Still, he never married and remained childless throughout his life, again, as far as we know."

When it appeared Noreen would say no more, McGarr reactivated the machine.

The title of the "Frollick" disappeared, and, as the screen brightened again, it showed Brian Herrick, sitting naked in the tall, padded-leather chair in which his corpse was found. But it was a much younger Herrick, the black-and-white film evidently having been copied onto the videotape prior to the taping. His hands were gripping the arms of the chair, and his legs were spread so that he was visible in all his completeness.

Charlotte Bing rose from her chair. "What is this—some kind of trick? That's Brian . . . twenty years ago."

"Please"—McGarr touched her arm—"hang on for a moment. All I need are a few identifications, and then you can go."

Said Ward in an undertone to McGarr, "You can say one thing for 'The Dean.' He had a Gulliver, all right."

Noreen began to giggle. "Very witty, Hughie. *Very.*"

"Leave it to you to notice that," said Bresnahan to Ward, shaking her luxurious waves of auburn hair.

"And you mean to tell me, *you* didn't? No matter what else he might have been, you can't deny he was well manned."

"Now you're being vulgar."

"Well—it's a vulgar performance, from what I hear."

But the camera had panned in on Herrick's face. With a wry smile and bright, mischievous eyes, he began declaiming:

Apollo, god of light and wit
Could verse inspire, but seldom writ:
As handsome as my Lady's page;
Sweet five and twenty was his age.

His wig was made of sunny rays,
He crowned his youthful head with bays:

Herrick pointed to the laurel wreath that rested on an art-
ful tangle of blond curls.

"Was he ever blond?" Noreen asked.

"Only for Frollicks," said Charlotte Bing. "He lived for
them."

And died, thought McGarr, as they would soon see.

Not all the court of heaven could show
So nice and so complete a beau.
Yet with his beauty, wealth, and parts,
Enough to win ten thousand hearts;
No vulgar deity above
Was so unfortunate in love.

For Corinna, pride of Hammond Lane
Is the nymph for whom he sighs in vain.

Herrick pointed to the stage. There, a strikingly beautiful
girl—or perhaps a diminutive woman—was shown climbing
the stage stairs and opening a door, as though entering a boudoir. She was dressed in eighteenth-century garb, complete
with a high-powdered wig, much facial makeup, and a décol-
letage bodice that made two bright mounds of her breasts.

Herrick's voice continued, narrating from off camera:

Years ago, she was no drab,
He loved her, then she turned to flab.
For his love she struggled, must be admit',
To stem the flux of thighs, tummy and . . . wit.

The stage darkened momentarily, and when the lights came back on, another, somewhat taller, older woman had taken the younger, diminutive woman's place. Otherwise, they were similarly dressed.

Now, never did the Black Pits boast
So bright a battered, strolling toast
Returning at the midnight hour;
Four storeys climbing to her bower;
Then seated on a three-legged chair,
Takes off her artificial hair:

The woman sat and proceeded to act out the verses that Herrick was reciting. Removing the hair, she was seen to be bald. She tossed the wig on the dressing table, then turned to the camera that panned in on her much-painted face.

Now, picking out a crystal eye,
She wipes it clean, and lays it by.

"What? No!" Ruth Bresnahan objected. "Did she really do that?"

Said Ward, "Either that, or she's a great woman for the long wink."

"It's sick!"

"Nothing of the kind—it's comedy."

"Bent!"

"Not yet. From what Bernie told me, the bent part is yet to come. Where is he anyway?"

Her eyebrows from a mouse's hide,
Stuck on with art on either side,

Pulls off with care, and first displaying 'em,
Then in a play-book smoothly lays 'em.

"Chief—do I have to watch this?"

McGarr only shrugged; Bresnahan had certainly witnessed more hideous sights in her now several years with the Murder Squad. He wondered what bothered her most—the patent ugliness of the women, or the fact that a *woman* was being sent up.

Now dexterously her plumpers draws,
That serve to fill her hollow jaws.

The bald, one-eyed woman pulled something from either cheek and laid them on the table.

Untwists a wire, and from her gums
A set of teeth completely comes.
Pulls out the rags contrived to prop
Her flabby dugs, and down they drop.

"Well—I've had quite enough of this." Bresnahan stood. "If you don't mind, Chief, I'd prefer to learn about this sec- ondhand, which I'm sure I will," she said directly to Ward, as she turned and left.

"Now—what did I do?" Ward asked. "What *am* I doing but my job of work?"

"And *loving* every sordid moment!"

"Ah, stay, Rut'ie—you'll be missing the best part."

Bresnahan stormed toward the bookshelves and the kitchen beyond.

Proceeding on, the lovely goddess
Unlaces next her steel-ribbed bodice;
Which by the operator's skill,
Press down the lumps, the hollows.
Up goes her hand, and off she slips
The bolsters that supply her hips.
With gentlest touch, she next explores
Her shankers, issues, running sores;

"There it is," said Noreen, "a major strain in the Irish comic tradition—the mind making fun of the body and pushing the grotesque to the point where it becomes macabre."

"That it is," said Ward.

"It was a treatment used by Gaelic poets long before Swift, but never more devotedly than he, who sent up human pride whenever he could—here women wishing to appear more beautiful than they are. But he's sending up women *in general.* What's that famous quote of his that rather sums up the subject of his shrift?"

Yet again McGarr paused the video.

" 'I have ever hated all nations, professions, and communities,' he wrote in a letter to Pope, " 'and all my love is towards individuals: for instance, I hate the tribe of lawyers, but I love Counsellor Such-a-one, and Judge Such-a-one: so with physicians . . . But principally I hate and detest that animal called man, although I heartily love John, Peter, Thomas, and so forth.'

"Of course, Swift wrote this particular poem in his dotage, when by all reports he was ga-ga."

Charlotte Bing chimed in, "Which doesn't diminish the fact that the Deans, both of them, were Freudian archetypes—misogynistic, anal-hoarding, necrophilic personalities. Neither of them knew their fathers, and may, therefore, have been in love with their mothers. Guilt-ridden because of their lust, they actually detested women and wished to vilify them any chance they got. To label them corrupt! To call them whores!"

It was the second time that she had used that word. McGarr pointed the remote device at the video and pressed the button.

Effects of many a sad disaster,
And then to each applies a plaster.
She takes a bolus e'er she sleeps;
And then between two blankets creeps.

"Corinna" popped something into her toothless mouth and then began settling herself into the low cot on the stage. Suddenly, she stopped. Raising her shiny pate, she squinted her one eye, trying to peer past the stage lights. Spake she:

Aye? What there? Who there think I spy?
With me one discerning, rheumy eye?
A peeping Sean methinks he is,
From his bony points and leering viz.
Or could it be me darlin' Apollo,
Ripe beauty he often follows.

Corinna climbed out of the bed and padded to the edge of the stage, her large, fallen breasts swaying on her protuberant stomach. Her nipples were the size of small targets. Her shanks were thin, her feet splayed.

Sure, 'tis he, I ken his member,
Bent, bedad, like in coldest December.

Ward turned and looked behind him, as though to see if Bresnahan was still in the large room, perhaps watching from the aisle between the bookshelves.

But we'll fix him up, and right the wrong
With some wily help from memory strong.

With that, like some Yahoo wench—McGarr could only think—she hopped off the stage, landing flat-footed in front of the camera. She smiled fully into the lens, baring her toothless gums and old, cracked tongue.

No trick of mine, I speak in trow
It's deep inside his laureled brow
Oft' times he sees what he will see,
When all along 'tis only me.

Gradually, the camera angle had been changing, as it followed the hag down from the stage toward Herrick. Now the picture was being shot from above the tall chair, looking down on a much older Herrick and not one woman but two standing to either side.

The younger, diminutive woman had reappeared, and she, too, was naked, apart from the long tresses of a blond wig and the heavy, eighteenth-century makeup that "Corinna" (the elder) had removed. The younger, however, had the figure and lustrous skin of a voluptuous girl, and the contrast between the two was startling and off-putting, like a "before" and "after" picture out of Hogarth.

Using the Pause button on the VCR remote device, McGarr froze the action. "The first thing I want you to note is the ring of keys beside Herrick on the table. Second, who are those women?"

"The young one, the *vixen*," Charlotte Bing said with some force, "is Joneux Ariane Danvers-Forde. Brian hired her a little over a year ago as an assistant in the Delmas Conservation Bindery. When I interviewed her for the position, she said she wanted the job desperately, that she was from Paris, and she couldn't stand life out in the country, where she lives with a husband, might I add. I suppose this attests to the level of her desperation, although Brian might well have understood that she shared his predilections when he took her on. He was quite acute at recognizing kindred spirits."

"Yourself included?" McGarr asked.

"God, no," Bing shot back. "I was hired by the former keeper. Before—*long* before—Brian took over."

"Danvers-Forde, you say?" Noreen asked. "There's only one Danvers-Forde family that I know of in Ireland. That couldn't be the little French girl that Nigel Danvers-Forde's son, Alastair, married, could it? Remember, Peter—we went to their wedding, three or four years ago in Dunlavin."

It must have been a dull time, since McGarr did not have the foggiest recollection. He would have remembered the bride, however, had she appeared as she was on the screen.

"His family was against the marriage. It seems that her origins are rather obscure. She's from someplace like Tunisia. As I remember the story, Alastair met her in a bar. Or a bistro. No—a cabaret in Paris, where she was a dancer." Noreen's memory for gossip was also capacious. "Oh, my," she said, staring at the screen.

"What about the other woman?"

Ward spoke up. "Her name is Teddy Baer. That's"—he spelled it. "She does a comic striptease at the Poop Deck, which is a bucket of blood in Stoney Batter." It was an old industrial area of Dublin. "Sunday mornings at eleven. You know, for the irreligious element in the city. She's supported, if you don't mind my saying, by a group of middle-aged rockers who used to play in show bands. *They* can play anything, and they're brilliant. Teddy's husband collects two quid a head at the door—kind of a sheepish little fella, ten, maybe twenty, years younger than she. He's called—are you ready for this?—'Bunny.' "

"Bunny Baer," McGarr said.

"That's right."

"How do you know that?" Bresnahan asked from the shadows of the bookshelves, where she had evidently been watching.

"What d'you think I did with me time when you were on your 'extended holiday'?" He meant the nine-month leave of absence Bresnahan took following her father's death the year past.

"You sought out women who would make fools of themselves?"

Ward cocked his head. "That's one interpretation, I suppose."

"You sought out women who would degrade themselves and confirm the poor opinion that men like you have of them?"

"I didn't *seek out* anything of the sort. I just went up there with the lads after a workout for a jar and a bit of a laugh. She holds up her breasts, like this"—Ward turned and held up his hands, as if he were grasping melons—"and says, 'Would any of yiz give me a second glance, if these was two fried eggs?' She continues on with the joke, mentioning her rashers, her puddin's, and her tripes. It's gas."

"So—you admit it then?"

"What—to *being* there? Yes, I was there."

"And *laughing*?"

"I roared! You'd have to see it yourself. She changes the show every week. It's never the same old soap."

"You've changed my entire opinion of you."

Ward raised a hand and pincered his temples. "I'd thought you'd left the room."

"Would that have made a difference?"

Said McGarr, "We'll skip through this next part," which was Herrick's last fling.

"Oh, really—why?" Noreen asked.

"What—you want to see them *work* on him?"

"Well, you did, didn't you? And I was hoping to get an idea of the entire . . . flavor of the situation."

"Trust me—it's *tangy*. But you can see it later, if you like. Alone." McGarr faded the picture and punched the Fast-forward lever. After just over two minutes had elapsed, he brightened the screen and switched to normal speed. Sated, eyes glassy, Herrick was seen slumped down in the large chair.

Suddenly, the diminutive woman—Joneux Ariane Danvers-Forde—appeared in the picture beside Herrick's chair. But for a pair of skimpy black tights, she was still naked. "I should be leaving you now, Dean. You know how Alastair gets when I'm too late." Her accent was slight but fetching, and Herrick's hand fell on her buttocks.

"She certainly is an attractive *physical* specimen, is she not?" Noreen said. "Tiny as she is."

"With the morals of a pit viper," remarked Charlotte Bing.

"Why do you choose to stay with that . . . Puritan dunce, when you can have me, freedom, and all I possess?"

"We'll see," she replied.

Said Noreen, "The Danvers-Fordes have bags of money, world-class money, more money than Herrick could ever have possessed."

"Will I see you tomorrow?" Herrick asked. As she moved toward him to kiss his forehead, Herrick's other hand came up and grazed her rosebud nipples.

"Perhaps. I'll have to see if I can get away. Don't get up, I'll let myself out the front." She moved into the room, toward the bookshelves, the kitchen, and the rest of the house. They heard the sliding pocket doors open.

"Don't forget to lock the front door," Herrick called after her. "Speaking of which." With an effort, Herrick tried to pull himself up in his chair and reach for the ring of keys on the table. "Bunny!" he called. "Bunny—where the hell are you, when I need you?"

Another man's voice was then heard to say, "Will that be all, Doctor?"

"For one night? Of course. I'm not as young as I used to be."

"What about a drink? Can I pour you another?"

"Now, *that* you can, Bunny, me boy. And one for yourself, as well—I hate to drink alone. You deserve a good belt." Herrick smiled weakly and turned his head to the decanter on the table beside him, which was empty.

"Ah now, you know me and drink, Doctor—I'm just not suited to it, nor it to me."

"You mean not while there's business to be transacted. You're altogether the brilliant pimp, is what you are. A natural. You don't drink. You don't even boff the help, from what Teddy tells me. But who can blame you—a toothless old Cyclopean termagant like Teddy. She's an acquired taste, she is."

Baer began to object, but Herrick cut him off.

"And I commend the strategy, Bunny boy. Why truck—for

want of the more appropriate word—with younger whores, when there's the challenge of selling that old shoe to miscreants such as I for more money than she ever made at one sitting in all her professional life."

"Ah now, Doctor—"

Herrick's temper suddenly squalled. "And don't ah-Doctor me. She's a whore out of hell, and you know it. Which is her attraction. Now fetch the fresh bottle of the good stuff in the kitchen and *two* glasses. The Glenfinnan. You'll find it on the side. And fill up the decanter while you're about it!"

They heard footsteps on the flagstones and the sliding pocket doors open farther.

While Baer was gone, Herrick dozed, but other sounds could be heard in the room, including Teddy's unmistakable, raspy voice grousing as she dressed.

A second man, obviously Bunny Baer, now appeared with a full decanter and a second glass. He poured a goodly measure into both glasses. Turning, he handed one to Herrick and raised his own—a small, balding man in his early fifties with a red, windburned face. He was wearing a jogging suit that said ARSENAL in white piping. His narrow eyes were pink-rimmed but quick, hence the name, McGarr assumed. Bunny.

They raised glasses to each other, and Herrick drank his off in a swallow. But Baer merely placed his glass on the table behind him and slid it toward the decanter.

"That the husband?" McGarr asked.

"That's him," said Ward, as the tape kept running. "The bunny. Sits at a table in the stairwell up to the Poop Deck with the line going halfway around the block. Takes the two quid from you like it's the last he'll ever see. Folds the bills neatly into a little strongbox he brings along, eyes gleaming like they are there on the screen. Hardly says two words. Acts like he's not all there, but—"

But McGarr could only agree; he seemed quick enough for "the business" he was in. Or just business.

"You sound like a regular," said Bresnahan.

"It's just me excellent memory."

"For *significant* detail. T. and A.—isn't that what you call it?"

"Not me—I never mentioned that sexist acronym in my life. And speaking of significant detail, since some of us are concentrating on extraneous matters—Chief, could you spin back to where the Bunny puts his glass on the table and slides it toward the decanter."

McGarr complied.

"Can you run it now in slow motion?"

McGarr had to hold the remote device a bit away from him and squint. He was at an age when, sometime soon, he would have to be fitted with reading glasses. He discovered the button and rolled the tape forward.

"See—the keys are on the table when Bunny returns with the decanter. But after he pours the drinks, he gets himself between Herrick and the decanter and, unfortunately, the camera. He pushes his drink away, and the hand, coming back, picks up the keys and—there! Still, we can't actually see it—it goes right into his trouser pocket. Now, when he steps away from the table to let Herrick reach for the check in the book, the keys are gone."

"Very good, Hughie," Noreen said. "Don't you think so, Peter? I would never have noticed that."

McGarr had the first time he viewed the tape, which was the reason he had asked them earlier to mark the keys.

Now the screen was showing Herrick reaching over to the

table to set the empty glass down and pick something out of the open book on the table. "That enough for you, Bunny man? It includes what I owe you from the last few times as well. I want to thank you for being patient. And *sticking* with me." Herrick began a chuckle that collapsed into a wet, hacking cough.

Slumped like that in the chair, he was not a pretty sight, and as different from his younger self who had been presented at the beginning of the tape as Teddy Baer was from Joneux Ariane Danvers-Forde.

Baer stared down at what was obviously a bank check and then flashed Herrick a smile of nakedly unselfconscious avarice. He looked for a moment like a small child who had been given a sweet.

"You bring that here, you greedy bastard," Teddy Baer bawled from off camera. "That's mine. *I* worked for it, not you. And I won't have you putting it on the nose of any damned dog."

"Not when it came from the tail," said Herrick loud enough to be heard by all.

Baer's smile fell. "Ah, now, Doctor—you shouldn't be slaggin' Teddy that way. She was a looker in her time, so she was. You've no idea of the life she's had to lead, through no fault of her own."

"Looking at her, me imagination riots. Admit it, Bunny boy, your Teddy is shot, gone, offal."

"Now, Doctor," Baer objected again.

"But, to be fair to the randy bitch, flesh is flesh. How can one orifice, *qua* orifice, be distinguished from another, except in the imagination? And, after all, as Augustine had it, *'Inter urines et faeces nascimur,'*" Herrick went on, suddenly very drunk, "which Swift harpooned thus:

Should I the Queen of Love refuse
Because she rose from stinking Ooze?"

Baer's eyes were now narrow and joyless, obviously under-standing only the intent of what Herrick was saying. Folding the check, he slipped it into an interior pocket of his ARSE-NAL warmup jacket. "Let me pour you some more, sir."

"Good Bunny."

"Don't think it's over," Teddy again called out. "You'll turn that over the moment we get home, Bunny Baer, or I'll give you da t'rashin' of yehr loife!"

A sparkle appeared in Baer's eyes, as though he enjoyed the prospect of the threat. Baer handed Herrick the fresh drink, then moved away from the table out of view of the camera.

They heard another door open, and Teddy say again, "Give it over!"

"Speaking of which." With effort Herrick pulled himself out of the chair and looked down at the table. "Bunny"—he called after the other man—"did you take my keys?"

"We'll put it away for travel money." It was Baer's voice. "*Give* it!"

"You know, that trip we'll be taking soon."

Herrick moved away from the table and toward the camera, his genitals swinging loosely in the shadow of his large stom-ach and between his thin thighs. When he had passed beyond the camera, they heard him shout, "Bunny—you sneaky little cunt, did you take my keys?"

"No, Doctor. Of course not, Doctor. What would I want with your keys?"

"What *wouldn't* you?" Herrick muttered.

Bawled Teddy, "Give it, or I'll break yehr fookin' head, so I will."

"Do I have to be subjected to this much longer?" Charlotte Bing asked.

"You've heard the last words," said McGarr.

There followed another two-minute interval, in which they heard car doors slam and a car start up and drive off. Then there was silence for a while, until the conservatory door was closed. Herrick reappeared, still plainly laboring under whatever he had drunk.

Yet at the table he reached for the decanter and poured himself another and drank that. Tugging the tall, heavy chair around, he then fell into it at the table.

McGarr froze the action. "Notice how full that decanter is. It's a half-gallon container, I'd hazard, with how much in it?"

"A little less than half-filled," said Noreen.

"Just about a full liter," said Ward. "Less, say, a pint."

"When I came across it last night, the decanter had only an inch or two in the bottom. Both liter bottles—we'll learn when we listen to the answering machine—were a gift, I found them in the kitchen. Empty."

Said Ward, "Bernie must have got here first."

McGarr switched off the television and the VCR. He stood. "Now, Ms. Bing—if you'll accompany me into the kitchen. Perhaps you can identify the voices on the answering machine."

"But what about the rest of the videotape?" Noreen asked.

"It's just of Herrick. Dying."

Noreen was plainly disappointed. "You didn't let us see the first bit, and now the second. How am I supposed to give you an opinion based on incomplete information?"

McGarr decided he would not remind her that he had asked her there to give him an opinion on old and rare books. "Whatever poisoned him was quick-acting but nasty stuff. It made him violently, convulsively ill before he actually expired. I don't think Miss Bing wants to see that."

Charlotte Bing closed her eyes and shook her head. "May I meet you in the kitchen?" She then left the room.

"But, as I said," McGarr went on, "you can see it yourself."

"When?"

"Later."

"Later when?"

"I'll have Bernie make a copy, and I'll bring it home."

"Well—isn't that a bit much? Can't I just rewind it and watch it here?"

"You mean you're not interested in the voices on the answering machine."

"I'm sure I wouldn't recognize them anyway," she said, taking the remote device from his hands.

7

A Nip o' the
Good Stuff

OUT IN THE KITCHEN, McGarr had some difficulty operating the player that the Tech Squad had left to enhance the voices. "Where's Bernie?" Being the squad's chief interrogator, McKeon was acquainted with most types of audio devices.

But before Ward could leave the kitchen to go look for McKeon, McGarr got the machine working.

The first voice was that of a man who spoke excellent English but with a slight accent that McGarr guessed was Dutch. "Brian, it's Jan." (Pronounced "Yah-n.") "It's Thursday evening, about quarter to seven. This afternoon I took the chance of leaving you a little present I picked up in Scotland. I put it in back of the Janus figure beside your front door. Thinking you might have left town on a little buying tour, I rang up Charlotte at the library, but she said you told her you were going home. I just don't want you to forget and miss it in the dark. It took some doing getting that lot through Customs. Drink it in good health.

"On another matter, let me remind you you're late again with your payment on that loan." There was a slight pause, and then, "What a shame it would be for you to lose all you worked so hard for these many years. I know you have the money or can get it. And we have our agreement."

McGarr stopped the machine. "Was that Jan—"

"—deKuyper," Bing supplied. "As I think I mentioned to you last night, he's the conservator of the Delmas Conservation Bindery. He's Dutch, originally, although he's been in this country quite some time. May I sit down?" Charlotte Bing pulled out a kitchen chair and eased herself into it, looking now as pale as she did last evening before her migraine came on.

Next came her own voice, inquiring, "Brian? It's Tuesday, half-five in the evening. We haven't heard from you now since Thursday last, which is unusual, and we're rather concerned over here at Marsh's. We had Dr. Drayton in from Cambridge to take a look at our Cicero's *Letters,* and he was disappointed not to see you again. He asked for your phone number, and I was embarrassed to have to tell him, as you requested, that it was unavailable. Please give me a call when you can."

The third call was from deKuyper again. "Herrick. It's Wednesday morning, and I still have nothing from you. As I told you when we first made our agreement—like it or not, you've involved my career in your project, and you must pay me what you owe me."

Said Charlotte Bing, "I'm so glad I phoned you," meaning McGarr.

McGarr switched off the machine. "Why? Because you think deKuyper was blackmailing Herrick?"

"It would appear so, wouldn't it? His mentioning his career. If, say, Brian had accomplished a removal of the best of Marsh's, and eventually it was discovered, people would want to know why deKuyper never suspected, him being the conservator. Or even me, being deputy keeper."

Noreen patted Bing's shoulder. "But you *did* suspect. In time, I should think."

"Let us hope."

McGarr activated the machine again.

Another man's voice was heard, saying in a decidedly lazy Oxbridge accent, "Dr. Herrick, this is Alastair Danvers-Forde. Would my wife be there? Would you or she give me a call? I believe we have several matters to discuss."

The final voice was Bunny Baer; it could be nobody else. "Doctor—we're not stoppin' round t'noight. Or any udder noight. Yeh're a filthy, fookin' bah-stard, so ye' are. Und dere's a end to it."

McGarr switched off the machine.

Charlotte Bing asked, "Do you really think Brian was poisoned?"

McGarr hunched his shoulders. "It would appear so."

"But . . . how?"

McGarr shook his head. "We're performing further tests. It might take some time."

He was both right and wrong.

Because upstairs in the master bedroom Detective Superintendent Bernie McKeon did not understand why he felt so ill.

He had found the ornate silver flask, as McGarr said he would, inside the Bible on a shelf beneath the nightstand by the tall, canopied bed in the master bedroom. When he unscrewed the shiny jigger cap and pulled out the cork, the mildly pungent aroma of rare, aged malt whiskey wafted up to his nose.

It was topped right up; nobody had taken so much as a sip. And tip-top whiskey it was in every way, he could tell.

Although usually a Powers man himself (an acceptable brand of Irish whiskey), he considered himself expert in the stuff. Whiskey and McKeon went way back to his youth in the hills of County Monaghan, where his father used to make his own.

Still, he only took the smallest sip, knowing he had the full day before him. Also, he had never yet breached McGarr's cardinal rule in regard to indulging while on a job. "If you find drink and drink it, don't get drunk."

Nevertheless, he had appreciated the pleasant bite of its going down. And then the warm-all-over feeling it gave him, the slight headiness (stoked by the fires of the night before), and the glow that only malt can impart. When he began to feel strange.

Strange how? he asked himself. At first restless, he guessed. He shuffled down the wide, curved staircase, thinking he would nip into the conservatory and view the skin flick for the third time.

But instead he looked into his "office" in the sitting room, hoping for any further information from the coroner or the report from the Tech Squad, which was still outstanding. But nothing. Not even the telephone had rung while he was there watching. And he wanted it to, which was strange, since the infernal gadget was the bane of his life. For some reason, he was feeling . . . anxious, and he stood there staring down at it for the longest time.

It occurred to him then that maybe he had not taken enough of the whiskey to settle his stomach, which was now beginning to bother him, and he would put down one more small belt before catching the videotape. Back up at his cache in the Bible, he could scarcely keep his shaking hands from spilling the precious elixir. But he tossed off a capful, and then another. The pain in his gut now felt like somebody had stuck him with a knife and was ripping it up to his throat.

McKeon barely got the cork back in and the cap twisted down when he grew suddenly, overwhelmingly nauseous and knew he was going to be sick. Tossing the flask on the top of the bed, he rushed toward the toilet as well as he was able. Now he was sweating, barely able to breathe, and something like froth was forming at the corners of his mouth.

Falling to the tiles, McKeon grabbed hold of the toilet and vomited for all he was worth. Worse, while vomiting, he believed he messed his trousers, but he was too ill even to check. Also, there was something very wrong with his heart, which was fluttering, and it occurred to him that what was now happening to him he had seen before—on the videotape. He was dying, poisoned, like the victim, Herrick. And he had better act fast.

Still retching, he twisted his bulky body around and pulled off a shoe. The effort to do only that took so much out of him that he blacked out for a moment, but the sharp pain of his face smacking the tiles brought him around. He had to tell himself, "It's the only thing you have left to do in your life, if you're to live," to make himself swing the shoe at the pipes of the sink. Once. Again. And again and again, before he passed out.

Down in the kitchen, where the tape of the answering machine had just ended, the others heard the banging.

Said Hughie Ward, "There mustn't be any tissue in the jakes." He glanced up at McGarr, then both men turned and sprinted for the stairs.

8

Containers and Keys

FOUR HOURS LATER McGarr and the others were allowed into Bernie McKeon's room in St. Vincent's Hospital. The only thing that had saved him was the suggestion of an African resident doctor that intermuscular injections of morphine might control his convulsions. "I've seen this kind of thing before when people have eaten wild berries and plants."

There followed a series of gastric lavages and other emergency medical procedures that McGarr and his staff were not allowed to witness.

"That the morphine worked," said the same resident doctor, "might narrow the field of possible poisons. Not all respond to such prophylaxis."

McGarr thanked the doctor and phoned the information in to the Tech Squad, which had already received the flask of whiskey from which McKeon had drunk. Results from the analysis of the fluid within should be forthcoming, McGarr was assured.

Now McKeon's wife—an older, child-worn woman who was given to much actual hand-wringing—said, "I don't know what we would have done, had we lost him." She turned to

Noreen and Ruth Bresnahan, who were standing on one side of the bed; McGarr and Ward were on the other, sharing a windowsill that looked out on a Saturday-busy Merrion Road.

"He never let me work a day in my life."

"I never knew that about Bernie," said Ruth Bresnahan. "And why is that?"

Ward's eyes met McGarr's before caroming off. Bresnahan's militant feminism was a cross that he would have to bear. The knowledge did not make the burden any more supportable.

"When we were young," Una McKeon went on, her eyes still reddened from her tears of the night before, "it wasn't the thing for a woman to work, not with a husband on the Guards. And then with the kids coming along, one right after another—"

To a total of twelve—no, thirteen, one having been lost tragically—McGarr recollected.

"—there was no time for me to work. You know, *work* work."

Having a fair portion of the same, albeit unpaid, woman's work at home. Fair? McGarr understood empathetically that there had been probably nothing *fair* about it. Either way.

"Still and all," said Bresnahan, who herself was scarcely thirty and looked like a model out of some haute couture magazine, "did you not feel as though you were being pre- vented from"—she crimped her long fingers, the nails of which had been manicured to the perfection of seductive blood-red talons—*"achieving?"*

"Quite the opposite," replied Una McKeon. "I kept saying novenas that I would *achieve* less, but the babbies just kept arriving. I'd only have to look at yehr mahn." She swung her chin at the figure in the hospital bed. "And there I was, blown up like a balloon."

Bresnahan's own eyes, which were the color of dark smoke, followed the gaze of the other woman; it was as though she were appreciating the perfidy of the man, who had been her mentor for most of her career, for the first time. "The rotter," she said. "Just to please himself."

"Well, let me say—Bernie wasn't the only party pleased," said Una McKeon. "He has a way about him, so he does. I hope this doesn't hinder him at all."

McGarr rattled the sheaf of papers in his hands. "Shall we get on with it?"

"If you'd like me to leave," Una McKeon began saying, but McGarr waved her back into her chair; she should know something about how her husband was nearly murdered. "What we have is this. Interrupt me if I leave anything out." McGarr began summarizing what they knew about the death of Brian Herrick:

Thursday week in the afternoon—as Charlotte Bing had related—Herrick had told her he would be taking some time off to do some private work at home. Herrick did not go there immediately, however (or, at least, if he did, he did not answer the bell), since Jan deKuyper had called in to the house in Shrewsbury Road some time later. Finding nobody at home, he left a packet behind a statuary on the porch; in it were two liter bottles of Glenfinnan whiskey, which deKuyper had purchased, evidently at Herrick's request, while in Scotland.

DeKuyper also rang up Marsh's Library, inquiring after Herrick, only to be told by Bing that she thought he was at home. Later in the evening, deKuyper rang up Herrick, leaving a message on the answering machine about the Glenfinnan, and also making a demand for a monthly payment on a "loan," or—

"Blackmail, I bet," said Bresnahan. "That second call with the carry-on about his career is a veiled threat."

Ward nodded, as did Noreen. McGarr tended to agree.

At any rate, by that Thursday night, when Herrick's "Frollick" was staged, Herrick had retrieved the packet from the porch and evidently opened both bottles.

"Why *both* bottles?" Noreen asked.

McGarr explained: because Herrick had obviously filled the flask in the Bible in the bedroom from the bottle that contained the poison. It was that bottle—the second bottle—that Bunny Baer got for him at the end of the film, filling the decanter with its contents. The first bottle Herrick had already consumed with no ill effect, either to him or to anybody else.

"Wasn't *that* fortunate," Noreen again interjected. "There would have been four deaths instead of one. The bloody poisoner didn't care how many people he killed."

Said Ruth Bresnahan, "Unless it was one of the 'Frollickers' who planted the flask, so as to make it seem that the bottle had been spiked either before it entered the house or before they arrived."

Ward nodded and smiled. "Good thinking, Ruthie."

"Please don't patronize me, Superintendent. It's demeaning—to you."

McGarr went on: In the videotape, they had witnessed Baer pouring one of the lethal cups, and, of course, Herrick self-administered another, after the "Frollickers" had left the conservatory. At that point, the decanter was a little less than half-filled, and Herrick, who then became troubled, depleted it no farther. But when McGarr viewed Herrick's corpse a week later, there was only an inch or two of Glenfinnan—

"And it *was* Glenfinnan"—in the bottom, and that "I consumed with no harm."

"That practice *must* stop," said Noreen.

"Aye. Forthwith," chimed in Una McKeon.

"And isn't it illegal?"

"Certainly—if the victim would choose to press charges," Ward observed.

"Conclusion?" McGarr asked.

Bresnahan and Ward both began speaking at once, until Ward deferred.

"Thank you, Superintendent," she said.

Said Ward, "The analytical skills of subordinates should be evaluated from time to time, right, Chief?"

"Whoever spiked the bottle returned to the house sometime after Herrick's death and purged both the tainted liter bottle and the decanter of the poisoned fluid."

"Correct," said McGarr.

"But why?" Noreen asked.

Said Bresnahan, "Either to remove the direct evidence that Herrick had been poisoned, or because the poison, whatever we finally discover it to be, can be traced back to them."

"Also," McGarr interrupted, "we know from our experience that murderers always try too hard." He squinted down at the Tech Squad report. "This murderer is no exception. He washed and then dried the bottles, the decanter that was found on the table, and the two glasses on the table—both Herrick's and the one Bunny Baer poured for himself, and which spilled while Herrick was convulsing.

"The murderer even laid the glass back down on its side. The one thing he didn't think he could do was to remove the poison from the cap of the tainted bottle, which I have an idea must be cork, and so he took *both* caps with him. The Tech Squad went back twice; the caps to the bottles of Glenfinnan can't be found anywhere.

"Nor could the murderer remove the spilled liquor from the table, and scrapings taken by the Tech Squad contain a substance similar to one found in Herrick's blood and—I should imagine—in the flask Bernie drank from."

"Which means that there was a significant time lag between Herrick's death and whenever the murderer cleaned up," said Ward.

"Not necessarily," Bresnahan corrected. "The room was hot, and the Glenfinnan is forty percent alcohol or thereabouts."

"And might easily dry overnight," said Noreen, eyeing McGarr, who had once marred a choice end table at her parent's country home in Dunlavin with a glass, the bottom of which had been wet with whiskey.

"So much for the time lag."

"Well—at least the cleanup didn't happen that night," Bresnahan noted supportively. "Also, that person wasn't well enough acquainted with Herrick to have known about the flask."

Meaning it wasn't somebody who had shared both Herrick's bed and his taste for malt whiskey, McGarr thought. "Along that line of thinking, the Tech Squad discovered the fingerprints of a small woman on the furniture around the bed in the master bedroom, in the toilet there, and on the headboard and one of the lower posts of the bed, 'gripping it like a pole,' it says here. 'The prints, which were old, were rather obscured by the force of her grasp.' I think we can assume that Herrick's relationship with Mrs. Danvers-Forde was rather long-standing, probably dating from her employment at the library.

"Which brings us to the matter of the keys."

Charlotte Bing had a complete set that, she said, Herrick had given her years ago, even though Herrick had been heard to say plainly on the videotape that he would have to change the lock on the conservatory door *again,* now that he believed he had lost his keys.

Joneux Ariane Danvers-Forde had keys at least to the front door locks, because Herrick had asked her to lock up on her way out.

And, of course, there was Bunny Baer, whom they had watched nick Herrick's set off the conservatory table. Again on the videotape.

"DeKuyper, we can assume," McGarr concluded, "obviously didn't have keys, otherwise he would have slipped the packet with the two liter bottles of Glenfinnan inside the front door.

"What time do we have?"

"Half four," said Bresnahan, glancing at her new watch that, she had told Noreen, was a present from an admirer (not Ward).

Time to fetch Maddie from play school, McGarr thought. He turned to his wife. "What about the idea of you and Ruth picking up Maddie and dropping in on your parents in Dunlavin for the weekend? You might look up the Danvers-Fordes," if, indeed, some horsy gathering was not already in the works. "You could make everything easier for Ruthie."

"And I haven't really had the chance to *speak* to Ruth since her return," Noreen enthused, pleased to be continuing on with the investigation.

"I'll tackle deKuyper, who lives here in Dublin, and stay close to the office"—because of the countless other open murder files, McGarr meant.

"Hughie—you take the Baers, since you're already known to frequent the . . . what's the name of that kip?"

"The Poop Deck," Ward said somewhat sheepishly. "You know, like on a ship."

"Of fools," Bresnahan offered.

"I heard that."

"I was hoping you would. And remember this—if you bring Teddy Baer back to your flat, it's over between us. I simply refuse to compete with a toothless, one-eyed woman."

Noreen and Ruth began laughing uproariously.

"Oh, I see," said Ward weakly. "It's all right if you make fun of other women, but not when men do."

But their laughter had brought Bernie McKeon around. His wife, Una, moved to his side. He blinked and tried to say, "Well, now—" He tried again, "Well, now, here're all of yous. Are we in . . . heaven?"

"If he makes a crack about how it can't be because I'm here, I'll kill him," said Una McKeon.

"You know what I'd like?"

Said McGarr, "If he says a double whiskey, I'll kill him first."

"There's gratitude for you," said McKeon. "Amn't I after hearing you say that but for me, you wouldn't know *what* killed that old Heresy."

"Herrick," Ward corrected. "And we don't know that yet, either."

"What I'd like is a nice cup o' tay. Other than being parched, I feel rather in the pink, so I do."

"With or without?" Ward asked, making for the door.

"Sure, he's had enough morphine to fell a bull," said his wife. "That's where the *pink* is coming from."

"Really?" McKeon was alarmed. "Drugs? I've never had a drug in me life."

"Well, you have now," she went on. "How does it feel?"

It took McKeon some time to answer. "A bit disturbing, if you must know."

$\mathcal{P}art\ II$

ON SNARES
AND POISON
IN THE
PROVISION
OF LIFE

9

Opening

IT WAS NEARLY DARK by the time Noreen and Ruth Bresnahan picked up Maddie at school and headed southwest out of Dublin along the N-7.

Noreen was pleased to have Ruth living back in town after nearly a year's absence, and she was eager to know how the young woman's relationship with the elusive Hugh Ward was progressing. Noreen had formerly considered Ward an eternal bachelor and practicing ladies' man.

"So," she said, once having settled Maddie in the backseat of the large Rover, which was a hand-me-down from her well-off parents, "how's life in tandem?" Up ahead on the dual carriageway, an articulated lorry was rolling slowly along, its many lights making it look like a small moving city.

"If you mean do I like life back in the city," as opposed to the South Kerry Mountains where she had spent her rustication, "I do. I'd rather camp out in kip in Coolock," which was a working-class area of Dublin, "with mots and gurriers like the Baers, than to live in comfort among the muck, the cows, and the Culchies."

Now they had hit upon a topic dear to Noreen's heart—a

love triangle or, at least, an erstwhile love triangle. "Speaking of Culchie—didn't I read that *your* Culchie pulled off a narrow victory in the recent election?" For the Dail Eireann, Noreen meant, the national parliament. "*The* O'Suilleabhain," Noreen added mockingly; it had been how Rory O'Suilleabhain's mother had referred to him, even though there were many in County Kerry with the same surname.

But, at least superficially, Rory O'Suilleabhain probably deserved the preferment. Not only was he tall and dark with sculptured features and shoulders so wide they looked padded, he was also clever enough to have made his farm prosper and to have achieved significant position at a young age. With thin hips and eyes the color of Noreen's own, which were turquoise, he seemed like the perfect catch, but the problem was—Ruth had related to Noreen—he knew it. "I never met a more impervious ego in all my life."

Both sets of parents had assumed that, one day, O'Suilleabhain and Ruth, who was an only child, would marry and consolidate their two farms, which were large and contiguous. And in truth Ruth had secretly pined for Rory O'Suilleabhain for longer than she cared to remember, before "*The*" O'Suilleabhain had finally turned his attention to her nearly in his thirtieth year. But only a few months ago she had broken off her engagement to him in favor of the short, dark Hugh Ward. It was the sort of story that tickled the strings of Noreen McGarr's perennially romantic heart, though she suspected the diminuendo was not quite over, with *The* O'Suilleabhain currently in town for the sitting of the Dail. "Has he looked you up yet?"

"Better than that—he gave me this." Ruth held out her wrist to show Noreen her new wristwatch.

"The light's not good. What kind is it?"

"A Vacheron—"

"—Constantine? And gold! My God—he must have paid a bomb for that."

"His note said it was just a little 'friendship' present to show me that he was willing to let bygones be bygones. And—as I probably told you—he has gobs of money, more now that he has the political connection. It seems that he just won a contract to ship an enormous amount of beef to Libya."

"Note? You mean you still haven't actually met with him?" Noreen could scarcely keep her eyes on the road, wishing to read Ruth's features in the glare from the passing cars.

Bresnahan shook her handsome head. "The note went on to say he wanted me to keep track of the time that we were spending in the same city. And would I mind if he were to use me as a 'resource.' You know, give him some advice, were he to ring me up and ask."

Note? Noreen thought. It sounded more to her like a love letter. "And what class of advice, pray tell?"

"Oh—where to shop, what to wear, whom to know, I suspect. He doesn't want to make any *Culchie* mistakes, I'm thinking."

As he did with Ruth before she broke off the engagement with him, thought Noreen. He might be a Culchie, but he was a clever Culchie, and he was learning. "And how're you to manage the advice? Over dinner and wine in his hotel suite, I take it?"

"No—he's been good about that. He rang me up, though. Just to make sure I got his present and consented to keep it."

Which I see you did, Noreen concluded. With no little willingness. "And what does 'yehr mahn' think about this?"

She lengthened the Dublin pronunciation so that there would be no mistake she meant Ward.

"What *can* he?"

Which Noreen interpreted as what *would* he; Ward was too much experienced with women not to know the corrosive effects of acknowledged jealousy.

"But, you know—I expected him to say *something*. When he picked up the phone and it was Rory, he didn't even blink. He said, 'Oh, certainly. Let me get her for you,' then took his jacket and went out to the gym. It was he who encouraged me to keep the thing." Again Bresnahan admired the gold spangle on her wrist.

"You mean he didn't even question you about the call?"

"Not a word."

Noreen smiled. It was a situation that would bear close scrutiny. "But are you happy with Hughie?" It was a leading question; after all, they were the closest of friends.

"Oh, yes—immensely. He's *Hughie,* you know." Ruth flashed her smoky eyes at Noreen, as if Noreen would understand Ward's advantages. "And then he's such pleasant company otherwise. Everybody knows him, and he always understands just where to take me that will be new and interesting, although most of the time we just stay home."

"Which is?"

"Oh, my place or his. Whichever is closer. It doesn't seem to matter, although I hate having to make another stop in the morning before coming in to work."

"You mean—you haven't actually moved in together then? You could save a rent," which in Dublin was bound to be exorbitant, especially considering the choice places that they lived. Also there was the idea of commitment with no "safe house" to flee to whenever they had spats, which were inevitable.

"Truth is, we've not been able to decide between the two places. He prefers his, which *is* so much larger." It was an entire floor of a former warehouse down by the quays that Ward had "retrofitted," his term, into a charming studio. "But I don't feel safe there. You know, at night."

Not even with a Glock automatic in her purse and a wall filled with commendations for marksmanship. Also, Ward was perhaps the single toughest man—in the best sense—whom Noreen knew, save her own husband.

"And he says my place is too small and the people too 'Dublin Four' in mentality." She meant the postal district "Dublin 4" that had been the subject of a series of short stories by a famous writer and much commentary in the press. Encompassing most of Ballsbridge and Sandymount, it was inhabited by comfortably-off retirees, government officials, and many other professionals. Bresnahan's own digs was a mews apartment above a carriage house that had been declared a national architectural treasure. It was just the sort of neighborhood where ... well, the Charlotte Bings of the city lived.

"Finally, there's my mother. She refuses to rent out the farm and come join me here in town, until such time as I'm 'happily married and settled.' Her words. But I've been trying to convince her, and I should imagine the isolation will get to her sooner or later. And I'm not at all sure, actually, that I want to be either married or settled."

So—Noreen thought, as she pulled the Rover off the highway at Naas and headed south toward Dunlavin—their indecision had provided a wily, stunningly handsome, and wealthy

Culchie T.D. with just the sort of . . . well, opening wasn't quite the word, that he would be quick to exploit. In his own profoundly country way, Rory O'Suilleabhain was a competent man and quite the romantic swain, she had heard tell. They would be hearing more of him; of that Noreen was certain.

10

Short Shrift in
Brobdingnag

MCGARR HIMSELF WAS THINKING of a love triangle, as he searched a lane off James Street for the residence of Jan deKuyper, conservator of the Delmas Conservation Bindery. Granted McGarr did not know much Swift, like Noreen, but he was well acquainted with old Dublin songs and ditties, one of which told the story of a "Twangman" who had murdered for love:

He lay in wait, by James's Gate
Till the poor oul' Bags came up
And with his twang knife he took the life
of the poor oul' gather-him-up.

McGarr paused to tighten the collar of his mac against his neck, as he searched the narrow laneway for the number. Across James Street he could see the royal-blue gates of the Guinness Brewery, where his father had spent all fifty-two years of his working life. On the corner was St. Patrick's Hospital, in which McGarr and his eight brothers and sisters had been born, and a stone's throw away was their first school. Yet he had not ventured down this alley since then, and he was curious which building would be deKuyper's.

It had grown chill and blear, as the night had come on, with another choking mist rolling up from the nearby Liffey. The sky was dark with cloud, and it would rain by morning.

And far from being a house or a flat, deKuyper's abode was a former church or temple that McGarr also remembered as a scary old place that he and his brothers used to stone. Invested in youthful intolerance by their own religion, they would wait until nobody was about and hurl bricks at the stained-glass windows that were even then protected by an impenetrable steel mesh. Only ball bearings, stolen from the scrap heaps in the nearby railway yards, could get through and puncture the panes.

THE TEMPLE OF WRATH had been chiseled into the granite lintel above the stout door, which opened even before McGarr could knock. Said deKuyper, introducing himself and ushering McGarr in, "I know. I keep telling myself that I should have that damn phrase hammered off. The place was built by a fundamentalist sect from the North with only the best materials and much careful zeal. The rest I wouldn't touch for all the guilt in the Old Testament."

A huge man by any standard, deKuyper had a great tawny beard and a mass of unkempt blond curls. He was wearing a baggy and stained fisherman's-knit jumper and dark trousers that were also streaked with some whitish substance that McGarr guessed was bookbinding glue. "I want to thank you for your warning phone call. It gave me a chance to clean up."

McGarr wondered what the place must have looked like before the cleaning effort, unless, of course, deKuyper was being facetious. Instead of pews, the interior of the former church was filled with tables and stacks of books on industrial pallets. In one wing, McGarr could just make out the prongs of a small forklift truck. In the other wing was what looked like a chemist's laboratory complete with sinks, Bunsen burners, and a modern microscope.

Where the altar had been was now a fireplace with several logs blazing. Two large stuffed chairs and a coffee table were arranged nearby. Above the mantel was a mural that had obviously been part of the original church—or "Temple of Wrath," McGarr reminded himself. Employing a three-dimensional illusion, it pictured the hilt of a sword piercing a storm cloud, while its blade appeared on the other side as a jagged lightning bolt that seemed to issue from the wall into the church.

"As I said, but for the 'Wrath' carry-on above the front door, it suits me fine. It has space." DeKuyper swung his arms. "And *immanence*!"

"But do you live here as well?"

"Of course!" Spinning around, the immense man cast one paw toward the front. "Where else but the choir, which is the place for an angelic spirit."

There above the door and surrounded by the brass pipes of an organ, McGarr could see additional domestic furniture— bed, table, chairs, some kitchen appliances.

"Truth is, it's warmer up there in the cold months. During the summer, I'm usually away."

"Back to Holland?"

DeKuyper's smile diminished. His eyes were a strange color, almost the same shade as his golden hair. "Not always. My mother is still alive, and I try to get to see her. But mainly I just travel. I enjoy traveling, don't you?"

McGarr only glanced toward the chair by the fire.

"Should we sit down? As you mentioned on the phone, you'd like to discuss poor Brian and his untimely death. Would you take something?" By which he meant a drink, McGarr supposed. DeKuyper pulled a watch from his pocket. "It's about the time of night that I usually have a wee one."

"That would be very good of you," McGarr replied, climbing toward the former altar.

"I must say that I was rather amazed both by Brian's passing and the reports in the papers that you think it's a homicide."

"I never said that," McGarr corrected, as deKuyper advanced on a small bar near the fireplace. "So far we don't know the exact cause of Dr. Herrick's death."

"Not even after the autopsy?"

"It was inconclusive."

"Really? In this day and age? How is that?"

McGarr removed his fedora and tried to settle himself in one of the chairs that seemed to have been custom-made to somebody of deKuyper's great size. When McGarr leaned back in it, he nearly lay down. Having to content himself with sitting on the edge of the cushion, he felt suddenly juvenile. He watched deKuyper closely to make sure he poured both glasses from the same bottle. "How tall are you, anyway?"

"A bit over seven feet."

"And your weight?"

"Ah—twenty stone or so. When Brian hired me, he bragged that I was bigger than Cam 'The Walker,'" who was a character out of ancient Irish mythology; legend had it that Cam was so huge, no horse could carry him.

In taking the seat across from McGarr, deKuyper again asked, "Are inconclusive results usual?" He handed McGarr a wide tumbler that contained at least two inches of whiskey.

McGarr could barely grip it with one hand and had to hold the glass in his palm. "Glenfinnan?"

"Why, yes. How did you know without tasting . . . ? Of course—the bottles I bought Brian."

"A splendid gift both in selection and generosity."

"Ah, but Brian was w-ery good to me." It was the first noticeably foreign utterance that McGarr had been able to detect in deKuyper's speech. Otherwise, he sounded rather like an American or Canadian.

"So I understand. Was he the one who hired you?"

"After a manner of speaking. He sent my name to the governing body of Marsh's, who approved me." DeKuyper reached for the glass that his huge hand readily encompassed.

"As conservator of the Delmas Bindery."

DeKuyper nodded.

"What will you do now?"

The huge man raised his glass to his lips, but he stopped. "I don't know what you mean."

"The position of keeper—it's open now. Do you plan to apply for it?"

The glass moved back to the table. "To be frank, the possibility has crossed my mind. I think from every point of view I'm the most qualified person presently on the scene. I know the governors will probably advertise the post, but who knows the collection better, *as well as* every other aspect of rare and antiquarian books?"

"By that you mean the *conservation* of books."

"Exactly." Now deKuyper drank. Setting the glass down, he added, "Unless you know something I don't."

McGarr stood and moved toward the table with the bar. "May I examine that bottle?"

"The Glenfinnan? Of course. As I mentioned, your warning call gave me a chance to clean up." There was a definite sarcastic edge to that.

McGarr thought of the other warning calls that deKuyper had put in—to Herrick, telling him he was late in his payments and might therefore jeopardize his career. "You wouldn't happen to have an unopened bottle of Glenfinnan, would you?"

The Dutchman shook his head. "Sorry—that's it. No trophies for the Garda Siochana tonight, I'm afraid." As if McGarr's request had been personal. The tone of the interview was rapidly deteriorating.

The cap of the Glenfinnan bottle was the traditional kind with a cork stopper attached to a solid wood top. Marks on the neck of the bottle showed that the cork had originally been sealed with a foil or plastic wrap. A tax stamp had probably been strapped to the top.

How difficult would it have been to have removed the stamp, seal, cork, and a quantity of the whiskey, and then added whatever potion it was that had killed Herrick and sickened Bernie McKeon? McGarr glanced into the church with its workbenches and laboratory wing. Probably not all that hard for a person who was used to careful work and had probably studied chemistry.

"May I ask you what you're looking for? Perhaps I can help you?" The voice came from directly over McGarr, deKuyper having followed him over to the bar.

"Why not?" McGarr had to twist his neck to look up at the large man. "Shall we return to our seats?"

"As you wish," but deKuyper did not move, and McGarr had to squeeze out from between him and the table.

Back in his seat, McGarr pulled a card from his coat pocket and slid it across the table to deKuyper. "That your writing?"

DeKuyper had to hold the note-sized card to the light from the fire. "You know it is. There's my name."

"What were you reminding Herrick of?"

The huge man finished his whiskey and set the glass on the table. When he looked up at McGarr, his yellow eyes were narrowed and hard. "Of a debt he owed me, which is none of your business."

McGarr cocked his head, as though to say, Not yet, but I could make it mine. "What sort of debt?"

"A debt, is all. He owed me money. Lots of it."

"For what?"

"For whatever he wanted. I didn't ask him. He said he needed money, and I had it at the time. Why the questions? Am I a suspect in your . . . *murder* investigation, like the papers say you're conducting? If I am, I can make a phone call, too. This minute. To my solicitor."

"How much money?"

"T'ousands." That was said like a Dubliner, evidently to mock McGarr's own way of speaking. "Great *gobs* of money, as you people say it. A veritable *bomb.*"

"Where did you get money like that? Are you wealthy?"

Something about McGarr's confident manner evidently gave deKuyper pause. He did not reply.

"A glance at your bank records says otherwise." McGarr again reached into his jacket. "And curiously enough, whenever you deposited money, it was just after Dr. Herrick had withdrawn either the exact same amount or close to it."

McGarr slid deKuyper a thick sheaf of bank statements that had been faxed to him extralegally by a helpful credit counselor who owed him a favor.

"How'd you get ahold of this?"

"Blackmail," said McGarr. "You're not the only one who's good at it." Next he slid deKuyper another sheaf of faxes, which were Herrick's bank statements. "If you ever loaned Herrick money, it never appeared in his accounts. Up until a few years ago, he received stipends from his father's estate on a regular basis in regular amounts."

"It was cash."

"Finally, there's this. From his jacket, he drew a small microcassette player. He switched it on, and deKuyper was heard to say:

"Brian, it's Jan. It's Thursday evening, about quarter to seven. This afternoon I took the chance of leaving a little present I picked up in Scotland in back of the Janus figure beside your front door. Thinking you might have left town on a little buying tour, I rang up Charlotte at the library, but she said you told her you were going home. I just don't want you to forget and miss it in the dark. It took some doing getting that lot through Customs. Drink it in good health.

"On another matter, let me remind you you're late again with your payment on that loan. What a shame it would be for you to lose all you worked so hard for these many years. I know you have the money or you can get it. And we have an agreement."

There was a pause before deKuyper's second telephone message to Herrick came on:

"Herrick. It's Wednesday morning, and I still have nothing from you. As I told you when we first made our agreement—like it or not, you've involved my career in your project, and you must pay me what you owe me."

McGarr waited until deKuyper looked up at him again. "Why should Herrick lose everything he worked so hard for?"

"Because I'd foreclose on his house, which he put up for security. If I had to. If I *have* to. You know, the estate."

"Really? You have that in writing? Can I see it?"

Again deKuyper did not reply.

"Also, there's the matter of your career and Herrick's private project. Were you working on that, too?" McGarr turned his head toward the work area of the former church. "Could you show me exactly what that was, either here or at Herrick's house?"

It was then that deKuyper's prodigious arm shot out and batted the microcassette player off the table. Like a bullet, it shot through the flames in the hearth and shattered on the fireback. Standing, deKuyper snatched up the two sheafs of faxes and tossed them on the flames. "And since you're not going to drink that, not in *my* company, we'll just add a little accelerant to your evidence." As he dashed the whiskey into the hearth, the fire exploded—the fax pages bursting into multicolored flame.

"They're just copies, you know," McGarr said evenly.

"Illegally obtained."

"Well," McGarr went on in the same even tone of voice, "you'll have a hell of a time proving that *now,* won't you? Having destroyed the evidence."

DeKuyper was looming over McGarr now, glaring down at him. "You are odious. Vermin. You try to pull everybody down to your own hideous level. Let me tell you something, so you know—Brian Herrick may have been many things, some not so savory, but one thing he had that a sniveling, conniving little wretch like yourself couldn't possibly understand was honor."

"Really? Are you telling me that there's honor among you thieves? Or is it that only a blackmailer like yourself can see the honor in a thief who is paying him *on time.*"

"*Had* I been his blackmailer, would I have murdered him? That's what this is all about, isn't it?"

McGarr hunched his shoulders and glanced past the man's thick legs at the fire. "At five thousand pounds a quarter, Herrick's money was running out. Then there was his post as keeper, which you've already coveted. Was it your intention to carry on with his *project* as well? After all, only you two seemed to know about it."

"That's *enough!*" the titanic man roared. Clapping the fedora on McGarr's head, deKuyper snatched him up by the back of his mac and rushed him down off the former altar, through the maze of worktables, and to the door. Like a child, McGarr could neither make his feet touch the ground nor swing his arms back to strike the man. And there McGarr weighed over thirteen stone; deKuyper possessed enormous strength.

In the open door, deKuyper said, "If you come back, make sure you have your troop of dwarfs and an order for my arrest. Otherwise, I'll have you up on charges of police harassment." With that, he booted McGarr *literally* down the stairs, which were wet and slippery from a now-driving rain. McGarr fell in a heap on the footpath.

The door closed with a solid clump, and the light was extinguished.

Maybe it was the language that deKuyper had used or the contemptuous ease with which he had dispatched him, but McGarr suddenly remembered the name of the place in *Gulliver* where the giants live. "Brobdingnag," he said, trying to pick himself up.

Suddenly, there was a hand under his arm, helping him to his feet. "I won't let on to a soul, if you don't," a woman said. "The blighter is only four of yeh. Or six and me."

"I like six better," said McGarr, trying to make out her face in the deep darkness of the laneway.

"Can I buy yeh a consoling pint, and we'll discuss it?" As she pushed the hair from in front of her face, he saw she was the young reporter who had tried to interview him that morning at Herrick's, and he felt as though he had been tossed—kicked—from the clutches of one giant to the tentacles of an even more relentless hydra. The Fourth Estate. Though he could hardly refuse.

Sore now, he limped up the laneway toward the lights in James Street, her hand still under his arm.

11

Lilly-Pat

AS OCCURRED MORE OFTEN THAN NOT on a dark, wet November Saturday night at the country house of Fitzhugh and Nuala Frenche in Dunlavin, a "wee party" was in progress. Noreen pulled her car off the road onto the serpentine drive that was lined with ancient beeches.

"How can you tell there's a party?" Ruth asked.

"From the number of lights on in the house and the smoke coming from the chimneys. If Mammy and Daddy were alone, there'd only be lights on in the sitting room. And at the front door, of course, in the event somebody should call in. They know most of the locals, and also they have their Dublin friends and their . . ."

Connections, thought Ruth Bresnahan. Fitzhugh Frenche had made his fortune, it was said, mainly by being a clever man. He was pleasant company, a good listener, wise when it came to advice, and utterly discreet. In some Irish circles, a timely tip over brandy and cigars was often the price of friendship.

And indeed the Frenches were established. It was Ruth's

first time visiting them there, and she was impressed, not so much by the size of the house as by its appearance. No mansion, it was instead a large Georgian country house of three stories with a graceful facade that featured rounded corners and tall, arched windows. A complex of stables and outbuildings, also constructed of white limestone, flanked one end of the building, a wide patio leading down a hill into a formal garden was on the other side.

"Probably something informal, like a race meeting, from the look of the cars," which were muddy. "Which is good. Nobody will be stuffy or pretentious."

Through open curtains, Ruth could see groups of men and women, dressed in riding or stylish sporting costumes. A wood fire was blazing in what looked like the dining room, the long table having been set but not yet used. In the kitchen beyond, a number of women were moving about, preparing the dinner.

"Your parents have servants?" Ruth asked.

"God, no—they wouldn't think of it. Even the *idea* of servants would destroy them. Times like this, they merely ask a few of the local women, who need work, to help out. And after dinner, when the plates are cleaned up, their husbands come to fetch them but stay. And we have a grand oul' time."

Ruth caught the archaic inflection and thought how nice it would be to own a place like this, down in the country but only thirty miles from town. Her own country house was nearly one hundred and seventy-five hard miles away, in Sneem, County Kerry. In November the only conversations Ruth had been able to scare up had been of cows, land, tractors, and manly sport among the men, and motherhood among the women. Ruth had pined for Dublin.

Noreen's mother answered the door.

"Granny!" Maddie shouted and ran into the skirt of the older woman.

Well preserved for a woman who had to be approaching seventy, Nuala Frenche always looked to Ruth like a slightly older sister of Noreen, who was herself no more than thirty-five. Apart from Nuala's hair, which she left snow white, the two women shared the same sea-green eyes, the same long, thin, straight nose and slightly protrusive upper lip.

And finally they were built alike, with nicely made shoulders, thin waists, and shapely legs. To Ruth the two women seemed like little dolls, and there were not a few successful men in Dublin—Ruth had heard more than once—who considered Fitzhugh Frenche the luckiest of men "and not just in business."

Ruth noted that Nuala was, as usual, costumed utterly à la mode—a "broomstick" skirt with wrinkle pleating. Above she wore a hand-knit jumper with delicate crochet stitching, a bateau neck, and drop shoulders, which not every woman her age *could* wear. Both were white and made of silk.

Ruth tried to imagine what the outfit cost and, more, where a woman of Nuala's age would have thought to purchase something at once so stylish, so understated, and yet so becoming. And without a word having been passed, Ruth understood that she had suddenly arrived in the *other* Ireland, which was the Great Divide. It had to do with the old saying that "good form" was everything; for in Ireland one was either a gentleman or gentlewoman, or one was not.

"And here you are, Maddie," Nuala said, picking up her grandchild. "Accompanied by the two most beautiful women in Dublin." Shifting Maddie to her other arm, the older woman offered Ruth her hand. "How *are* you, my dear. And what a wonderful way you now have your hair." Nuala had to reach up to touch a lock of Ruth's deep auburn waves. "We've missed you. It's been an entire year, hasn't it? Noreen has kept me up to speed, of course, but I don't know who's happier to have you back—Peter or us."

It was a nice thought, but they all knew the real answer, which was that Hughie Ward was the happiest to have Ruth back.

"And is Hughie not with you?" Nuala asked, glancing out the door that Noreen was closing.

"We left him in town. He's to attend a comic striptease tomorrow at eleven."

"Is it business or pleasure?"

"Well, there's some doubt about which."

"On Sunday morning? Has Dublin gone Yahoo altogether?"

Noreen laughed. "You have it right there, mum—the pub is called the Poop Deck, appropriately enough."

Nuala began laughing. "Go over, now. Is there such a place? Wait till Fitz hears this. On second thought, you better not tell him, or Hughie is sure to have company. There's nothing Fitz likes more than a bit of a laugh at *our* expense, if you know what I mean."

"I do," said Ruth. "He's another unreconstructable male."

"And where is the sexist boar?" Noreen asked.

"Ach—holding forth in the sitting room from the sound of it." Nuala turned her head to Maddie. "Will you come with me into the kitchen, luveen. Knowing your mother, who can live on dank air, she hasn't fed you yet. You must be famished, and I want to hear all about your school."

Noreen and Ruth hung up their coats and followed the sound of Fitzhugh Frenche's voice into a long room that was filled with people. And suddenly the aroma of burning beech-wood, fine cigars, and the spices in the mulled wine and hot whiskey that were being served at a drinks table reminded Ruth of Christmas, which was the only time that her frugal father had plumped for a cigar. It would be the first holiday she would spend without him.

She also thought of her mother, who was now living alone in the large farmhouse in Sneem, refusing to come to Dublin unless and until Ruth married Rory O'Suilleabhain. No other would do. Sometimes old people could act like spoiled children. Pity all of them were not like Nuala and Fitzhugh Frenche.

He, too, was a small person—once dark and still robust, though well into his seventies. A sportsman all his life, he had a complexion that was windburned and sanguineous, especially, as now, when he was in his cups. Bushy eyebrows the color of steel hooded dark bright eyes, and his paunch was considerable. Tonight he was wearing a black cashmere jumper over a white shirt. Gray slacks and sturdy walking shoes completed his garb.

Frenche was relating a story in dialect, evidently about some tenant of his in another part of the country, probably Bresnahan's own Kerry, from the sound of his voice. "You two'll like this story about one of my tenants, who discovered a giant.

"So this time, he rings me up about six in the morning," Frenche went on in a breezy manner, swinging the silver cup from which he was drinking. "I hadn't been down there in a dog's age. 'Fitz, is it choo?' he asked. I allowed as how I wasn't sure, given the hour. 'Are ye gettin' yehr wear?' "

Some of the others chuckled, "wear" being a Dublin term for sexual relations.

" 'Not at the moment,' says I.

" 'That's grand, because I don't like to disturb a man when he's about the business. I wouldn't think of it, if it wasn't so important. Fitz, the cows has gone off their milk.'

" 'How long?'

" 'Ah, a fortnight, I reckon. But we could be wonderful lucky in this. It could mean TV, radio, tourists. I'm talkin' a roaring trade. We'll become famous and rich.'

"Now he had me.

" 'Do y'know the long field?'

" 'Which one?' I asked, since the farm has an even dozen.

" 'The green one.' "

Noreen and Ruth now joined in the laughter.

"Well, it *was* spring.

" 'The one with the gorgeous grass down by the river. I took a look at it this morn', like to check things out, and there, begob, wasn't there some footprints in the dew. Never seen anything like 'em in me life. And *big*.'

" 'How big?'

" 'About the size of . . . a loose cow pat. No, *two* loose cow pats, I swear on me mother's grave. But, you know, *joined*.' "

Now all were laughing heartily.

" 'And the trail coming up from the river. Says I to meself, I never seen a print like that from man nor beasht, but I had me rosary with me and Bert.'

" 'Who's Bert?'

" 'Me *dog,* Fitz. This *is* Fitz, is it not?'

"I swore it was.

" 'So into the bush I plunged, Bert in the lead. But didn't he come lashing back to give out in me face. Worried, like. Honest to God, Fitz—I will not venture down there again. Not in this lifetime. Not without two big men and some sh-ticks! I'm fifty-three years old, and I've seen all the birds and beashts in Ireland, but this one's as tall as a house, and you know what it leaves behind?'

" 'Footprints?' I asked.

" 'No—sh-lime. And the sh-tink of it! Why, it reminds me of the famous ballad from the North. The one the Ulster Symphony Orchestra is always playin'.'

"I thought for a moment and was about to ask him if he meant—" Frenche surveyed his audience and asked, "Any guesses?"

The others waited expectantly.

" 'Derry Aire.' When didn't his wife come on the line to harangue me for encouraging him. It seems he'd been on the 'quare sh-tuff' the night long and was having one of his visions. 'Isn't it always giants and Druids in Ireland,' says she, 'when it isn't the little men?' And what in the name of Sweet Relief was I doing up at such an hour of the morning?" Frenche sipped from his cup, the story being over.

Said Noreen, "But you haven't mentioned the best part, Daddy—his name."

"Well, now—somebody might know him. I can't be the only person he rings up."

"Sure, if they ever heard it, they'd never forget."

Said Bresnahan, looking off into the room with affected nonchalance, "It's Aengus O'Boyle. The 'G' is silent. He's a noted greyhound breeder who advertises on Kerry radio, guaranteeing a 'bingo' every time your bitch is serviced by his longtime champion stud, 'Pocket Rocket.' "

"Bingo!" Fitzhugh Frenche cried. "I'm skint! She knew all along, but, then again, it wasn't quite fair—the woman is a professional."

"Dog breeder?" another man asked. "No offense, miss, but, looking at you, I'd hazard you'd be rather more capable within your own species."

Now the group roared their approval.

"Crack!" piped Fitzhugh Frenche between laughs. "*Great* crack! I haven't laughed this hard in a greyhound's age." 'Crack' being a term used in Ireland to describe playful conversation or any good time.

Frenche then kissed his daughter and began introducing Ruth to the others nearby. Apart from some young man in the farthest corner of the large room who had his back to them, Bresnahan was the tallest and certainly the "broadest" person in the room. Standing six-feet-one-and-a-half inches in her stocking feet, she weighed a svelte 9.2 stone.

And it was while she was shaking hands and trading pleasantries that she noticed the woman she had come to see. Joneux Ariane Danvers-Forde now entered the room, accompanied by a young man who could only be her husband, Ruth decided.

The dark, exotic-looking woman—tiny, really—immediately collected all eyes, not only because of her diminutive size, which had to be well under five feet, but also because of the dress she was barely wearing. It was a black-and-gold Jacquard print with a drop-waist that clung to her coltish frame like second skin, before flaring at the knees to random pleats. Tipped at a rakish angle à la Napoleon, she also wore a black cockade hat with a spray of peacock-feather eyes laced through the felt. It was trimmed with gold braid to match the dress, and the combined effect of the costume was stunning.

Especially when compared to her husband, who looked almost seedy in an old, if once fine, tweed suit and brogues so aged that the polished leather was cracked like old paint. A man in his early thirties, he had regular features and might even have seemed handsome had he attended to his appearance. His blondish hair, which was long, had not felt the tooth of a comb in days. Walking in back of his wife with his hands in his trouser pockets, he turned to this one and that without saying a word, as though contemptuous of their obvious interest in his wife.

When they stopped at the drinks table, Bresnahan saw her opportunity. "It strikes me that we're the only two people in the room without a drink," she said to Noreen.

"Oh, let me amend that," said Fitzhugh Frenche. "I'm a deplorable host. What are you having?"

"No, no, Daddy," Noreen interjected, knowing what Ruth intended. "We'll fetch our own, thank you. And yours." She reached for his cup.

"But you don't know what I'm having?"

"Ballygowan, isn't it? As prescribed by your cardiologist."

"What does he know?" said Frenche sourly. "I'm the one with the heart."

"As we understand all too well," Noreen replied, taking the cup from him.

"The least you can do is put a touch of color in it."

Nearing the drinks table, Noreen met other people whom she had to greet, and by the time they reached their goal, the Danvers-Fordes had their drinks in hand and were turning away from the table.

"Ah—Joneux Ariane and Alastair," Noreen said breezily. "I have somebody for you to meet."

"Really, Noreen?" replied the young man. "And there when I thought we had met *everybody*"—in the world worth knowing, went unsaid. His eyes swept Bresnahan from her black Hermès shoes that gave her three inches that she did not need, to her black patterned stockings and purple velvety spandex dress that made the most of her angular figure. His eyes lingered on the black velvet necklace with its large amethyst stone—a gift from a wealthy uncle in South America—before stealing briefly to her dark gray eyes and deep red hair. She was two of him, at least. In everything, she decided.

"This is Ruth. Ruth, I'd like you to meet Joneux Ariane and Alastair."

"Pleased," said the diminutive Frenchwoman.

"You wouldn't have been out riding today?" asked her husband.

"I only just arrived from town. What about you?"

Danvers-Forde waved a hand. "I gave it up. Now I let others ride for me. It's not only pointless in this day and age, it's perilous." His eyes surveyed the several people in the room who were wearing splints or casts. "It's a shame there's nowhere to sit. I always hate coming to these affairs that keep one on one's feet. We'll eat when?" he asked of Noreen, who hunched her shoulders and tried to look as though she were not offended. "They always leave one so drained in the morning."

Bresnahan's gorge rose. Danvers-Forde was a type, not a person—a throwback to the self-consciously shabby, talkative, and fey "young bloods" who lazed about the pages of Somerville & Ross and Maria Edgeworth novels. She tried to tell herself that there were only so many ways of being a gentleman in a society that required it. And when one had plenty of money, no real purpose in life, limited intelligence, and lived in the country . . . No, she still wanted to throttle the little bastard. She could feel the flush in her cheeks.

"And what do you do—obviously in town?" he asked, again letting his eyes slide down her body.

His wife, meanwhile, sipped from her drink and smiled at the several men in the room who were still regarding her.

"I'm with the police," which brought Joneux Ariane's head around.

Danvers-Forde sighed. "I don't suppose you're here felicitously, Noreen's husband being that"—he raised a slim hand and wiggled his fingers—"McGarr person, who's always—" he wiggled them some more—"in the papers."

Noreen's chin came up, and she turned to a man who was passing, "Hello, Prionsias—Noreen Frenche. You remember me?"

Prionsias did indeed; she took his arm, and they walked toward the dining room.

"How tiresome this all is," Danvers-Forde went on. "And in what capacity are you tonight—is it Ruth? Are you *with* the Guards or *with* yourself?"

"If you mean . . . would I like to ask your wife a few questions? I would."

"What if she's not up to it?"

"Then tomorrow, or the next day. She might prefer to speak to me at Dublin Castle. It's all one to me, but I should imagine it would be less painful here." Bresnahan attempted a smile that translated, I could—and *would*—eat you, had I the chance. Old shoes, baggy suit, and all.

Suddenly, Danvers-Forde's temper squalled. "Can't you just leave the dead lie!" he blurted out petulantly. Heads turned to them; he pulled off his half-glasses. "I mean, it's *obscene* the way all you jackals are allowed to pick over the remains of the dead! Fitzhugh," he fairly shouted across the large room, "how could you have let this person in here?"

Danvers-Forde's diminutive wife did not hesitate. Taking Ruth by the arm, she led her away. "Perhaps we should find a quiet room where we can speak."

Which turned out to be the library that occupied one end of the large house.

12

L i l l y - P u t a

"I'VE NEVER BEEN IN THIS ROOM BEFORE," said Joneux Ariane Danvers-Forde, moving toward the bookshelves. "I didn't realize that Fitz collected books."

"Actually, I believe it's Nuala who's interested in books."

"In Irish, in particular. Here's Brian Merriman's *The Midnight Court,* which looks to be a first edition. In excellent condition. I don't believe I've ever seen one of these before. But"—Joneux Ariane turned to Ruth—"you didn't come to speak about books, did you?"

Not unless you wish to, Bresnahan thought.

"They're saying that Brian was murdered, but I jus' can' believe it." Her French accent was scarcely apparent.

"Well—the papers will say any scurrilous thing, just to sell a few extra copies, without concern for anybody's reputation." Ruth sat to put the diminutive woman at her ease; the size difference was so great that Bresnahan had the feeling that she was interviewing a small child. "It's just that when the cause of death cannot be pinpointed, we must investigate, but discreetly, which is the reason I attempted to look you up here. Quietly."

The Frenchwoman's eyes met Bresnahan's for the first time, as though petitioning her understanding. "Alastair is so juvenile, sometimes. He has no understanding of the world."

Or of some of the creatures in it, like Brian Herrick and Teddy and Bunny Baer, thought Bresnahan.

"He thinks everybody should be good and *rationnel*," she said, pronouncing it in French, "when people are ..."

Bresnahan would wait until the cows came home for the woman to say it.

"... just people."

"And Brian Herrick was just being *people* during his 'Frollicks?' "

"*Mais oui.* Why not? Like Montaigne or even Swift, it's possible to subscribe to rationality, whenever possible, yet still embrace one's humanity in all its guises."

Including Herrick himself and Teddy Baer? Bresnahan wondered. She doubted the woman's sincerity. In order for her to have *embraced* either, she would have to have been impelled by a more powerful, less intellectual urge. Like the threat of death. Bresnahan now wished she possessed the intestinal fortitude to have watched the entire videotape, as had Noreen McGarr.

"For instance, there's a statue of Montaigne in Bordeaux, picturing him naked as an old man with a protrusive stomach and useless penis. It's *not* the Montaigne of the *Essays* with his rapier intelligence and legendary sexual prowess. But rather the Montaigne who accepted *everything,* good and bad, about being human with neither contempt nor illusions, knowing life's limitations and richness. At the same time, he encouraged humanity to *be* better, whenever the opportunity arose. When one was tested.

"Or your own Swift. What was your Swift? He was an

injured moralist who never forgave the world for not being what the optimistic philosophers, whom he had read in his youth, said it would become. Far from improving the lot of all humanity, man would use the tools of his rationality for individual ends. Or for the ends of class, country, or race. In that, Swift prefigured much of what has proved, in this century, to be the lasting legacy of the Enlightenment."

Again Bresnahan waited; here she had a little French *philosophe* on her hands, as opposed to the *poule* that Joneux Ariane Danvers-Forde had appeared as in the videotape. "How so?"

"Why, in that people are *rationis capax.* By that I mean *capable* of rational thought and action, but they seldom choose to exercise that capacity. And then mostly only to satisfy their desires."

Which brought them to the point. "Were you satisfying your desires the night that Dr. Herrick died?"

Joneux Ariane Danvers-Forde's chin came up. "Did he actually die *that* night?"

"We have it on film or, rather, tape."

"His *death?*"

Bresnahan nodded.

A smile seemed to flicker across the woman's pretty features, as though she would not mind seeing *that*. "But how did he die?"

"The official explanation is respiratory failure, but we've reason to believe Dr. Herrick was poisoned."

"How?"

"By something he drank."

"But—he drank only whiskey. At least while I was there."

Bresnahan waited. The dark hair of the little woman was wiry and lustrous; in a cascade of finger waves it fell nearly to

her waist. Her skin was olive in tone, her nose slightly aquiline, and her cheekbones were high. Her dark eyes flashed at
Bresnahan. "And I—I drank some of that whiskey as well."

"When?"

"Well—you know, *before* the frolic, while Teddy and I were
dressing. I find it always helps to be a little drunk."

"You mean—to dance? You're a dancer, I take it."

The small woman only shrugged before continuing. "And I
also took a glass up to the bedroom, where I showered and
dressed before leaving."

"From the bottle in the kitchen?"

She nodded.

"Were two bottles there?"

"Yes—but one was finished. I had to take my drink from
the second."

"Why didn't you pour your drink from the flask in the
bedroom?"

"You mean the one in the Bible? Brian used that only for
emergencies, or when either of us was too weary to walk
downstairs for more."

"Emergencies?"

"Often, after he'd been drinking, Brian couldn't sleep
through the night without more. Or he'd have nightmares
and—"

"Hallucinations," Bresnahan supplied. "You mean he was
an alcoholic?"

Another shrug. Joneux Ariane sipped from her own glass,
which appeared to contain a goodly measure of whiskey. "Call
it what you will—it was his house, his whiskey."

But not his wife, thought Bresnahan. "Did you return to
the kitchen before you left?"

"You mean for yet another drink?" She shook her head. "I

considered it, I must say, but it was late, and I had a long drive. Also I saw Mr. Baer pass by the kitchen door on his way from the conservatory."

"And you . . . ?"

"Left."

"Why? Don't you get on with Baer?"

"I've never cared for his type."

"Which is?"

"A *maquereau*, what else?"

"Meaning you've had experience with pimps?"

The small woman did not reply. Nor was she upset by the question, which led Bresnahan to conclude she had been interviewed by the police before and likely on such a matter.

"When you left, you left by the front door?"

"Yes."

"Locking it after you, since you had keys."

"Of course. Brian had asked me, and, then, when he's drunk, he's—he was not very careful of such things."

"May I ask you something quite personal?"

The Frenchwoman gave Bresnahan a look of frank resignation, as though there was nothing she would not answer.

"What was the appeal of Herrick for you?"

Joneux Ariane shrugged and stepped toward the bookshelves again. "I suppose it was that he was *not* my husband. Also, we had books in common—their care and conservation—which I have trained for and is not just a hobby of mine. And then Brian was large—did you get a look at him? Which mattered—*matters!*—to me in men. He had imagination and *technique*." She said the word in a decidedly French way. "Also friends, who made it more entertaining still." She turned her head back to Bresnahan, a thin smile on her pretty lips, which were daubed with gold lipstick to match the gold in her dress and on her hat. "I assume you want the truth. I hope I'm not shocking you."

Bresnahan shook her head, but—country girl that she was—she *was* plainly shocked. "Like Teddy Baer."

"Especially Teddy Baer. There we are speaking of experience. Teddy is the mistress of the carnal. Brian swore that in the dark he could not tell which one of us it was, though he always seemed to prefer Teddy's ministrations more completely. And I, too. Sometimes I preferred Teddy myself."

Fighting to keep her moral outrage in check, Bresnahan went on, "And your husband knew about your relationship with Dr. Herrick?"

"You know he did. He rang him up sometime later, which must be on Brian's answering machine."

"A *week* later, when he thought you might be there again. Were you?"

Joneux Ariane shook her head.

"Did you go over there and, say, find him dead, and, not wishing to involve yourself . . . ?"

"I said no."

"Where were you, then?"

"That's my business. If Brian was already dead, how can it matter to you where I was a week later?"

"Why weren't you moved at least to ring Herrick up during that week?"

"I had no need for him."

"Didn't it strike you as curious that he didn't come into his work in the library?"

"It crossed my mind, but I had my own duties to attend to, my husband, and my other interests."

"Then you *were* concerned for Herrick?"

Joneux Ariane finished her drink. "As I said, it crossed my

mind, but when I phoned, I reached only his machine but did not leave messages—in the interest of discretion. And, as I said, I'd had enough of him, at least for a while."

"But with your keys mightn't you have stopped round just to check on him?"

"Well"—her eyes again flashed at Bresnahan—"my husband took away my keys the night I got back, so stopping round, discreetly, was out of the question."

"But you might have otherwise? You had not . . . broken things off with him?"

Now the smaller woman turned to face Bresnahan. "Why do you seem to be so interested in my . . . adventures? Are you in need of adventure yourself? A woman, like you—you need only say the word."

Bresnahan was in some doubt as to whether she meant to her or to some other person. She stood. "Well—thank you for your time."

"What a shame. Just when we were getting acquainted."

"You must certainly have a tolerant husband?"

"There is no other kind worth keeping."

"Doesn't he complain about your—"

"Peccadilloes?"

"Now, there's a word I hadn't considered."

"Of course he complains. But then, he loves me. At least he tells me he does. And, of course, I've encouraged him to have his own little flings, were the urge to strike him. Do you find him appealing?"

Bresnahan could not keep her nostrils from flaring. "I should imagine that you would be rather more adept at initiating something like that than he?" She opened the library door for the woman.

"Perhaps. But that only proves I married well. Alastair and

I were made for each other. And there he is—the *very best* husband a sybarite such as I could possibly possess."

And what should be behind Alastair Danvers-Forde than the hulking frame of Rory O'Suilleabhain. "Ruthie, I declare to God you are the prettiest sight I've seen this many a long day."

Ruth was flabbergasted. "How did you manage to get here?"

"Well, Fitz and me—we got a little somethin' goin', like, and he invited me down for the weekend. I understand he's well connected; would you say that's right? I mean, one Kerry person to another. It's the very divil dealin' with these slippery Jackeens"—by which O'Suilleabhain meant Dubliners.

Thought Ruth, *The* O'Suilleabhain would be well up to them, at least in regard to turning a profit. She had never known a man more fit for the sharp deal, be it cattle, sheep, politics, or women. In addition to his startling good looks—his height, build, lustrous black hair, sea-green eyes, and features that might have been drawn by a fashion artist—he was clever. Nothing seemed to escape him. And he was forever acquitting himself favorably in any contest or exchange. Save with her. "I think you'll find Fitzhugh Frenche an honorable man."

"That's all I needed to hear. From your lips." It was dark there in the hallway, and the only two other people around were the Danvers-Fordes, who seemed like dolls or children, compared to Ruth and the nearly six-foot-six O'Suilleabhain. When he bent to kiss her, Bresnahan's right arm shot out, and the slap resounded down the long hallway like a gunshot.

Several people actually stuck their heads out of other rooms to see what had happened.

Said Ruth, "I didn't mean to hit you so hard, but it felt good." She moved toward the light of the sitting room.

Seeming to take neither injury nor offense from the blow, O'Suilleabhain said, "Well—it woke me up, it did. I thought I was going to sleep with all this Dublin chat."

He carried on in that fashion throughout the rest of the evening, trying to isolate her, Bresnahan thought; the attempt was to make the two of them seem like big, handsome, but definite Culchies against all the small, swift, pretty perhaps but obviously canny, gurriers who were gathered there in the Frenches' country house.

Later, he said to her, "You know, I've come to realize in the last few weeks that Dublin is really only one small part of Ireland, and the people who live here might seem sharp and opinionated, but most of them are only confused. They'll tell you one thing one moment, and another another. Not like people in the country, every man Jack and Jill of us, who have had to deal with the reality of work and the land on a daily basis. Which makes our politics *right.*"

Literally, thought Bresnahan, who knew better. Having *worked* on a daily basis with the Serious Crimes Unit for over five years, she understood that there was no denying the problems of the cities, no matter how much rural-dominated Irish politics wished to dismiss them.

O'Suilleabhain even had the audacity to ask her where, in the large house, she would be sleeping, and could he "nip in" for a "chat?"

"With Noreen and Maddie," Bresnahan had replied, not expecting that would be the case in the large house. "I'm sure you can find some other woman here who wouldn't mind your nips and chat."

"But you have me on the wrong foot altogether, so you

have. By chat I *meant* chat. And there can be no other woman. For me there is only you." His eyes had fixed hers. "I say this from the bottom of my heart."

Or at least bottom, thought Bresnahan. Although secretly flattered, she turned away from him in exasperation and sought out other company.

Later, over milk and cookies in the immense kitchen, still warm and fragrant from the dinner, Nuala Frenche, who also could not sleep, gave Ruth some advice. "It seems that you have a choice facing you, my dear. An interesting choice that other women would beg for. I wouldn't mention it, other than I think of you as a daughter."

Ruth nodded, knowing that the older woman had only her best interest at heart.

Nuala continued. "You can continue on with your Hughie Ward, who will achieve high position—perhaps the highest—in the Garda Soichana. He might even move on and become one of the leaders of the country in an *administrative* way. On the other hand, you have *The* O'Suilleabhain, whom my Fitz, who is a great judge of men, says will do something big for himself.

"Hughie? He's a handsome man, an accomplished man, a *good* man. It could be that Rory isn't a good man, but he will probably become a *powerful* man in due time. I've seen men come and go.

"I won't say any more, other than you'll have to choose. I don't think either will be content to sit on the fence. Which isn't to say you *must* choose. I've often imagined what my life would've been, had I remained single and stayed in university."

After a contemplative pause, Nuala Frenche added, "But if you do choose, remember that a man needs a woman to *confide* in, a woman who will not break his confidence and put him down. The best kind of woman can build a man up and make him go. Men are all just grown-up boys, who need to have their confidence pumped up by a mammy. Who *isn't* their mammy. And the bigger they become, the more they need."

It occurred to Bresnahan for the first time that she might not choose; that she might continue as she was now, living alone, since she did not believe there would ever come a day when she would again give up her career. And the idea of *being* a mammy—well, she was not ready for that just yet. In any guise.

13

Ya-boo! (s)

DETECTIVE SUPERINTENDENT HUGH WARD made sure he got
to the Poop Deck before its Sunday 11:00 A.M. opening,
knowing there would be a crowd.

Just after sunup, when Ward began his jog out to Dun
Laoghaire—just over ten miles, round trip—it had begun to
rain. By the time he got back, a needlelike sleet was raking
the quays, and the skies had turned a gloomy dun color,
almost as though night had returned. It was Ireland in winter.

Ward knew how Dublin pub crawlers would react. Those
with any readies left over from the night before would make
straight for their favorite pub and camp out, maybe for the
rest of the day, if they were flush. The Poop Deck with its
excellent rock band and live (or was it barely alive?) strip
show would top the list among the class of topers that Ward
thought of as hard-core Dubs—those who would prefer the
ripe comedy and fallen flesh of Teddy Baer over the chance of
some future, unknowable, and perhaps heavenly reward. Of a
Sunday morning.

The location of "The Deck," as the pub was known to regulars, was in Stoney Batter, an old commercial and industrial

area of Dublin, and there were only warehouses and trading establishments nearby. On a blear winter morning, it had the look of a battered and tatty ghost town with only a few cars parked in front of the pub, since most of the patrons would arrive on foot.

"The Deck" itself was appropriately on the second floor, and the stairway up was already crowded. With a large camera bag swinging from a shoulder of his black leather jacket, Ward was the final petitioner at the shrine of Teddy Baer to get in out of the freezing rain.

At the top of the stairs, he could just see the balding pate of Bunny Baer, already positioned at his card table with his little money box before him. Ward would let Baer complete his collections, before taking him aside. The last thing Ward wanted was any commotion that might make the Bunny go to ground or leave the country, as Baer had hinted at in the videotape. But Ward would squeeze the Bunny some this morning. Gently.

The hallway was thick with cigarette smoke, and Ward, who was extremely health conscious, was glad he was standing in the open doorway. In front of him were five "chippies"—he thought of the type—young, working-class women who were dressed in cheaply stylish costumes and sported raffish coiffures, much makeup, garish jewelry, and were wearing so many different perfumes, pomades, and lotions that, Ward suspected, the mix was even more noxious than the smoke.

Although styles had changed over the years, Ward could remember "chippies" from his own youth—shop girls, hairstylists, waitresses, factory workers, and the like—circulating in groups on the weekends, all looking for a "fella" or a bit of a laugh. Anything that might be considered adventure enough to be hashed over throughout the coming work week. Dates might even be made to meet a fella and perhaps a few of his mates at some venue or other, but, if the "chippies" showed up, they would be in number—for strength, safety, but mostly for sororal solidarity, so Ward had always thought. A date was never a "date" with a chippie; the unexpected inevitably occurred.

"What's in the bag?" the nearest one asked. Dressed all in black, she looked anorexic with her skinny, bowed legs and thin arms and chest, and her makeup—much eye shadow against some floury cosmetic base—made her seem cadaverous.

"Camera," said Ward noncommittally. He had long ago learned that it was a form of self-abuse to engage in conversation—to say nothing of "chat"—with groups of more than two Irish women, since the assumption was that you could only be interested in one, and the others, feeling slighted, would inevitably have you off. Verbally. Or they would have you off (still verbally) as part of the (blood?) "sport" that existed between young Irish men and women.

"What's he say?" another asked.

"Says he's got a camera in the bag."

"Sure, he can take *our* picture." She pulled open her jacket and placed her hands on her hips.

And a fine pair of . . . eyes she had, thought Ward, looking away and smiling slightly. The young woman had either full, buoyant breasts or a miraculous padded brassiere.

"Ah—he's not interested."

"Probably a bleedin' seacher," muttered the one with the pair; it was Dublin argot for homosexual.

"Can't yeh see—Teddy's more his type. He's come to snap her."

"And more his age."

Ward's nostrils flared; Teddy Baer was probably older than his own mother.

"See—yeh slagged him off," one critiqued, pointing at Ward's face. "It's Teddy he's come for, right enough. Pity her oul' one won't let him bring it in."

Ward glanced at her.

"Won't let nobody bring a camera in," she went on conversationally. "Shoots all her videos himself, he does. Ten quid apiece at the top of the stairs."

"Get the one called 'An Immodest Proposal,' " another said.

"Or 'The Drapier's Litters.' It's a gas. We play it all the time for laughs."

"You got a name?"

Ward glanced down at his boots, which were Western style and covered with snakeskin. In addition to the black leather jacket, he was also wearing jeans.

"No—can't you see from the tan? He's either over here from the States for a fil-m, or he's scoutin' locations. If he was to tell us his name, we'd probably faint."

She must be the reader in the group, Ward imagined— movie mags.

"Me arse," said someone of the others. "He's a brazzer"—by which she meant pimp. "Them's brazzer's boots."

"I don't care what they are, they're fookin' deadly."

"He'll make a demo of Teddy, and next week she'll be playin' Las Vegas."

"And his willie in her spare time!"

They all laughed.

"Nah, yiz're all wrong. I know who he is now," said the first.

"Who?"

She gathered the others to her and whispered.

"Ah—you're talkin' t'rough yehr hole."

"You think so? And there's this." They grouped round the knowledgeable one again, then turned and regarded Ward once more.

"That little fella?" one said. "Why, he's barely tall enough for a decent *vertical.*"

Some of them began giggling again, while the source of the information added something else that sounded to Ward either like, "Me da' t'inks he's fookin' rapid" or "rabid." He decided it was the former, and she was discussing Ward's erstwhile career as an amateur boxer. Ward had twice won the European amateur championship in the seventy-kilo weight class.

"That's shite, it is. There's not a mark on his puss."

"And you think he's fookin' gorgeous, I suppose."

"Well—don't you? I'd throw a leg over him anytime."

The others gave out a group wail and tried to shove her toward him.

There, thought Ward, he hadn't said a word, and he had already seduced the best-looking one of them.

"Watch—I'll prove it," said the one who thought she knew who he was.

From out of nowhere—it seemed to Ward—the punch came and caught him just below the belt of the tight-fitting jeans. Not expecting to be hit, he was surprised, and his stomach muscles were relaxed. But the blow did not strike him *exactly* in the stomach, either. On came the pain, and he went down.

"Jaysus—I don't believe it!" one cried joyfully. "She dropped the fooker with one punch!"

"He went down like a sack o' shit!"

"Yah ballocks, yah. Yeh caught him a bit low." That one reached for Ward's arm. "Gather round, girls. Just like on a rugby pitch when it happens, we'll make a circle and rub it up for the poor mahn."

Ward thought he might vomit, the pain was so intense. He was on his knees, his forehead resting on the floor. Two of them were trying to pick him up.

"Yehr da' 'll be proud of yeh, Flossie, when he hears this."

"Jesus—I'm sorry. Christ Almighty, I better get out of here. When he comes to, he'll give me a toompin'."

When Ward felt another hand at the small of his back, where he kept a 9-mm Glock in a kidney holster, he snapped back his own right hand and caught somebody's wrist.

The girl screamed, "He's got a gun!"

"Didn't I tell yiz?" said the one who had done the punching. "He's 'Whipper' Ward, the boxer and the cop."

Ward staggered to his feet, as some of the other would-be patrons of the Poop Deck began rushing down the stairs. So much for anonymity, Ward thought. He could see Bunny Baer at the top, trying to prevent a few others from storming into the pub proper. The mention of a gun combined with a man carrying a bag was enough to throw any Irish crowd into an uproar.

He pulled his Garda picture I.D. from a pocket and tried to raise it above his head. "I'm Garda Detective Superintendent Ward. Don't panic! I'm only wanting a word with yehr mahn." With the other hand, he pointed up the stairs at Baer. "Now, if you could let me through."

Shouldering his bag, Ward stepped by the chippie who had done the damage, her eyes wide with fright. "Tell your father he owes me a pint."

"Fair play to you," several of the others said, clapping his shoulders and back.

"Sure, if that's all you want," she said, "come and see us near the bar, after yehr done with that malignant little bastard." She meant the Bunny.

Who said to Ward, "But who'll collect the head charge?"

"I don't know, I don't care. Get somebody!"

"But couldn't yeh come back later? Yehr deprivin' me of me living."

Ward shook his head.

Baer's pink-rimmed eyes flashed into the bar, where the band and the barmen were setting up. But obviously there was nobody he trusted.

"Do you have tickets?" Ward asked.

Baer nodded.

"Are they numbered?"

Again.

"Take down the number of the first ticket. When you get back, make a count."

"But the bank." He glanced at the little green strongbox.

Ward took the man's arm. "We'd better do this up in the Castle."

"No, no, no—I'll get somebody."

Five minutes later in a storeroom with Baer sitting on a chair in front of him, Ward held a video recorder in the palm of his hand and played Baer the portion of the Brian Herrick death tape that showed Baer stealing Herrick's keys. "Why?"

"Why not? I hated his fookin' guts, I did. Always. And after what he said about Teddy, I decided that was it. Teddy wouldn't perform for him again."

"Being the sensitive type," said Ward. "So to get him back for the insult, you took his keys."

"Something on that order."

"Or on the order of needing them, knowing he'd soon be dead."

Again the bunny eyes flickered up at him. "I don't understand."

"Let me show you. You went into the kitchen to fetch him more drink?"

Baer nodded.

"You filled the decanter, then poured two drinks."

"I don't know. I guess."

"You didn't drink yours."

"I don't drink. I *hate* the fookin' stuff."

"Herrick drank his."

Baer wagged his head from side to side. "Ah—he was drunk. He would'a sucked horse piss from a trough, the state he was in."

"Dead drunk, as it turned out." Ward showed Baer the footage of Herrick drinking, then—skipping forward—Herrick's dying.

"A heart attack?" Baer asked.

"Down on his hands and knees vomiting."

"Shittin' himself blue." Baer allowed himself a thin, unlovely smile.

"Does the date eight, nine, eleven, mean anything to you?"

Baer shook his head.

"Or the numbers?"

"What was they again?"

Ward repeated them.

Baer had slumped back in the seat. "You mean—there was som'pin' in the drink?"

Ward nodded.

"That killed him?"

Again.

"But there couldn't've been. Teddy, the little one—they had some of it, so they did. To loosen them up. I poured 'em meself."

"From the decanter."

Baer had to think. "Now that you mention it—I think it was. There was a decanter on the library table when we come in, lookin' nearly empty. But it's a big yoke, like we just seen on that." He pointed at the screen of the camcorder. "There was still a good lot in it."

The ring of baldness on the back of Baer's bent head looked like the tonsure of a monk. He was wearing another warmup suit that said, HOTSPURS; the stark white runners on his feet were by New Balance. Well used, they had been touched up with white polish. Baer was a careful man.

"What about out in the kitchen when you went to fill the decanter?"

Baer glanced up at him, not knowing what he meant.

"The whiskey."

"Oh—the one bottle was empty, the other fullish. I can remember saying to meself that I never heard of Glen—"

"—finnan," Ward completed.

"—and it must be some off-brand that he picked up in a bin in Dunne's Stores," which was a supermarket chain with a large liquor section.

"The top was off, as always."

Ward waited, trying to read the small, pink-rimmed eyes that were some dark shade of blue.

"A put-on it was. A . . . affection."

"Affectation."

"That's it. The fookin' blighter was always puttin' on, that's maybe what I hated most. Even drunk, *more* when drunk. Som'tin' out of a fookin' John Wayne movie, or maybe it was the way Dean Swift drank way back in . . . whatever century it was. Pulled the top off a bottle, then t'rew it in the bin, like the whole shaggin' t'ing had to be drunk off at a swallow. Wine, whiskey, small bottle or big, like them two yokes. I can remember sayin' to meself, seeing them in the kitchen—maybe they'll do the job, and good riddance. Which they did. With some help, like. As yeh said."

"How 'fullish' was the second bottle?"

Baer sat up again; out in the bar the band had begun to play, and Teddy could be heard crooning an off-key rendition of "Young Blood." "More than half of it was still there, but I can remember thinking at the time that the little one must 'a took a sup herself for the road home, and I was worried about her."

Ward raised an eyebrow.

"She's class, she is. The way she looks, the way she moves. French even. She could . . ." Baer shook his head and looked away wistfully. Thought Ward: Make a packet of money for some lucky promoter or pimp, whichever Baer was. And then she had proved on the videotape that dancing was not the only act in her repertoire; she was not averse to doing the business on film, at least with Herrick.

"So you poured the decanter, then the drinks, and we're back to the keys. You stole Herrick's keys in order to—"

Looking trapped, Baer glanced at the door where Teddy was singing,

Then I met yerh maw,
She was raw,
* She said, "You better leave wee Willie alone."*

Ah—young blood! I say, young blood!
Young blood—I can't get yiz out o' me moind!

An extended drumroll with much thumping of the bass completed the song.

Baer pushed up the sleeves of the warmup jacket and ruffled the bald spot on the top of his head.

Said Ward, "So far I've got you procuring and promoting an indecent act. And theft. Shall we add murder to it? No jury, watching you fetch, then pour the potion that killed Herrick, will acquit you. Not with your record."

Ward pulled out a computer printout of the Bunny's rap sheet that began with a child-molestation charge at age eighteen and ran a steady gamut of vice offenses, including atrocious assault upon a woman for whom he had been pimping. It was dismissed when the woman refused to testify. The Bunny was much less mild than he seemed, at least with women. Ward scaled the sheet down at Baer's New Balance runners.

Baer did not touch it. "Well—I figured the gobshite owed me. Every time we went over there, he had his camera runnin', and what happened there *tops* anyt'ing that could happen here." He waved a hand at the door, where Teddy could now be heard delivering her monologue. "And the roights"—Baer thumped his chest—"was mine!"

Ward assumed he meant the rights to Teddy's performances.

"Who knows what he had in mind for them. I t'ought maybe I'd get some blokes I know to take them back for me."

Too careful to do it himself, thought Ward. "Their share being . . . ?"

"Whatever they could take away from the place, which would be their business. There was some nice things in that place."

"So, you made a couple of copies of the keys."

Baer's eyes rose to Ward, who with his leather jacket, jeans, and snakeskin boots looked young and inexperienced; obviously, he was at least several steps ahead of Baer.

"Remember, it's murder."

Baer sighed and muttered, "I still have two sets." He reached into a pocket of the warmup suit and pulled out two key rings. "The originals and this other. I laid the third off on a bloke I heard of. But you know as well as me nothing's been taken. Before I could set things up, Herrick died, and you put a bleedin' guard on the house, front and back."

"What bloke?"

"Ah—" Yet again the hand passed over Baer's shiny pate. "Christ."

Teddy had begun another song:

Gimme a little kiss, won't yeh, hon?

"To?" Ward demanded, his tone now rough.

"To a Dutch fella who collects books. He's known, y'know, *on the street* to be interested in old books. Paid twenty pound once, I hear, for a little book a' poems."

"You mean he fences books."

Baer's hand shot out. "I'm not sayin' that now. I *wouldn't* say that. Ever. He's into books, he is, but it's not like he's the bookish type, if you know what I mean?"

"Jan deKuyper," said Ward. "Lives on James Place. The old 'Temple of Wrath.' "

Baer looked sick. "How can I get out of this? I only took

the fookin' keys. I don't know what he did with 'em, probably nuttin'. Far as what Teddy and me and the little one did with Herrick in his own house—we're consenting adults. He invited us over. When I left him, he was still walking about, you saw that yehrself. I don't know nuttin' about any poison or whiskey. I can't stand the stuff. I don't go *near* it!"

"What about your phone message to Herrick a week later?"

Baer brightened. "See—that's proof I t'ought the bastard was aloive a whole effin' week after you say he died."

Out in the bar, Teddy wailed,

And I'll give it roight bah-ck,

Bah-boom, roared the bass drum.

I'll give it roight bah-ck,

Bah-boom.

Chew you!

Or, at least, so Ward heard. *Bah-boom, bah-bah-boom, bah-bah-boom!* The crowd cheered, whistled, and catcalled.

Said Ward, "I want several things from you." He opened the camera bag and fitted the camcorder into its slot.

"Anything." Baer plainly sensed a deal.

"First, the keys."

Baer handed the two sets over.

"Also a copy of each and every video you have of Teddy. That your stock?" He pointed to the videotapes that were stacked in neat groups on some shelving at one end of the storeroom. "I'm sure any magistrate would be interested in them, to say nothing of the tax man." It would keep Baer on a string, coming to him with anything he heard that might get him off. "Finally—not a word to deKuyper." Ward thought he knew how McGarr would handle the situation. "Not a hint. Nothing."

"You must be daft if yeh t'ink I'd tell him I grassed on him. You ever see the yoke? He's the biggest bastard in maybe all of Ireland. A giant. Flaming blond beard. T'irty stone at least. Worked with Herrick, so he did."

"The tapes," Hughie said, pointing to the open camera bag.

Baer scrambled up from the low chair. "You'll like these, you will. Teddy's a great, undiscovered comic geen-us. Herrick might've made up some of the stuff and the titles, like. But on her own she's even better. You'll see so this morning. She'd make a hit in London or the States, if I could just get the word out."

Or get Joneux Ariane Danvers-Forde into the act, thought Ward. What the act needed was relief, if only visual, from the nakedly comic.

By the time Ward got out into the bar proper, Teddy had already selected her young "goat," as it were, from the audience and was sitting in his lap, one arm wrapping his neck. He was a large, obviously country bachelor around forty, who was wearing an outmoded overcoat and heavy black shoes. He had clipped his graying hair himself in front of a mirror, and the back was scissored with lines, like shingles.

To be a good sport, he was trying to smile, but the look of acute embarrassment was frozen on his windburned features, while Teddy demanded of him,

"And just how long *has* it been, Colm! Girls," she shouted over to the chippies, who now occupied a corner booth near the bar and had been joined by at least a half-dozen others, "have yiz copped onto his name? And it's true!" Teddy gave a little shriek and jumped out of his lap, while with the other hand she patted at him, as though fluffing a cushion. "He's a *hard* mahn, I'll tell yeh. You couldn't ride that yoke from here to—where was it you said you was from, Colm!"

The man said something.

"Leitrim!" Teddy shouted. "Not without serious damage."

Whether it was the effect of the soft, theatrical lighting, or Teddy's own ministrations to her physiognomy, she looked decades younger than she appeared in Herrick's videotapes. She was wearing a black lace top with full sleeves and a wide red dress with something like crinoline below. Her wig was honey blond, (Marilyn) Monroesque in cut, and she even sported a beauty spot on one cheek. Whenever she spoke, her red lips gleamed like fresh red paint.

But, then again, Ward thought—the whole point of Herrick's "Frollicks" had been to denigrate the human body, from how he looked in the early footage, as compared to later, to the obvious suggestion that Joneux Ariane Danvers-Forde would one day look something like Teddy.

Sitting back down in the man's lap, she said, "Now for your answer, Colm—and don't. *Don't* even t'ink of lying to yehr aunt Teddy, or she'll *punish* yeh, she will. How *long* has it been?"

The man muttered something, but Teddy spun suddenly and pummeled his face with her immense breasts. "Get cheeky with me, will yeh? Girls—how's that for a one-two punch?"

The chippies cheered.

"Now, when I ask yez summtin', Colm, I want yeh to answer in a loud, clear, *truthful* voice. We're all friends here, havin' a bit of a laugh, is all. And who knows—yeh tell us the truth that we know is true. Whoy, some manky lass might take pity on yeh, and yeh'll slump back to Leitrim with a big smile on your face and yehr column *not* in yehr hand!"

Colm made the further mistake of muttering something else.

"Louder!" Teddy demanded.

He said it again, though still not loud.

"How long did y'say? Twenty-two years?"

"No, no"—he tried to correct—"two. *Two* years!"

"You heard him yerselves, girls. Two, two—twenty-two years! That makes the poor dear agricultural sod a near virgin. His fookin' hymen has probably grown back altogether!

"And now for the big, *big* question, Colm. The one for the jackpot. Will we ask it together, girls?"

The chippies and other regulars cheered. The drummer struck up another drumroll that ended with a clash of cymbals. The entire bar, it seemed, roared, "HOW *LONG* IS IT?"

Added Teddy, "Yeh can give us the measure in feet or meters, we're all bleedin' engineers here." Again she leaned into him, her breasts splaying to either side of his face. "A *meter,* he says. At least! Jaysus, girls—it's our lucky day. Will I t'row a leg over him, just to see if he's lying?"

"No—ME FIRST, ME FIRST!" the chippies began to chant.

And in a dexterous feat, given Teddy's age, she swung a leg over the man's head, so that she was now straddling him with her wide red skirt and all the fluff beneath covering his head. Grabbing at her hem, she pulled it down. "And would yiz credit it, girls," she called over her shoulder. "He's not only BIG, he's one o' 'dem! A—"

"MUNCHKIN!" they all shouted.

Naturally, the man began struggling, but Teddy held him fast in the skirt.

"SO MUNCH!" the chippies roared.

The man's shiny, black shoes were now working the floor, pushing Teddy and him back until the chair finally toppled over.

"YA-HOO!" the chippies chorused. "RIDE HIM, COWGIRL!"

Ward slipped out the door and down the stairs.

♦

$\mathcal{P}art\ III$

BY

APPETITES

ALLURED

14

The Fatal Cup

HUGH WARD GOT A SURPRISE when he awoke the next morning—there in bed beside him.

He had thought Ruthie would be coming back Sunday night, and, not having seen each other for over a day, they would have some "catching up" to do. But when Ward rolled over, she was not there.

He snatched up the bedside phone, thinking that she had probably got back late and, not wanting to wake him, had decided to bunk in her own place.

The second surprise hit him when the phone answered on the first ring, and it was a man. "Who's this?"

"Well—you rang up, chum. You should know who you're calling. What number did you want?"

Ward said Bresnahan's number.

"And who are you wanting to speak to?"

Ward was catching on; there was no way of disguising a Kerry brogue that thick. Ward made his own voice as soft and slick as warm butter, although his heart was racing faster than it ever had in the boxing ring. "Ruth Bresnahan, please. Would she be there?"

"I'll see if she's out of the shower yet."

Shower! That was fast. There she had been away only a day and a half, and she was already showering with the Culchie bastard she said she had thrown over last summer. Maybe that's how relations were down in the mountains of Kerry, which—Ward reminded himself—had never been thoroughly civilized. But it was not how they (Ruthie and he) had agreed to behave toward each other.

He then heard O'Suilleabhain say something low, and Ruth giggled before coming on the wire with her patented, cheerful but sultry, "Hah-loo? Is it you?"

Ward managed a neutral grunt.

"It's not what you think. Noreen had to leave early last night, so she could get Maddie in bed and ready for school this morning, and I was having such a good time with Nuala and Fitzhugh, I decided to stay over when they needed a fourth for bridge."

The third being O'Suilleabhain, no doubt.

"Rory said he'd run me into town early enough to change for work. Which reminds me, will I see you there?"

What a curious question. Where else would she see him on a Monday morning? "I only called," he began to explain, "because—"

"Really. I must go. I'll be late if I don't. Tah."

She did not even give him time to respond before ringing off.

Ward could picture where she was standing between her bedroom and sitting room with his nibs only a few yards away. And what could she be wearing—a bath towel, a bathrobe, or perhaps some one of the more alluring presents that Ward himself had given her that made her look like a goddess. *If* she could be believed, and she had not already thrown herself at her former playmate, present neighbor, ex-fiancé, and fellow South Kerry Mountains savage.

Ward had to tell himself that she had never lied to him. Ever. Which was cheering. But—it dawned on Ward, as he threw back the covers and hopped out of bed—that she could hardly have said in front of O'Suilleabhain, "Look—I just spent the weekend with Rory, and I'm afraid it's all over between us." Or worse, "I just spent the weekend with Rory, but I'd like to continue to see you, too." Or worse still, "I spent the weekend with Rory. I had to get him out of my system. I hope my telling you this doesn't make a difference."

Ward would lose it completely, if that were the case. More than a few times, Ward had said exactly that to a woman, and the confession had inevitably begun an ugly and attenuated process of breaking apart.

Ward glanced at the clock. How much time would it take Bresnahan to dress and get into work in O'Suilleabhain's big Mercedes? Making for his closet, Ward decided those two were made for each other. Him with the Merc, her with her BMW, both . . . behemoths, both from the same rural background, and now in Dublin together where—it was true—she could help the ambitious wanker more than a team of publicists. She had taste, she knew the city, and she now had contacts—all courtesy of him. Ward.

He could see them together (the delight of press photographers), being snapped while attending some affair in Leinster House or the Shelbourne or some one of the charity balls that would be coming up now at Christmas. He tall, dark, and handsome with position and money; she tall, angular, and auburn with the looks of a kind of ancient Danaan queen, or so Ward himself always thought. They could become the toast of young Dublin society, especially with people like Fitzhugh and Nuala Frenche guiding them along. Fitzhugh must have been feeling O'Suilleabhain out, inviting him down to Dunlavin. They probably had some deal in the works.

Twenty-five minutes, Ward decided. At the inside. He would have to beat her there just to assess what sort of "cushion" of time she would provide herself with, because of O'Suilleabhain's presence. He couldn't keep himself from imagining how easily the towel might drop off her glorious body for a "quickie" before work, which was a common occurrence between Ward and her. He'd have to run, literally, which was the only way he could get cross town in twenty-five minutes during rush hour—on foot.

Ward reached for his runners and sweat suit. Maybe McGarr would have something undercover for him to do today. It would be the first time that Ward had arrived at the Castle either not impeccably attired, as was his wont, or, at least, dressed for an assignment.

He scarcely felt his legs or noticed the traffic that he dodged in and out of, the thick fumes from the fleets of buses that were conveying commuters to their jobs in the city center, the crowds that had already gathered near O'Connell Bridge. Rather than fight the throngs around Trinity College and along Dame Street, Ward kept running along the Liffey until he reached the Parliament Street, where he struck south.

Taking the stairs in the Castle entry three at a time, Ward hit the timer on his sports watch just as he bumped through the door into the battered old office that had been converted from a former British Army barracks. And there she was, sitting at her desk and already on the phone.

Ward checked the watch: twenty-two minutes, thirty-one seconds. "How'd you get here so quickie?" he blurted out.

"Quickly," he quickly corrected, glancing around to see if anybody else heard.

Bresnahan lowered the phone. "I thought you were going to run only every *other* day, like the orthopedist advised." Because of his knees, the joints of which had collected some calcification after all his years of violent physical activity.

"I dunno," he replied without thinking, "I thought maybe I'd give the ring another go." Suddenly, he crouched, pivoted, and threw a flurry of rapid punches at an imaginary opponent. "Y'know, maybe move up another weight class." Like to two-hundred-and-forty-pound, jumbo Culchies, he thought.

"If you do, when will I see you?" She had the phone on her hip, which meant she must be speaking to her mother, perhaps telling the perfidious, plotting crone of her "wonderful" weekend with Rory. "With all the training and the foreign trips. And consider the fact that you're no spring chicken."

That alone made Ward, who had been talking just to have something to say, want to do it.

"You told me before," she went on, "that at thirty-two, there has to be somebody out there who's younger, quicker, stronger, *tougher* even."

"Yah, but I decided it's the skill, the artistry, the ring savvy that really matters, and why throw that away?" Ward feinted, dodged, and jabbed some more, then straightened up in front of her desk, the sweat rolling down his face. Yet for maybe the first time ever after a workout, he felt miserable, betrayed, and there she probably had not even held the big bloody bollock's hand. "How?"

"How what?"

"How'd you get here so fast?"

"Rory. He's installed a brace of blue, blinking lights in the rear window of his Merc. Says it's one of the—"

"Perquisites of his profession," Ward put in.

"No, actually, one of the 'prerogatives' of his 'commission,' he calls it, being a member of the Dail and all. He uses it in combination with the car horn to great effect."

Ward smiled. O'Suilleabhain *would,* being a total, roaring, flaming, bloody gobshite; only an ego-crazed, power-hungry, agricultural sod would do something so . . . garish, and Ward was unable to keep the contempt from his face.

Bresnahan smiled. "A bit much?"

Or to keep himself from blurting out. "Not at all. For him? It's perfect. I wouldn't have him change a blue blink or a horn beep. Be a pity if he traveled up North," where somebody might actually mistake him for the police.

And curiously, Bresnahan's own smile grew more complete. "What's this I'm hearing? Could it be . . . ?"

"It's McKeon, I think," Ward said, cutting her off. Ducking down and spinning again, he threw a few more shots at McKeon's voice, which they'd been hearing from the direction of McGarr's cubicle.

"Yo—Ali, me mahn," said McKeon. "When you're through fighting smoke and shadow, could you and your sparring partner do a coupl'a turns in here. We'd like to begin."

McGarr was seated at his desk, a pile of folders before him. Over the weekend, there had been a party at a flat in Ballymun, a notorious, high-rise housing scheme on the outskirts of Dublin. Some neighbors, returning home from a pub and hearing the music, tried to join in but were denied admission. They returned with reinforcements, and a melee broke out.

"T'ugs and louts," McKeon branded them.

"Three dead," McGarr went on. "One by cleaver, the two others by defenestration."

"De-who?" In spite of his recent brush with death, McKeon's dark eyes were shining. His thick blond hair had been recently clipped and was parted carefully at the side.

"—fenestration," explained Sinclaire, who was the only one of them who had attended university. "It means they were chucked out the *fenestra*. That's window to you with no Latin."

"Nah, nah, nah—that's not how it happened, Hippocrates. The one t'ug had the other t'ug by the craw, like so." McKeon rounded on Sinclaire, who made for the door. Mc-Keon then demonstrated on himself. "And they was on this balcony. So he gets the idea to push him over, but doesn't the railing come away, conveniently relieving the roles of two welfare spongers. It's all on videotape."

"What—another one?" Delaney asked.

"I tell you—it's the answer to the crime problem country-wide. We just get the government to issue everybody a video camera and some tape, and there we have it—instant, incontrovertible evidence to all crime committed in the Republic of Eire." He pronounced it "ear."

"And you'd be out of a job," said Swords from the top of a file cabinet where he was sitting like a pooka; in all there were fifteen people packed into the cubicle. Bresnahan, who was least senior of all, was standing in the door.

"Non-sense—*you*'d be out on your arse, of course. But me—I'd be watching the videotapes."

"With the clicker in one hand and a jug of *cicuta* in the other," said McGarr. "Johnny"—he closed the Ballymun file and scaled it at Swords—"you and Sinclaire handle that one. I want it all wrapped up with the videotape, statements from all participants, and a confession from yehr woman with the cleaver by midweek at the latest."

"Kick—who?" McKeon asked.

"Something must have happened to his brain while he was in that coma," said Ward.

"But not to me nose. Have yeh never heard of Sunshine Soap? Imagine the b-galls of him—sorry, Rut'ie—comin' to work in that condition."

"Says he's going to change his line of work anyhow," she said.

"What's it this time?"

"Says he's going to follow your recent lead, Bernie." And to the others, Bresnahan advised, "Nobody help him. He's on his own with this one."

McKeon only had to think for a moment. "The first mucker who says 'punch-drunk' will find himself joining Swords and Sinclaire in Ballymun."

"Well, there's proof the poison did nothing to destroy his mental associations," somebody else put in. "He's still got wet on the brain."

"Some form of *cicuta maculata,*" McGarr went on, as though speaking to himself, "has been identified as the poison that was contained in the flask that heroic Detective Superintendent McKeon volunteered to test for the Garda Siochana.

"It's a family of mainly American weeds, which are considered by many authorities to be the most virulent, poisonous plants in the North Temperate Zone. The juice from some varieties, namely *cicuta maculata,* can kill an adult in twenty minutes. Horribly, might I add. The juice, extracted from the roots, is soluble in alcohol, and its taste is reported to be smoky and thus can be obscured in something like whiskey that is distilled over a peat fire."

"So much for single-malt, pot-stilled whiskey."

"Sure, there's always brandy."

"Or porter."

Said McKeon sourly, "I wouldn't rub porter on a sore bruise."

"Not with your lips in plain view."

"*Cicuta maculata* is not to be confused with *conium maculatum,* which is the Eurasian herb that produced the cup that Socrates quaffed. Members of the *cicuta* family are known colloquially as cowbane, wild parsnip, snakeroot, snakeweed, beaver poison, muskrat weed, spotted hemlock, spotted cowbane, musquash root, false parsley, poison hemlock, water hemlock, wild carrot, fever root, mock-eel root, spotted parsley and *carotte à moreau* in French Canada.

"The profusion of common names gives some idea of the ubiquity of the family, and its confusion with other nonpoisonous plants indicates the difficulty in identifying its varieties."

"Except that *cicuta* plants are not native to Ireland." McKeon, of course, having been nearly killed by the plant, had read all about it.

McGarr nodded. "But would grow here readily, though the chief botanist at Trinity tells me there have been no reports of them in over fifty years. So much for the means by which Herrick was murdered. Let's ramble on to motive and opportunity."

McGarr checked his watch, which said five of ten. He had to be in court on another case at ten-thirty. "I have Hughie's report following his visit to the Poop Deck."

"Did she have her eye in or out for you?" McKeon asked.

"I forgot all about that," said Bresnahan.

"Being otherwise engaged." It was Ward.

"There it is again, raising its ugly, untrusting head."

McGarr went on. "My own report of my visit to Jan

deKuyper, the conservator at the Delmas Bindery, is here, and Rut'ie had the goodness to phone me last night with what she learned in Dunlavin about Joneux Ariane Danvers-Forde and spouse." He quickly summarized what they knew so far.

DeKuyper had purchased two liter bottles of Glenfinnan as a gift to Herrick. That alone was curious, since McGarr had made some inquiries, and deKuyper was known to be an unabashed skinflint. Along with the gift of the whiskey was a notecard advising Herrick to "save the best for last," meaning the bottle that had been aged longer. Herrick did the opposite, which perhaps averted the deaths of at least two other people.

"But why would deKuyper kill him, when Herrick was providing deKuyper with five thousand a quarter?" McKeon asked.

McGarr hunched a shoulder. "Charlotte Bing has it that Herrick was tapping both the principal and interest of the bequest his father had left him, and his funds were getting low."

"But even so," Bresnahan put in, "the house and contents must be worth—" She glanced at Ward.

"Two-three hundred grand."

"Four, I bet," she said. "A foreign embassy or some EC commission would snap that place up all found—make the lower floor an office, the upper a residence."

McGarr carried on: DeKuyper had told him that he intended to apply for Herrick's now-vacant post as keeper, which might be motive enough. Hadn't they known of murders committed over the price of a pint? In any case, what deKuyper did not have, at least at the time that he dropped off the packet with the whiskey, was a set of keys to the house. Which he did now, Bunny Baer having "sold" him a duplicate set.

"Why, the cagey Bunny," observed McKeon.

Joneux Ariane Danvers-Forde had the opportunity to spike the second bottle when she left the "Frollick" to dress and go home. She could also have filled the flask and placed it in the Bible. Either way, deKuyper would look like the poisoner, having spiked the longer-aged bottle and advised Herrick to drink it last. But then, why would Danvers-Forde have said she took a drink from *that* bottle? Or told Bresnahan that some whiskey had already been taken from it?

"About a pint flask gone?" Ward asked.

"Exactly," confirmed Bresnahan, who had interviewed the woman.

But Bunny Baer also described the second bottle as having been not quite full, so that—if Danvers-Forde were telling the truth or was not mistaken about pouring from the second bottle—the bottle must have been spiked sometime between her taking a drink and Baer filling the decanter.

"Who could only be Baer," McKeon concluded.

Said Bresnahan, "What's the chance of Bunny Baer knowing about the poisonous effects of *cicuta*"—

"—*maculata*," McGarr supplied.

"And its solubility in alcohol, the smoky taste, etcetera. What's his motive for having been so well prepared to slip the stuff into the decanter? Herrick's slagging of Teddy?"

"Maybe—no *maybe* about it—he was in for a cut of whatever his mates, the ones he was goin' to lay the keys off on, could take away from Herrick's. He's got a record as long as yehr arm."

"But would he—Bunny Baer—actually commit murder

himself for a cut of a burglary?" Ward asked. "Once it was known to be murder, once his mates put it together that Baer must have got hold of the keys around the time of the murder, Baer would be meat for them—either in a direct tip to us or whenever they got in a jam. It's the reason he only 'offered' the keys to deKuyper, who's an outsider."

"Doubtless anonymously, or through some intermediary," Bresnahan put in.

Said Ward, "On the other hand, can you think of any motive whatsoever for Joneux Ariane Danvers-Forde wanting to murder Herrick, who had hired her and with whom she was sharing so much else?"

"Delicately put," said Bresnahan.

"By a delicate sensibility," said Ward.

Said McKeon, "Only when upwind. And have yous two whiz kids not considered that maybe she didn't *want* to share herself with that oul' bag of goods?"

"You mean—as in *sexual harassment?*" Bresnahan asked with no little amazement. "Did she look like an unwilling participant to you?"

"Maybe it was just a put-on, like, to t'row us off."

"Then she deserves the Academy Award."

McKeon cocked his head; he had more police experience than Bresnahan and Ward combined. "Whoever did this t'ing planned it to a tee, and we don't know enough to discount anybody. Yet."

McGarr was staring down at the two rings of keys on his desk, the "originals" and one of the two copies that Baer had made. McKeon was right; what they were missing was a convincing motive for Herrick's murder, and it had something to do with the keys.

"Then there's Charlotte Bing," said Ward, as though reading McGarr's mind. "She had keys. She also knew about the delivery of the whiskey, since deKuyper had told her about it on the phone."

"But why would she murder Herrick?" Bresnahan asked.

"The old wrath of a woman scorned," Ward replied.

"You're only thinking of your former flames," she muttered, adding in a louder voice, "And Charlotte Bing's affair with Herrick was nearly twenty years ago. Certainly, she was well shut of that dirty old soak."

"To become keeper of Marsh's Library?" McKeon asked. "Maybe she knew what he was up to with the books. It's the reason she rang us up, as I remember."

Again there was a matter of preparation—obtaining the *cicuta maculata* and waiting for the opportunity to use it. For Charlotte Bing, that would have also meant stealing into the house while the others were still there, if the scenario about the second bottle was accurate. And Bing did not seem like the type of person who would be up to an adventure of that sort.

"Would she have known about the flask in the Bible?" Ward asked.

Bresnahan shook her head. "Herrick couldn't have been drinking like that for twenty years. When she had known him, his alcoholism had probably not been as severe."

"Which shows what you know about alcoholism," said McKeon. Suddenly, everybody in the cubicle was staring at him. "Well, don't look at me," he complained. "I'm not one to kiss and tell. And I want all of yiz to know that I haven't had so much as a whiff off a ball of malt since my . . . misadventure."

"Someone wheel in the polygraph," said Swords.

McGarr scooped up the keys and tossed one set to McKeon.

"Give me two hours to finish up here and go home and pack a suitcase, then remove the guard from the house." With all the keys that were still out there, somebody was bound to come poking about, and he was interested in knowing who that would be. Also, he still had the feeling that they had missed something in the house itself.

"Will you need a hand, somebody to spell you?" asked McKeon.

"I'll have Hughie stop round sometime after the sun goes down." As in, you're benched, for the moment.

McKeon looked away toward the grime-encrusted window, having expected no more.

"I'll also need two pair of infrared sensors, the kind that can be fitted to doors, and an ear monitor. The pitch of the warning signal of each sensor should be different"—so he would know which of the two doors in Herrick's house was being opened. "That's for you, Bernie.

"Your second assignment is to find the police report of the death of Charlotte Bing's mother. You can fax it to me at Herrick's. Third, ring up a reporter at the *Press*. One"—from his billfold McGarr dug out the young woman's card— "Cecilia Gill. Tell her you've got a scoop—that we've decided Herrick did actually die of natural causes, and we're scrubbing our investigation, as of noon today. The guards will be taken away, and Herrick's solicitor will be allowed to proceed with the disposal of the estate, according to the terms of his will. If you act fast, she could have it in the evening edition.

"You two"—McGarr meant Bresnahan and Ward—"should take a closer look at Baer's allegation that deKuyper would fence stolen, rare books. Nuala—Noreen's mother—might give you the loan of a few interesting volumes from her collection. We might set him up."

"And deport the bastard," said McKeon.

"You have there in your hands some idea of what the *cicuta* family looks like." McGarr pointed to the photocopies. "Also, while you're down in Dunlavin, you might pop in on the Danvers-Fordes and look around, if you can. It's a long shot that a person would use a plant to poison somebody and then not destroy it, but I have an idea that whoever did this thing thinks we're—"

"Thick," said Ward, glancing through the copies. "There must be twenty plants here, and they all look different."

"*Cicuta maculata, cicuta californica, cicuta douglasii, cicuta vagans, cicuta bolanderi, cicuta curtissii, cicuta bulbifera,*" Bresnahan read, leafing through the pages.

"Well, yes and no. Most of the varieties grow in wet or boggy ground and along streams and swales."

"That should help you a great deal, here in Ireland," said Sinclaire. "We'll be thinking of you while we're out in the concrete jungles of Ballymun."

"And some varieties can grow quite tall—over ten feet. But not at this time of year. As I said, it's—"

"A long shot," McKeon repeated with malice. "G'luck, children."

The meeting continued.

15

The Romance of a Chequered History

TO BEGIN THEIR INVENTORY of Marsh's Library that morning, Noreen McGarr and Charlotte Bing drove there together, unfortunately in Bing's car. Noreen already had a premonition that her experience with Charlotte Bing would be a *travail,* and a means of escape might prove desirable.

Noreen, of course, had visited the building several times. She had even once used the collection while writing a paper as a raw undergraduate.

She now said to Charlotte Bing, "It's a handsome building, I'll give it that." They were standing outside.

"Indeed. It's perhaps the finest example of a seventeenth-century scholar's library anywhere. And it remains essentially unchanged since its construction in 1701."

"Wasn't it built by Sir William Robinson, who was earlier responsible for the magnificent Royal Hospital?" Noreen's area of expertise was art and architecture.

"Shall I give you the tour?"

"Why not?" Charlotte Bing's obvious delight in the details of her profession, which had to be old stuff to anybody after twenty-plus years, rather intrigued Noreen.

"It was built, as you can see, in the shape of an 'L'."

Noreen looked up at the tall, gabled structure that was situated in a narrow laneway not far from busy Patrick Street. The twin steeples of St. Patrick's Cathedral, where Swift had been dean, loomed above the structure.

"The lower level with the entrance there"—she pointed to a gap in a high wall—"was meant to be the living quarters of the keeper. Now we use it for other purposes. But the object, I believe, was to get the library reading areas of the building up into the light and, certainly, away from the rabble." Bing began climbing the stairs toward large, aged oak doors.

Narcissus Marsh, Bing went on, had been an Englishman who had been educated in Oxford. After his ordination, he was sent to Ireland as provost of Trinity College. But he soon wearied of looking after "Three-hundred-and-forty young men and boys in this lewd and debauch'd town."

Part of the reason for the waywardness of Trinity undergraduates at that time was the fact that no student was allowed to study in the library unless accompanied by Marsh himself or one of the fellows of the College. When Marsh was unable to get the rule changed, he decided to build a "public" library, the first in Ireland.

Once the building was constructed, Marsh acted quickly to stock its handsome shelves, acquiring the library of Edward Stillingfleet, once dean of St. Paul's Cathedral and later bishop of Worcester. The ten thousand volumes were described at the time as "The best private library in England." By then, Marsh had become primate of the Church of England in Ireland, and when he died a few years later, he willed his own books to the library.

"Not long after, the collections of the Huguenot emigré

Dr. Elias Bouhereau and John Stearnes were added," Bing continued, locking the heavy outer doors behind them. "And because the main body of work dates from the same period, it's a rather unified collection of about twenty-five thousand books relating to most branches of learning in the sixteenth, seventeenth, and early part of the eighteenth centuries. The collectors possessed eclectic tastes, and there're books on medicine, law, the physical sciences, botany, travel, mathematics, music, surveying, and classical literature."

After climbing another flight of interior stairs, they entered the library proper through a pair of tall glass doors.

And suddenly Noreen's mind was flooded with the recollection of the three or four days she had spent amid the beautiful oak bookcases, each with a carved and lettered gable, topped by a mitre. As a first-year student at Trinity, she had been researching a paper on the troubled history of the city of La Rochelle in France, and she was allowed to read the documents that Bouhereau, who had been a prominent citizen of that city, had brought with him in a strongbox when he fled to England in 1686.

It had been Noreen's first experience dealing with primary historical materials and had whetted her appetite for academic research. She still contributed regularly to several journals that dealt with art history and criticism.

"It was Marsh himself who in 1712 insisted Bouhereau chain at least the two lower shelves of books," Bing went on, closing the door.

"Why?"

"Because of thefts. But it didn't help much. in 1738, the Reverend John Wynne, who was then keeper, reported to the governors that a large number of books had been stolen or vandalized. Tracts, maps, and pictures had been ripped out. Yet the thievery continued until in 1779 the governors ordered that no book be taken down or read, except in the presence of the keeper or his deputy."

Said Noreen, "So, in spite of Marsh's good intention in establishing the library, it was back to the practice of Trinity."

"Worse—in 1828, after the first book thief was caught and banished from the library, the governors decreed that in the future the public would be allowed to read books only in the librarian's room."

Which had been where Noreen had perused the Huguenot archives. "So, if Dr. Herrick did remove books, he was not the first."

"Far from it. In 1849, a House of Commons report on public libraries stated that from the time of its foundation to that date, Marsh's had lost some twelve hundred books, one way or another." Bing led Noreen toward her "office," which was really the main reading table of the building; from there both wings of the library could be seen.

"Throughout our history, we've also been plagued by the lack of necessary funding and by cranks, fools, and knaves."

Noreen cocked her head; Bing's phrasing sounded like something out of Swift. Or Herrick.

Bing removed her heather-colored tweed coat, and Noreen noted that Charlotte Bing was still a shapely woman at—how old could she be? Forty-five or so? With her high pile of ashen hair, pale hazel eyes, and fair features, she might even appear rather beautiful, were she to soften her image. Fitting wire-rim spectacles over her ears only increased the severity.

"One keeper in the nineteenth century," she went on, reaching to help Noreen off with her coat, "was as ignorant as horse droppings and resented anybody who came to use the collection, even to locking his own deputy out on numerous occasions. He had the only key.

"Another time, the governors nearly agreed to a proposal to remove the books from the Marsh's for a proposed 'Gallery of Learning.' Only an offer from one of the Guinnesses—of *stout* fame, don't you know—saved us. He built a new road outside and placed a thousand pounds in trust for maintenance.

"More recently the Kennedys stepped in when it appeared the *public* would no longer continue to support this national institution!"

"The bread people?" Noreen asked, meaning Kennedy's Bread, which was marketed throughout the country.

"No! The bloody Americans." Charlotte Bing's hand came up to her mouth, and she nearly dropped Noreen's coat. Glancing toward the door, she said in a whisper, "I'm afraid I'm just an opinionated old shrew, and they've been so generous, Americans or not."

"Do you get many Americans?" Noreen looked to see if there was a window open, suddenly realizing how cold it was in the building.

"May through September. They come in here stunned, like they've never seen so many old books in one place at one time. And they ask the most obtuse questions. Often it's difficult to be civil."

Noreen glanced at the packed shelves of books and immediately felt very American. She had remembered Marsh's as a small, cozy place, but twenty-five thousand books and Charlotte Bing for a day? Or two or three! How long *could* it take?

She also thought of Brian Herrick's *copy* of Marsh's Library; there were far fewer books on those shelves. "Wouldn't it be easier if we simply went to Dr. Herrick's house and determined what from the library he might have taken there? Then—"

"But what if he already sold or otherwise disposed of some of his thefts? There's no knowing the perfidy of such a . . . *deviate*. We'll start with the Z's and work forward. Not only will it make the work seem to go faster, that wing of the building is presently catching the sun." She stepped toward the back wing of the library.

"Did you know that during the Easter Rising in 1916, Marsh's was in the direct line of fire between British troops and the I.R.A., who had taken over Jacob's factory? Machine-gun bullets shattered the glass doors in this room and *pierced* many of the books, as you'll see today. You know"—Bing grasped her elbows and tightened them to her, almost as though hugging herself—"sometimes I wish I had been around then. It was such an exciting time, and so romantic."

Noreen reached for her coat. If she had to endure the unromantic process of inventorying Marsh's Library in an unromantic age, at least she would do so warm.

16

Two Halves of a Donut

RUTH BRESNAHAN would not let Hugh Ward drive her new white BMW that she had bought with a part of the bequest from her father's estate. "I didn't pay an outrageous *bomb* of money for this chariot to sit and watch other people drive it."

Ward winced, not entirely from her driving, which was outrageous by his own careful standards. He was not exactly *other* people, at least not from his point of view. They were *us,* or us was *them.* Together. And there should be no differentiating between them.

"It's not like I'm the man from the moon," he complained, reaching for the dash, as she shot past an errant cow that was gorging on the lush grass by the side of the dirt road.

"Light o' me life," she replied, squeezing the gray linen of the summer suit he had changed into, "you are to me. What's more, if you drive, we wouldn't get there by nightfall."

"Well, you drive like a bat out of Kerry," which to Ward was like a kind of hell. He was also thinking of O'Suilleabhain with his blocklong Merc and the blue-flashing lights. Did everybody from Kerry with a few quid and a German automobile drive like a Grand Prix aspirant?

"No slaggin' now, or I'll do a donut."

"A what?"

"A donut. It's a maneuver done with brake pedal and accelerator."

"Where'd you get something like that?"

"A donut? On the teley and in the papers, although I was with Rory when he did one on St. Stephen's Green this morning."

Now Ward began to laugh; he clapped his hands. "That's perfect! I can see it in all the papers. Bulletin caps–

THE O'SUILLEABHAIN T.D.

DOES *DONUT*

ON ST. STEPHEN'S GREEN

"Observed by a cast of thousands walking to work," Bresnahan cried, warming to the crack. "And we're not messin'!"

Now they were both laughing.

"The shameless bastard," muttered Ward, when he had caught his breath.

"Though I'm only supposing," Ruth put in. "I was beneath the dash, me eyes squeezed tight."

Hoping nobody would see you in his company, Ward thought. "Where *are* we, for Jesus' sake," he asked, if only to change the subject; the less said about that wally the better.

But it only brought up another point of difference between them—Bresnahan always knew exactly where she was in the countryside, as though she had a gyroscope in her head. Whereas Ward needed a good map, the moment he left environs of Greater Dublin. Fields, cows, trees, and rock walls all looked the same to him.

"Nearly there," Bresnahan replied. "This way is faster, you'll see. What time is it?"

"Just after two."

"Whoops!" At a crossroads, Bresnahan swung the wheel, hit the brakes, then tromped the gas, and the responsive car showered an oncoming lorry with a howitzer blast of dirt and gravel, before veering down an even narrower lane at a torrid pace. "Well—that was *half* a donut. I'll give you the rest on the way back."

Now the Frenches' country house could be seen in the distance. "Told you—in *record* time."

Ward felt as though he had not swallowed the first bite yet.

After Nuala Frenche gave Bresnahan and Ward the loan of three rare and valuable books, she insisted they stay for lunch.

"Thanks, but we can't," said Bresnahan. "We're to pop in on the Danvers-Fordes and see what sort of plants they have."

"Well, that will take you all afternoon. Alastair's an amateur horticulturlist, you know. He employs a team of gardeners in the greenhouse alone, which is the reason he bought the property. The *orangerie,* he calls it—an immense old crystal-palace type affair made in the shape of a wheel. They say he's well known in the field, contributing articles on plant growth and so forth to specialist periodicals.

"You can do me a favor—take back Joneux Ariane's campaign hat, which she left with us the other night. I wonder how her war is going without it?"

"Which war is that?" Ward asked innocently.

"Why, the bloody war between the effing sexes, my dear. If you haven't noticed that she's a Napoleon or, at least, a Clausewitz in the struggle, then you're either unobservant, which you're not, sexless, which I hear you're not, or just a patently obsequious wretch in present company, and I commend your

tact. Were I not to know better, I'd hazard that you and
Joneux were brother and sister, you look so much alike."

"There you go—if all else fails," said Bresnahan, meaning
herself, "you can always come down here and commit adulter-
ous incest, while the husband is hip deep in horticulture."

An hour later, Bresnahan and Ward were invited a second
time to lunch—in the Danvers-Fordes' large ornate greenhouse. Five glass-covered spokes radiated from a central hub
that was shaped like a tulip. Four had been named after
a continent or two: "Eurasia," "Africa," "The Americas,"
"Down Under," while the fifth spoke was the entrance corri-
dor, and was lined with plants that Ward had seen before and,
he assumed, were native.

A long table, laden with platters of viands, bottles of wine,
and whiskey enough for a small army, had been placed in the
middle of the central hub. And the Danvers-Fordes' rambling
Tudor manor house—which could only be a re-creation in
Ireland—could be seen in the distance.

"This place reeks of major money," said Bresnahan.

"Millions," said Ward.

"More like billions," Bresnahan corrected.

"How do you know?" It rather irked him how she was getting "up," as it were, on the holdings of this one and that.

"Actually, he's Australian, or his father is. His mother was
Irish."

"What's the father do?"

"Cattle, I believe."

"Like yehr mahn," Ward said, meaning O'Suilleabhain.
"He ought to become better acquainted with the filthy-rich
poisoner."

"Already has. Rory's good, like that. You know, with
people."

In other words, he can exploit them by some means, being a nakedly ambitious Culchie *Wunderbuck.* It was Ward's term of derision for the jumped-up farmers in double-breasted suits who annually descended upon Dublin to hee and haw in the Dail Eireann and impose their narrow view of rectitude on the rest of the country. "Imagine," he said, "*The* O'Suilleabhain, beef baron of Kerry, Libya, and New South Wales."

"Perhaps you should have some wine to dampen your spleen. Here they come now."

Through the panes of the greenhouse, they could now see the Danvers-Fordes crossing the lawn, Joneux Ariane looking like a waif in a white muslin smock, white lacy ankle socks, and flat white slippers. There was a white silk bow in her hair, and she was wearing white fingerless silk gloves that rose to her elbows, evidently in deference to the cold, since her arms were otherwise bare to the shoulders. But, in all, the effect was meant to be—

"Sexy, say what?" Bresnahan asked. "Nuala was right on both scores. I don't believe I've ever seen that woman unprepared for battle. Or at least a good skirmish. You know, in the war between the effing sexes. She's dark, she's fine, she's built. If you were to knock off a few pounds and pump up your pects—there you are, my man, in highly seductive drag."

Ward shook his head; in former relationships it had always been he who had passed judgments. "You have a way of putting things."

"From my mouth to God's ear. In five minutes and without saying more than two words, she'll have you eating out of her . . . well, let's say slipper, just to be polite. But, of course, you've studied the video. Uninitiated men are more of a challenge, I should think."

For all his millions (or billions), Danvers-Forde himself was wearing the same rumpled tweed coat that he had on when Bresnahan first met him, or another very much like it. Added to that were jodhpurs and riding boots, although he had told Bresnahan he did not ride.

A thin smile of—was it satisfaction?—suggested that he was admiring his wife, who was moving ever so gracefully a half-step before him. With a weak chin and plain features, Danvers-Forde was not a handsome person himself, and he seemed to be taking pleasure in knowing he possessed, if only on paper, such an exotic creature.

"Back again so soon, Inspector Bresnahan?" he said upon entering the hub of the greenhouse. "You must be hot on the trail." He kept his hand on the door so that his wife could enter, and the servant, who had been waiting there, could leave. "This time with a one-man hit squad, so to speak."

As he moved toward the table, Danvers-Forde turned his head to each wing of the greenhouse, until he discovered his gardeners busy in "The Americas" section. He watched them for a moment, while Bresnahan introduced Joneux Ariane to Ward.

Under her long, dark eyelashes, her equally dark eyes flickered up at Ward; she then smiled in a way that was both shy and laden with promise. It was as though she were saying, You know, because you've seen what I sometimes do; perhaps, if we're careful, something might be arranged. Or so Ward imagined. He wrenched his eyes away.

"Straight through the plastron," Bresnahan remarked while extending her hand to the smaller woman. "In the future, keep your guard up." And then, "Joneux! How delighted I am to see you again. You look fetching."

Said Danvers-Forde, "Well, then, Ward—it *is* Ward, isn't it—would you care for some wine? Or whiskey."

Ward glanced at the brimming table that looked like something devised for a bacchanal. Only if you drink half the bottle first, he thought.

"Or are you in training? You *are* the pugilist policeman, are you not?"

It was a phrase that had sometimes been used in the papers and had always irked Ward. His being a guard did not give anybody the right to abuse him, verbally or otherwise. They would get right down to business.

Stepping toward Danvers-Forde, he opened a folder that contained photocopies of the information McGarr had assembled on the *cicuta* family of plants. "I'd like you to go over these carefully, sir, and tell me if you have such plants growing on your property. Or if you've come across plants like these in the recent past." It was Ward's official tone that he had learned from McGarr: the one that put an interviewee on notice that the visit was not social.

While Danvers-Forde was fanning through the material, Bresnahan turned to his wife. "Will you be attending Dr. Herrick's funeral?"

"When will it be?"

"Tuesday, I believe. Did you not know that we've called off our investigation? We're only cleaning up"—Ruth decided not to say "loose ends"—"a few details. The announcement will be in the evening papers."

"Of course she won't attend Herrick's funeral," her husband snapped. "Do you think Joneux *willingly* consorted with that old reprobate?"

The wife only looked away, so that Ward could not read her face. It had appeared to him that her performance on the videotape had seemed willing enough, unless playing the *put* was second nature to her. "By that you mean your wife was *forced* to have sexual relations with Herrick?"

"I don't mean anything of the sort, now that some generous soul has relieved the world of his presence. In fact, there's now no reason we should ever have to mention his name again."

His wife only continued to study the floor.

"These plants"—he handed the photocopies back to Ward—"aren't plants at all. They're weeds, and the only place I've ever glimpsed one such plant is in Herrick's own house. He's got—he *had*—a great bloody bush of water hemlock in a pot in the conservatory. That's *cicuta maculata*." Danvers-Forde tapped the top page that Ward was holding. "It's one of the 'exotics' he inherited from his father, who, incidentally, was another sort of individual altogether. I have all his books."

Ward waited.

"A sterling botanist and pharmaceutical innovator. If by showing me these"—Danvers-Forde indicated the photocopies—"you are suggesting that Herrick died of *cicuta maculata* poisoning, which can be a gruesome death, I can only say he got what he deserved. And, if he had one iota of common decency in him, which I doubt, it was suicide.

"So, my hat is off to whoever devised the brilliant plan of poisoning his cup, of which he was overly fond. I don't know if it says there"—again he waved his hand toward the photocopies—"but *cicuta maculata* is soluble in alcohol and produces a violent, agonizing death. One such poisoning was described as early as 1697 by the Swiss naturalist Johann Jakob Wepfer."

Danvers-Forde then turned his head to Ward. "But if

you're calling off your investigation, you must think it was self-administered."

Said Ward, "We're trying to find out where he might have gotten the stuff, but I guess you've cleared that up for us. Would you mind if I asked your gardeners if they recognize any of these plants? It's just a formality. Now."

Danvers-Forde gave out a short, mirthless laugh. "I only wish I had thought of it myself, eighteen months ago. Be my guest. The head man—Seamus there—will give you the tour. Take as much time as you need. And, of course, help yourselves." He meant the table that was brimming with food and drink.

Danvers-Forde turned to his wife. "Come along, Joneux. Now that we know what they're about, there's no sense in taking up any more of their time." Or wasting ours, went unsaid.

Passing Bresnahan with his arm around his wife's shoulder, he added, "Really, you should try the wine. Alcohol content around twelve percent or so—hardly enough to dissolve *cicuta maculata,* the taste of which is rather like burnt parsnips, enough like most whiskey to be a good match. Of course, there's some of that, too."

None of the gardeners had ever seen such plants.

Driving back through the thin, winter-afternoon light along another series of dirt roads, Bresnahan pulled the car down a cart track barely wide enough for goats. There was nothing to be seen in any direction but gorse, bogs, and heather, since they were deep in the desolate beauty of the Wicklow Hills.

"This looks like a suitable place," she said, switching off the engine.

"For what?" Ward asked, looking out on a cloud formation that was sweeping over the dun winter peaks just above them.

"Whoi, da udder half of the donut, yeh ninny," she replied in Dublin argot, wrapping an arm over his seat and tugging at his shoulder. "Aren't you goin' to give me me wear, little fella? Or are yeh all worn out from yehr sessions at the Poop Deck?"

"Better—'pooped out from yehr session on The Deck,' as it's called." Ward was trying to act nonchalant, but he twisted around and looked behind them. "What if somebody . . . ? And isn't this car rather small?" When they had two big beds waiting for them back in Dublin, he meant.

"Then I guess we'll just have to get out and use the bonnet." With her other hand she reached for him in a way that made saying no impossible. "Could it be you're getting a little stodgy in your elder age?"

Seconds later Ward asked, "Is this something you've done before?" Considering the ease with which they were now entangled.

"No, but I've been thinking about it. What about yourself?"

Ward kept his counsel, since it wouldn't take long. Never did, like that, out in the country where any gannet-eyed gorsoon forking an ass-rail of turf in one of the nearby bogs might see. Or the passengers in the airbus that now thundered only a few hundred feet over their heads, as it angled in on Dublin Airport to the north.

"Oh—look, Granny. What are those two people doing down there?" he imagined a child asking.

"Why, they're—let me adjust your safety belt."

It was dark by the time they got back to Dublin and Bresnahan's mews apartment, where they would drop off the car. And who should be waiting at the curb in his big black Mercedes but *The* O'Suilleabhain.

"Shit," said Ward, "what's this—old home week?"

"Nothing of the kind. He's just being persistent, and it's good for my pride, having him off. Many's the time the shoe was on the other hoof."

By which she meant?

"You go on now. I'll deal with him and ring you after."

After what—some shady lane? Ward wondered, as he climbed out of the BMW and made for the Shrewsbury Road, which was a short walk away.

O'Suilleabhain powered down the window. "How're ya, lad?"

"Evening, sir," Ward replied neutrally, his hands forming fists in his trouser pockets, as he moved by the car.

"And a fine evening, it tis," O'Suilleabhain went on, as though attempting conversation in his thick Kerry brogue.

Let's hope you'll not discover *how* fine, thought Ward. But he was worried, O'Suilleabhain being "good with people" by Bresnahan's own report.

17

Risus Purus

EVEN AT HALF FIVE IN THE EVENING, Charlotte Bing's enthusiasm for her "investigative inventory" (her term) of Marsh's Library showed no sign of flagging.

She had taken to employing a pocket torch to examine the physical characteristics of a book against the description of the book in the Marsh's Library provenance files, and even with that aid Noreen suspected that Bing's eyes must be bothering her as much as Noreen knew her own were. The *Book of Kells* could suddenly surface here for all Noreen presently cared; she was ready to go home.

Over the course of the long day, however, the two women had many opportunities to converse, and Noreen had learned several interesting things. For instance, they happened upon the subject of Jan deKuyper, the conservator of the bindery, and how he must have known what Herrick had been up to.

Asked Noreen, "I wonder why, then, deKuyper didn't blow the whistle on Herrick?"

"I should imagine that Brian made it worth Jan's while, as

I believe was the import of the telephone message deKuyper left. As you know, your husband asked me to identify his voice. Jan deKuyper may be a master artisan, but he is a thoroughly despicable character."

Noreen waited, but she finally had to ask, "How so?"

"Without resorting to supposition about his activities as conservator or gossip about what he's done since he arrived in this country, I'll have you know that he got into a fix over in Holland even *before* Brian hired him. It had something to do with his trying to pass off forged books and manuscripts on unsuspecting private collectors."

"But why, then, did Herrick hire him? Or, for that matter, the Danvers-Forde woman. Certainly, there must have been more than a few qualified Irish applicants for those positions."

"There were Irish applicants to be sure. But in considering anything about what Brian did or said in his lifetime, you must think Swift. Swift was Brian's mania, the other half of his bizarre, schizoid, delusional behavior. I think he truly believed himself to be Swift, when he was deep into the drink. Which, in these latter years, was more often than not."

Said Noreen, "So, deKuyper with his immense size was—"

Charlotte Bing nodded her golden head, "Brian's Brobdingnagian. I knew from the moment he walked in to be interviewed he would get the job."

"Which made Joneux Ariane Danvers-Forde his—"

"Pretty little Lilliputian, to say nothing of what else he may even then have known about her."

"Like what?" Now Noreen was all ears, as it were.

"I'll say no more. Gossip revolts me. Only that, if your husband conducts a complete search of the Shrewsbury Road house, he's certain to understand more about that relationship. I shan't do his job for him."

Noreen thought for a moment about the Swiftian framework in Herrick's personal dealings. "Then Teddy Baer and her husband were Dr. Herrick's Yahoos?"

"I should imagine. From what I saw on that wretched videotape and what I know of the 'Fourth Book' of *Gulliver,* they rather fit the bill."

"Then who was Herrick's Houyhnhnm?"

Charlotte Bing sighed and shook her head. "The moment he called me his 'gentle and reasonable Houyhnhnm,' I should have known that the man was deranged and left him." Color rose to Bing's face, and she touched the back of her bun. "I mean, Marsh's.

"But then I thought I had my mother to support, and jobs for librarians in Ireland were then scarce indeed."

"Didn't your mother die rather recently?"

"Two years ago this summer. During the holidays. I was away."

"That must have been difficult for you."

"No, actually. It was her time to go, and from all appearances, she passed away peacefully. I discovered her, when I got back."

Rather as she had discovered Herrick's corpse, Noreen thought. "What was the cause?"

"The doctor wrote down cardiac arrest, but she was an incontinent old woman who insisted upon having nobody but me wait on her hand and foot. I also had to support the house and pay for every bloody thing she got a whim to buy. Mail-order and telephone solicitations are a bane to society and should be outlawed! But"—Bing shook her head and pursed her lips in a way that made her look suddenly old—"she certainly had the last laugh on me."

Noreen waited.

"All those years that I had to put up with Brian Herrick, thinking that I couldn't possibly leave since I was the sole support of my doddering mother—and there she was sitting on a stack of New Zealand National Bonds that her prosperous, sheep-farmer brother had left her when he passed away thirty years earlier. She had the interest paid into an Auckland bank, and the annual accounts sent to her solicitor. I always wondered why in the name of God a woman who had no contact with the outside world other than me would need a solicitor. Whom *I* had to pay, mind."

Bing paused, as though reflecting on what she had just revealed. "Life can be strange. What is that wonderful definition in Beckett of the last laugh? I think it goes, 'The last laugh, the *risus purus,* the laugh down the snout—Haw!—at that which is (silence please!)—*cruel.'* Beckett, of course, owed much to Swift. I often think of them as being the same mind inhabiting different bodies, three centuries apart. With life, the *real* life that people must live within themselves and in society, having changed not one whit."

And a bitter experience, Noreen could only conclude from her tone.

But it was nearly a half hour later, after insisting that they leave off for the night, that Noreen chanced upon her only substantial find of the day.

In helping Bing switch out the lights, Noreen tripped over and spilled a carton of catalogs of former exhibitions that had been held at Marsh's Library during the tenure of Keeper Herrick. In picking them up, one caught her eye:

THE ENCHANTED HERBS

An Exhibition of Rare Botanical, Gardening,
and Herbal Books in Marsh's Library, Dublin

The exhibition had been held some two years earlier.
Noreen slipped the thin volume into her coat pocket.

18

A   P u n c t i l i o u s

A r c h i v i s t

AFTER SPENDING MOST OF THE DAY IN COURT, Chief Superintendent Peter McGarr caught a quick bite in a nearby pub and arrived at Brian Herrick's house on the Shrewsbury Road just as night was falling. Letting himself in by the conservatory door, he used his penlight to find his way to the desk in the study where Herrick seemed to have conducted the business of his life—wrote letters, made phone calls, paid bills.

An hour or so went by, as McGarr—still working by the thin light of the pocket torch—pieced through Herrick's accounts and tried to fill in the sketchy picture he had of the victim. That is, apart from the Herrick who had been *The Dean.*

Charolotte Bing had been right about Herrick's being careless of the details of daily life—his out-of-pocket expenses, his checkbook, even his appearance. In the desk were recent snapshots taken of him in various stages of boozey disarray, while others as few as five years earlier showed him to be neat and often natty. In those shots, his long hair—that he had kept permed? (there were paid receipts from "Choice Cuts," a "Uni-sex Hair Botique," for "Wash, cut and set")—made his round, jowly face and pale eyes look the very likeness of the portraits of Swift that were hanging in the house. Also dating from that time were bills from Brown, Thomas, an upmarket clothier in Grafton Street. But Herrick had purchased almost nothing of that sort since.

To stretch his legs, McGarr climbed the rosewood staircase to the master bedroom and examined the contents of Herrick's closets. Most of his excellent suits and jackets were thread-bare, the shoes worn, the shirts fraying. McGarr wondered if Herrick had mimicked Swift more than he knew and had become—what was the word Noreen had used?—gaga in his old age. But Herrick had been only fifty-nine, McGarr reminded himself, whereas a title plaque of one of the Swift portraits that Herrick had hung on the walls of the house, said:

Jonathan Swift,
b. 1667, d. 1745
Dublin

Which was nearly twenty years longer than Herrick. Conclusion? Beginning perhaps five years earlier, the drink or something else had taken Herrick down, precipitously and prematurely.

Yet back at the desk, McGarr discovered that, in regard to his property—the house and its furnishings—Herrick had continued to be (how had Charlotte Bing phrased it?)—a "punctilious archivist." In a folio ledger, Herrick had listed where he bought the accoutrements of his household, along with the date, the price, and a finely detailed description of each item. He had noted flaws, if there were any, and giving his estimation of the worth of the thing, as opposed to what he had paid. Seldom too much by his own estimation.

Also—verifying Charlotte Bing's earlier statement that Herrick had been on the ropes financially—was a thick folder of letters from the solicitor of Herrick's father's estate, warning him against and then acknowledging Herrick's decision to sell various financial instruments.

Those sales began about seven years earlier, roughly a year after Jan deKuyper had been hired into the Delmas Conservation Bindery. An admonition from the senior-most member of the law firm alerted Herrick to the possibility that such regular withdrawals would in time result in the dissolution of his inheritance. Yet the sums continued regularly and unabated.

The most recent letter from the solicitor notified Herrick that all funds left him by his father were now exhausted, apart from the annual legal fee, which was deducted, leaving a balance of some two hundred Irish pounds. "Check enclosed." *You fool* was not written, only suggested by the terseness of the missive.

There followed correspondence from other relatives, all evidently siblings, sending Herrick various amounts up to thirty thousand Irish pounds, either as outright gifts around Christmastime or as loans. Herrick was into one brother for over sixty thousand pounds.

McGarr got up from the desk and rigged the two infrared sensors, which operated on the principle of an electronic eye, to the front and conservatory doors. Once either beam was broken, a signal would be sent to a receiver that McGarr now attached to his belt. A cord ran to an audio device that he fitted into his ear.

Still using the penlight, McGarr then began to search for the repository—a safe, a hidden compartment, maybe even a false wall or removable floor slat—where a secretive, vain, and perhaps even a cunning man, such as Herrick, would have stored his most secret possessions. There had to be one. A man who had appropriated one persona, not his own, to front the world, while donning quite another during his "Frollicks," would not have trusted the secrets of his nightwatch to any place other than his lair.

Which had been the real Herrick? McGarr mused; or had both been masks? And how much by design had Herrick been like Swift? Noreen had said Swift seemed to have purposely obscured the details of his life. To this day, it was not certain whether Swift had been celibate throughout his life or a womanizer, a confirmed bachelor or secretly married perhaps to his own half-sister and the father of a child by her. All while simultaneously conducting at least two long-term affairs with other women, one of whom might also have borne his child. In other words, he had been a "master of disinformation"— Noreen's phrase.

Could it be that Herrick had chosen the Swift persona *because* of that ambiguity? That the central enigma of Swift as a human being had appealed to Herrick more than he knew? McGarr had not read much Swift—only *Gulliver* and a few of Swift's essays—years ago and because his schoolmasters made him, but he remembered having been confused by the quote "happiness . . . is a perpetual possession of being well deceived." And that what people valued most in life were the pleasures "that dupe and play the wag with the senses." And finally that accepting the surface of things was preferable to "that pretended philosophy, which enters into the depth of things, and then comes gravely back with information and discoveries, that in the inside they are good for nothing."

McGarr realized even back then, of course, that Swift had

been satirizing such a superficial point of view, but he wondered now by how much? Certainly, some . . . buffer of delu-
sion was necessary to deal with the reality that was presented
in graphic detail on the evening news, or in the newspapers,
or—more personally—what McGarr himself confronted on the
job. *Vide* Herrick's corpse. And McGarr's own buffer was? The
often unavailing presumption that people could be (and were
more often than not) better. Or, rather, that how they acted *in
extremis* was an aberration, which was not likely to recur with
any frequency. Still, as long as there was the possibility . . .
well, there would have to be somebody to examine the inside, as it were, and come back with discoveries and information. Society demanded it.

While continuing to *toss* Herrick's house and belongings,
McGarr came upon another disturbing Swift statement: "Mor-
tal man is a broomstick (which) raiseth a mighty Dust where
there was none before; sharing deeply all the while in the very
same Pollution he pretends to sweep away." In Swift as in life,
McGarr decided, there were no easy answers, and perhaps The
Dean—the *real* one—appealed to him more than he was willing to admit.

Three hours later, after nearly abandoning the search,
McGarr came across a false front in the books on the top shelf
of the H case in the conservatory library. (Why, he asked himself, had he not thought books to begin with, given Herrick's
obsession with them? And, of course, the "H"s considering
the man's ego?)

Sliding back the accordion fold of "book bindings," he
found roughly fifty thousand pounds in Irish currency, an old
canister of 16-mm film that said "Stella" on a piece of adhe-
sive tape, the deed to the Shrewsbury Road house. Herrick's
D.Litt. degree from Oxford, and a report dated three years

earlier from a Paris private-investigation agency concerning one Joneux Ariane El Kef, which was the name of a small city in Tunisia, McGarr seemed to remember. He had once spent a holiday near there. Perhaps she was a bastard as well, having been given, as a surname, the name of the place of her birth.

With the beam from his penlight, McGarr, who had worked in France for over a decade, quickly skimmed through the document.

It said that the young woman had been born in Tunis of a Tunisian mother and a French father, who was unknown. Emigrating to Marseilles, the mother was resorted to prostitution, in order to support herself and her daughter. The child proved to be intelligent, and her mother did everything in her power, including sending her to private schools in Avignon and later Paris, to keep her from the same fate.

Yet after taking two degrees at the Sorbonne and finding no suitable employment in her chosen field of book and manuscript conservation, Joneux Ariane LaBrecque (she was calling herself at the time) turned first to exotic dancing to make a living, "and then casual prostitution of the call-girl sort," which was much more lucrative.

It is supposed that while engaged in that activity she met Mr. Alastair Danvers-Forde of Dunlavin, County Kildare, Ireland, and also of Dublin, London and Paris, whose mistress she soon became. They were married about a year later in Dunlavin; nobody from the bride's side of the marriage attending the ceremony.

McGarr was about to replace the document when he heard an insistent beeping in his right ear. Quickly, he doused the penlight and pulled his Walther PPK from under his belt.

But after the door closed, he heard, "Chief, it's only me, Hughie. To spell you, like you said. And I think we got ourselves a break."

"I'm over here in the 'H's." McGarr shoved the automatic back under his belt, then began replacing the items he had found in the false front on the top shelf.

Said Ward, "You'll never guess where the *cicuta maculata* is?"

"At Danvers-Forde's?"

"No, but he knew about it, chapter and verse. And he also knew where it was."

McGarr waited.

"Here—it's one of the potted plants along the wall."

"Which one?"

"Dunno. We'll have to check. I got the descriptions here." Ward flicked on his own penlight. He read, '. . . a perennial herb with jointed stems and purple spots. It grows to eight feet tall. The flowers are small and white. When the root stock is split, drops of yellowish aromatic oil appear, which gives the plant a peculiar odor, like burned parsnips or—"

"Peat," McGarr supplied.

"Exactly. And soluble in alcohol. Says here that even in high concentrations it won't cloud alcohol."

Together they checked every plant until they found it, thriving. "And, look," said Ward, "unlike most of the other plants that are dying in the heat, it's been thinned out recently, or at least tended. The soil is loose, and"—he dug a finger down into the pot—"even a bit damp."

But it was then that they heard a car pull up in the alley beside the conservatory door. McGarr and Ward only made the cover of the tall bookshelves before the infrared monitor sounded again. The door opened.

" 'Ere we are," said Bunny Baer in his guttural and unmistakable Ath Cliath brogue. "I'm tellin' yeh, Ted', I've sussed it out. There's a feckin' fortune in these t'ings. We'll mail one out to Sir Alastair in Dunlavin—anonymous-like, tellin' him that the next one goes to Mum and Dad. And while we're bleedin' him white, we'll take that little trip I told you about—to London or Amsterdam or Paris. And flog copies of the tapes to all the poxy old wankers, like Herrick was."

" 'Wha'd'yeh mean by poxy old wankers? There's others that get off on this fare. Real men. *Young* men."

"But wankers all the same," the Bunny croaked on, like some round, dark carrion bird, as he slapped the plastic-cased videos into the carton. "Then we'll have two fiddles playin' at once. A feckin' *duet*!"

"I hope yehr roight."

"When was I *ever* wrong!"

Ward touched McGarr's sleeve to ask if he should move around to the other side of the room, in order to cut off their passage to the door. But McGarr shook his head. He had arranged for McKeon and two teams of squad staffers to cover each end of the alley. They would wait until the Baers got well shut of Shrewsbury Road before pulling them over.

Also, even though Baer had the opportunity to murder Herrick on the night of his death and perhaps even the motive—as they had heard from his own lips and were now seeing—would he have had the intelligence to carry it off? Whoever had extracted the poison from either the plant in the room or some other water hemlock was operating on an entirely different mental level from Bunny Baer and his hag. Although McGarr had been fooled before.

"And da best part?" Bunny rejoiced, as he staggered under

his load toward the door where Teddy now was standing, "they'll feckin' t'ink it's the jealous hubby what nicked 'em."

"Yeh mean—the lovesick Alastair?"

"Sir Wally-Wanker himself!" Bunny was having fun, that much was plain.

"Imagine, fallin' in the cess over that little tart who's probably t'rown a leg over half the tossers in Europe."

"Hush, now," Bunny warned. "Let's not make a balls o' this t'ing when we're nearly home free." The door closed, and McGarr moved into the kitchen to use the phone there.

Part IV

ON

HUMAN

BRUTES

19

Rationis Capax

or

On Enhancing One's Own
Natural Viciousness

MEANWHILE, Noreen McGarr was ensconced in a fleece-lined wing-back chair in the bedroom of the McGarrs' Belgrave Square town house.

There was a tall, mounded peat fire hissing agreeably in the hearth, and her slippered feet were up on the brass hob where they were toasting agreeably. Maddie had long since fallen asleep in the "big bed," as the child called her parents' sleeping accommodation, and Noreen had made herself a hot whiskey—*not* with Glenfinnan—which was steaming on the table beside her.

The book in her lap, which she had just finished reading, was none other than *Gulliver's Travels*. Around her were other texts that she had not opened since her school and university days, and in a way the past few hours' study had been like reacquainting herself with a portion of her past.

What had she learned?

Certainly the "Frollicks" of Brian Herrick could be considered mere sexual escapades of a rather burlesque/grotesque sort. But those videotapes also seemed to depend on what some critics called Swift's "excremental" verse.

By that was meant a handful of poems ("The Lady's Dressing Room," "Strephon and Chloe," "Cassinus and Peter," to name three) that parodied poems of romantic love by showing a woman who has been idealized earlier in the poem performing some bodily function.

Most quoted by the "excrementalists" was the final couplet in "Cassinus and Peter," in which poor Peter, who has extolled the perfection of his beloved, is then driven by jealousy to spy on her. Peeking into her boudoir while she is about her ablutions, he cries out:

Nor wonder how I lost my wits!
Oh! Caelia, Caelia, Caelia shits.

George Orwell, writing as late as 1929, thought Swift presented a diseased and negative view of humanity and life in general. With leaden irony (it is to be supposed) in no way up to the standard of his target, he declared,

Swift's greatness lies in the intensity, the almost insane violence of that hatred of the bowels which is the essence of his misanthropy and which underlies the whole of his work.

The Freudians, of course, were quick to hop on the excremental bandwagon, for Freud had written:

All neurotics, and many others too, take exception to the fact that "inter urines et faeces nascimur." . . . That we should find, as the deepest root of the sexual repression that marches with culture, the organic defense of the new form of life that began with the erect posture.

By the Freudians' measure, therefore, Swift had been repressed. They dragged out how often, it seemed, dung (or the hatred of dung) was the subject of Swift's shrift. There was a direct connection, they contended, between anal organization and human aggression, which was labeled the anal/sadistic phase. Defiance, mastery, the will to power first developed through the manipulation of excrement. As the child came to gain mastery over his bowels, he substituted symbols for feces. Thus, weapons, property, and money were merely consubstantiated dung.

And Swift and his characters seemed so perfectly anal. His Yahoos, for example, used excrement for aggression:

Several of this cursed Brood getting hold of the Branches behind, leaped up into the Tree, from whence they began to discharge their Excrements on my Head.

They also employed feces as part of the ritual that organized their society:

. . . this Leader *had usually a Favourite as* like himself *as he could get, whose Employment was to* lick his Master's Feet and Posteriors, and drive the Female *Yahoos* to his Kennel.

his Successor, the Head of all the Yahoos *in that District, Young and Old, Male and Female, come in a Body, and discharge their Excrements upon him from Head to Foot.*

Even books (or at least some books) qualified as mere manipulated dung. In *A Tale of a Tub* Swift wrote:

> *When writers of all sizes, like freemen of cities, are at liberty to throw out their filth and excrementious productions, in every street as they please, what can the consequence be, but that the town must be poisoned and become another jakes, as by report of great travellers, Edinburgh is at nights.*

But such stuff was tricky, and it was difficult to separate symbol from referent.

> *Everything spiritual and valuable has a gross and revolting parody, very similar to it, with the same name. Only unremitting judgement can distinguish between them.*

Like Swift and Herrick? Noreen wondered, flicking back through the books to several pages that she had turned down. The analogy seemed more than simply apt. After all, what had Herrick been but an anachronistic parody of the true Dean, even to having present at his "Frollicks" both the decrepit Teddy Baer and lithesome Joneux Ariane Danvers-Forde, whose at once delicate, childlike, but utterly sensual beauty could in no way be burlesqued.

Perhaps Herrick had merely been holding a "glass up to life," as some eighteenth-century writers, including Swift, had presumed to do. After all, the "death" tape began by showing a youthful Herrick, then ran on to the false Joneux/Teddy, to Teddy "Bare," as it were, in all her decrepitude. And finally it pictured Herrick's own fallen self with his musculature wasted, his stomach protuberant, and his genitalia pendant.

Following which—his most horrific death. Noreen had never seen a film so . . . riveting, since all was real. The man had died atrociously.

On the other hand, save for the death scene, Herrick himself had appeared to be taking a kind of drunken, sick, debauched fun in the entire proceeding. And certainly the "point" of the "Frollick," if there was one, was a demonstration of how disgusting the appetites of the species could be. All, including Joneux Ariane Danvers-Forde, who was playing the ingenue, partook in that, and there was no acting. The event was real.

Noreen kept thinking of Charlotte Bing having told her that Herrick had considered her his Houyhnhm, that is, a creature who was guided only by reasonable impulses and was disgusted by the antics of the yahoos in Houyhnhm Land. And yet the life of reason, as led by the Houyhnhms, seemed insipid, unfeeling, and dull.

Apart from their anger and hatred of things that were unreasonable, the superior horses displayed no emotions. Love was an abstract feeling, manifested mainly in the care taken for the young and the consideration given to the old. They took no pleasure in sex, the sole aim of which was procreation. And Houyhnhms did not feel particularly, not even for their own colts or foals.

By contrast, Yahoos for all their degeneration and dung seemed the more interesting species, *if only*— the reader was led to conclude—they might follow the dictates of reason at least some of the time. If not, their venality was assured. But once back in Yahoo England, Gulliver saw no hope of human improvement.

Yes, Yahoo man had the capacity to reason, but he almost

always placed reason in the service, rather than in the command, of his emotions. Used in such a way, reason was no longer reason, but rather some other

> . . . *Quality fitted to increase our natural Vices; as the Reflection from a troubled Stream returns the Image of an ill-shapen body, not only larger, but more distorted.*

As Herrick had distorted the image of Swift or—with Herrick directing—Teddy Baer had that of Joneux Ariane Danvers-Forde?

Noreen sighed. Perhaps she was tired and making too much of the Swift-Herrick connection. Checking the clock on the mantel, she saw that it was well past eleven, and she would have to get up early to continue her assault—led by Master-Houyhnhm Charlotte Bing—on the inventory of Marsh's Library. She would have to glance again at the book over breakfast, to see if her conclusions were as definite.

It was then, while inserting the bookmark at the beginning of the crucial Fourth Book, that a passage caught her eye:

> *We set sail from Portsmouth upon the 7th day of September, 1710; on the 14th, we met Captain Pocock of Bristol, at Tenariff, who was going to the bay of Campechy, to cut logwood.*

Noreen had skipped over most of the notes about the journey, since all those details had been included by Swift mainly to mimic the style of Defoe's *Robinson Crusoe*, of which *Gulliver's Travels* was a satire. But, given how leisurely ocean voyaging had been in the eighteenth century, 7-9-'10 was not much earlier than 9-5-'11, which was all that Brian Herrick had managed to write as he was dying.

And there it was on the following page:

Upon the 9th day of May, 1711, one James Welch came down to my cabin; and said he had orders from the captain to set me ashore.

It was the date on which Gulliver's mutinying crew had marooned him in Houyhnhm Land, and he encountered first the Yahoos and later the Houyhnhms.

But what did it mean, if the Baers had been Herrick's Yahoos and Charlotte Bing his Houyhnhm? That they had murdered him together? No. Bing would have had nothing to do with Teddy and Bunny Baer.

Switching out the light, Noreen noticed the catalog, *Enchanted Herbs,* that she had taken from Marsh's Library. That, too, would have to wait until morning. After all, it was her husband's profession, and she had had quite enough of excrement and mayhem for one night.

20

The Bigger
They Are

A DAY WENT BY, during which McGarr dealt with the details of the squad's many open investigations from the kitchen of Herrick's house. There he could be neither seen nor heard by anybody approaching front or back doors.

As night fell, Hugh Ward again joined him, and they began their second vigil. McGarr napped first. Around ten, he was jarred awake by the signal from the infrared sensor that had been positioned by the conservatory door.

"It's deKuyper," Ward whispered, when they had positioned themselves behind the row of bookcases farthest from the conservatory door. "And prepared. He's got a handcart, some stout cartons, and a van in the alley." Ward had been in communication with the surveillance team that was posted a few streets away.

"Come for the books, from the look of it," said McGarr. "He'll know what's valuable and what's not." And he'll save Noreen and Charlotte Bing some work, he thought. McGarr nudged Ward, and they moved silently out of the conservatory toward the front of the house. "We'll walk round and catch him, just before he leaves." McGarr had a personal score to settle with the large man, who might not be so formidable outside of the "House of Wrath."

DeKuyper. What did they know about him?

Surely, he was an unsavory character and had probably only been selected as conservator because of Herrick's obsession with Swift and the man's Brobdingnagian size. But could deKuyper have murdered Herrick?

It had been deKuyper who had delivered the Glenfinnan to the house. But not having keys, he had left the packet of two liter bottles on the porch outside of the front door. If, say, he *had* poisoned one of the bottles with *cicuta maculata*— recommending it to Herrick on the enclosed card by saying "Save the best for last"—why, then, had Joneux Ariane Danvers-Forde not died, too, having drunk from both bottles by her own admission?

McGarr had no idea, although she could be lying and be the murderess herself.

Also, deKuyper seemed to have been blackmailing Herrick, since he knew Herrick had been systematically substituting "period forgeries" for the most valuable books in Marsh's Library. But deKuyper had to have known—because Herrick would have told him—that Herrick's money was running out, at least the money that Herrick had inherited from his father.

There was, however, the cash—some sixty thousand pounds— that Herrick had evidently borrowed from his brother and sisters. Could deKuyper have known that Herrick was holding out on him and decided it was time to do away with him and take the rare books for himself? Charlotte Bing had intimated that there was a market for those items. And lucrative. They were worth thousands, perhaps hundreds of thousands of pounds.

But how, then, did the glass and decanter get washed after Herrick drank from them? And the decanter filled with several inches of uncorrupted and veritable Glenfinnan? McGarr had tasted Glenfinnan before; it was Glenfinnan. And would deKuyper have known about the flask in the Bible in the bedroom?

Now entering the alley where they could see deKuyper's van parked beside the conservatory door, McGarr asked Ward, "Were you offered drinks, when you were down in Dunlavin?"

"If you mean Glenfinnan—we were. It was there on the groaning board. Unopened, untouched."

McGarr made a mental note to have McKeon ring up the distillery in Scotland and learn where Glenfinnan was marketed in Ireland. Because of its high price and all the duty and taxes, little was probably sold, and then only in pricey, upmarket shops that might be canvassed in a day.

The conservatory door opened, and McGarr and Ward stepped into the deep shadows of a wall door to the back garden of another house.

DeKuyper appeared in the alley, pushing his handcart toward the van. it was stacked tall with cartons of books. He stopped, closed the door, and then checked to make sure it was locked, evidently having taken all he had come for.

"He's mine," said McGarr. "We have a little something to work out between us."

"Be careful. He's an oaf and strong."

They watched the huge man toss the cartons into the back of the van, his great gray beard flaring in the stiff breeze that was sweeping up the alley.

"You only jump in if I'm getting the piss beat out of me."

"You sure you don't want to just double up on him? That yoke must weigh thirty stone."

But it was dark, and McGarr would have the advantage of surprise. Also, Olympic rules would not apply. It was something McGarr had to do for himself as a matter of pride. Swift be ignored.

McGarr waited until deKuyper had all his crates loaded, the handcart secured within the back of the van, and was closing the doors. Running low with his head down, he made for the large man, like a rugger breaking from a scrum.

At the sound of footsteps, deKuyper spun around, and McGarr drove his head deep into deKuyper's immense stomach. The man let out a roar, and his hands jumped for McGarr's neck. But McGarr's arms were flailing into deKuyper's thighs, his groin, his lower stomach. He punched and punched and kept punching.

DeKuyper's hands found McGarr's shoulders. Pushing him away, they slid to his neck. Suddenly, McGarr could not breathe; it felt as if his throat were being crushed. Worse still, deKuyper now picked him off the ground, so that McGarr's own weight was added to the pressure of the huge man's hands.

Ward rushed forward, but deKuyper swung McGarr, like a doll, at him, fending him off. He threw McGarr this way and that, hurling him at Ward and snapping him back. As McGarr felt himself fading, his foot touched down for an instant, and, summoning his last bit of strength, he launched a punch at deKuyper's face. His fist collided with something soft, and in his shoulder he felt the man's nose fold under his knuckles.

DeKuyper's grip suddenly relaxed, the fingers opened, and

the arms dropped away. McGarr collapsed at the man's feet, his own hands jumping to his throat, which felt as if it had been broken.

Ward tried to pull him away. "Look out—he's about to fall."

McGarr glanced up.

DeKuyper was still standing, propped against the back of the van with his great feet spread wide. But his eyeballs had floated up into his head, and only the whites were showing. Blood was pouring from his broken nose.

"It's here we begin counting," said Ward. "Eight, nine, ten."

McGarr staggered to his feet and stepped away.

Herrick's Brobdingnag came down in a piece, his face bouncing off the cobblestones of the alleyway.

"He'll wear that pattern for a good few months to come," said Ward.

McGarr found his voice. "We should get him out of here." In case they had another visitor. The Danvers-Fordes also had a set of keys, to say nothing of Charlotte Bing.

21

Necessity Is the Mother of Invention.
(Jonathan Swift)

SEVEN HOURS EARLIER, Rory O'Suilleabhain had said to Ruth Bresnahan, "Ah, Ruthie—you've got to help me out. I've got this charity ball at the Burlington, and you know me. I don't dance a sh-tep. Everybody who's anybody'll be there—movie stars, politicians I should get to know, even U2. I'm at a loss. Utterly. I need your help."

Ruth listened more to O'Suilleabhain's tone than what he was saying, and in his voice she heard terror of the most exquisite sort, which was social terror. And to witness him, *The* O'Suilleabhain, the Cuchulain of the South Kerry Mountains, trembling at the thought of having to attend a social gathering delighted her. "What seems to be the problem, other than the footwork? I'm sure you can fudge that."

"How?"

"Just stand in one place, lean over the woman, fix her with your sea-green peepers, and give her your best smile. She'll think you're Fred Astaire."

"See, Ruthie?" He gesticulated a massive mitt at the windshield. "I need you. You know what it takes." He snapped his head to her, fixing her with said peepers. "Incidentally, how do I look?" The hand tried to pat down his flaring black tie, which had been knotted all wrong and made Ruth certain that he was not seeing anybody else.

Not that *she* was seeing *him.* But she reveled in the idea that even with his drop-dead good looks, his burgeoning "loot" (as he shamelessly called his new wealth), and his "prospects" (another of his terms), he was *bereft* in Dublin with nary a clue how to *get on,* which he had been a master of while in Kerry.

"Apart from the tie, which you might ask some other *gentleman* to rearrange for you, you look smashing." Which was true. With his jet-black hair, the eyes, his yards of shoulder, his deep chest, and narrow waist, he had been made to wear a black tuxedo. Also, the tailor to whom she had sent him had spared no expense and had created a masterpiece. It looked like something that might be worn to meet a queen. Or pope.

"In fact," she went on, "I can imagine at least several of the females in the gathering there eating you alive. Tux, boutonniere, and that deadly smile included. Give it to us one last time."

Like her puppet, O'Suilleabhain complied, bearing his white, even, and gleaming teeth. Unlike most Irish men, he had never smoked in a day of his life; in fact, he had no bad habits beyond the sins of his ego, which were manifold.

"There, that's it. You won't even have to utter a word. By morning they'll be ringing up all their other friends, telling them you're brilliant, a genius, a wit, and perhaps even a decent human being."

"Meaning you don't think I'll survive the ordeal, either." He looked away again, plainly worried.

"It depends on how you define the 'survive.'" Bresnahan was not about to let him off the hook, not after all the years that he had treated her cavalierly as the girl-next-door whom he could have for the asking. "Years from now, you'll look back on this occasion with humor. Like Fitzhugh Frenche, you'll be able to regale whole sitting rooms with the gorsoon you made of yourself your first night at an important social function.

"Of course, you'll be the talk of Dublin, or at least that part who won't wish to take you home to their beds or marry you to their daughter. Men mainly. But console yourself with the thought that Dublin talks and *must* talk about somebody, and why not you? When you become Master of the Universe or, better, C.E.O. of O'Suilleabhain Enterprises Unlimited, you'll realize that Barnum was right—even bad publicity is better than being ignored altogether. But by that time you'll have moved on to New York or Frankfurt or Tokyo, where the real money is made, and you won't care a fig about your reputation with Dublin wags."

"Now you're sending me up."

"You should get used to it. In your present social condition, you're definite quarry. But, sure, isn't it always better to laugh at yourself."

"You mean something like, 'Laugh, and the world laughs with you'?" he asked hopefully. "You know, generally I'm a happy person."

Bresnahan nearly felt sorry for the big, handsome piece of self-absorbed baggage; they would have him in bits in an hour. "Now that's the very ticket, I'm thinking. Since the last thing you want to do is show any anger. If they think you're vulnerable, why, they'll pounce on you like . . . Yahoos from out of a tree." Noreen McGarr had given Ruth the loan of her *Gulliver's Travels*.

O'Suilleabhain suddenly grasped her hand.

"Which is why, Ruthie, I need your help. I need you *with* me. *By my side.*"

Bresnahan shook her head. "Not a chance. Not on your life. You sink or swim or—in this case—drown in a sea of derisive laughter on your own. And if you don't open this door this instant, I'll . . . arrest you, so I will."

"Please, Ruthie. I'm *beggin'* yuh," O'Suilleabhain went on, squeezing her hand so hard she thought she might cry out in pain. "All I want is for you to come with me tonight and break the ice. The introductions and so forth. You get all dolled up, the way you knock people out. They won't even see me. Then, once I get everybody's name straight, and I'm not etting gobsful of hoof, why, we'll call you a taxi, and you won't *have* to leave with me."

Before she could object to that, he hurried on, "You know how I am when I get *in* with people."

Bresnahan knew that, too, though she hated to admit it. O'Suilleabhain was actually rather charming, once the ice was broken and he could forget himself. And as long as he did not make some irredeemable blunder or gaffe, his prospects of being accepted in social Dublin were excellent.

But now she had him in her power, as much as he had her hand in his mighty fist. And while that feeling might be wrong, it was pleasurable. Still, having to let him go (even though she no longer loved him) *would* be difficult, and she should enjoy herself as long as she could. Also, she had nothing better to do with her evening, her significant other being otherwise employed.

Sensing a change in her mood, O'Suilleabhain released her hand. He reached over into the backseat and produced an enormous box that could be filled only with roses from its size and shape. "You might as well take these. They'd only go to waste otherwise."

Bresnahan pulled off the silver ribbon and opened it. "My God, there must be two dozen long-stem roses in that box."

"Three. Two didn't quite get your age right."

"Nor does three."

"I figured I'd err on the side of excess, being me."

"What, is it my birthday?"

"Well"—O'Suilleabhain looked away—"given how I'm goin', every day might be your birthday, if you was to stick with me."

"Really, now? Can I tell you something?" She closed the box and opened the door. "Spout something like that tonight, and you'll be going all right—straight back to Kerry on a tide of sneering laughter. Now, tell me what you would have done with the flowers had I not been home—given them to the next lucky lass on your checklist?"

"Ah, shit, Ruthie—after all the years you *still* don't know me. It's you and only you, and has always been." Turning his dark head to Bresnahan, he fixed her with his sea-green peepers.

Ruth went upstairs to dress. When she returned, she was wearing a simple black shirtdress of rayon and gabardine with a surplice notch collar, an elastic waist cinched by a jewelry belt, and a slim skirt that was slit in front to midthigh. Gold-tone buttons matched the belt, and the skirt fell to midcalf. With gold cowrie-shell earrings and a filigree of gold around the toes and heels of her half-height shoes, her costume was the equivalent of O'Suilleabhain's tuxedo. In all, they looked nearly like brother and sister, he dark and she— with her billows of auburn hair and smoky gray eyes—light.

"Now try to smile and nod a lot," she advised, as he pulled the Mercedes up to the marquee of the hotel and a valet rushed forward to open the doors. "What you're trying to create is a certain mystique. You know—tall, dark, handsome, and *reserved.*"

O'Suilleabhain's brow glowered. "But what if I'm asked a question?"

"Mumble."

22

Never Seek;
Never Expect

BEING AN AMATEUR THIEF, Alastair Danvers-Forde waited until well after midnight, when he was probably the only person afoot on the Shrewsbury Road, before inserting his wife's key into the alley door of Brian Herrick's house and stepping in.

McGarr and Ward moved out of the kitchen into the conservatory, where they took positions on either side of the rows of gabled bookshelves.

Danvers-Forde walked straight by them to the "F"s. There he played the beam of a pocket torch over the shelf that had held the "Frollick" videotapes. "Oh, damn!" he lamented. "The bastards beat me to them."

Spinning around, he splashed the wide beam across Ward, who was standing in the opposite aisle, but he passed on to the "H"s, where he tugged over a reader's ladder and climbed to the top. After some rustling about, he was heard to say, "Well, at least that's something." They then heard him replacing the false front over Herrick's cache.

McGarr stepped forward; Ward switched on the lights.

Caught at the top of the ladder, Danvers-Forde snapped his head to the other end of the aisle, but there Ward stood. "I can explain everything."

"And you will," said McGarr, holding out a hand so Danvers-Forde could give him the papers that he had removed from the false front of books on the top shelf.

"*If* you promise to keep it to yourselves." Twisting his head, he again glanced at Ward.

McGarr took the papers from him, which turned out to be the report that the Paris private investigator had sent Herrick regarding Danvers-Forde's wife. "Why didn't you take the money?"

"I'm no thief." Danvers-Forde was dressed in something like a Special Op's outfit—black beret, black jumper, black trousers and shoes.

"What d'you call that?" Ward asked, pointing at the document.

"A way of ending my wife's torment."

"Which could only happen *after* Herrick was dead. Do I ring up the Castle, Chief?" Ward asked. "Given the hour, we might able to slip him in the barracks entrance without any reporters."

They were playing good cop/bad cop with a person who had probably never had a run-in with the police before.

"Let me ask him a few questions first. But ring up the office and tell them to get ready for processing."

"They'll *like* this at half-one." Ward turned toward the kitchen.

"Where were you the Thursday night that your wife was last here? And if you lie to me, I'll see you hang, one way or another." McGarr waved the report.

Danvers-Forde seemed suddenly pale and drawn. "I was outside in my car. As always."

"You mean you waited outside every Thursday night, while your wife—"

He nodded. "In case she needed me. Herrick was a drunk, as you probably know, and . . . unpredictable. I parked down the block a bit, where she could signal me from the front windows, if he abused her."

"What time period are we discussing here?"

"*Years,*" said Danvers-Forde. "Nearly three."

"How did you feel? Didn't that make you . . . ?"

"Angry? Enraged? Psychotic?"

McGarr said nothing.

"Of course, but what were my options? He had that—" He pointed to the report. "My hands were tied."

"How did Herrick get on to your wife's past?"

"He knew from the moment she walked in the door at Marsh's, applying for the assistant's post in the bindery. He'd seen her more than a few times, he later told her—when she was performing in Paris."

"Performing how?"

"*Dancing,* of course. It was much before she had to resort to . . . the other."

Practicing which she met *lucky* you, thought McGarr, but who was he to judge?

"Herrick might have been a sot, but he had a mind like a steel trap."

"Didn't your wife complain?"

Danvers-Forde shrugged. "She said that it was only one man, one night a week. You don't know the life she's had to lead, and what it took her just to survive."

Before she met you and hit the jackpot. And just what sort of life had her former life been? McGarr did not know enough about Joneux Ariane Danvers-Forde née El Kef. Perhaps she had killed before. "Hughie," he called.

Ward appeared immediately from the shadows near the steps to the kitchen. "Have Bernie get on to Criminal Justice in Paris. We need a complete rundown on Joneux Ariane El Kef."

"Actually, her name is—*was*—Jeanne El Kef. She took Joneux Ariane when she went on the stage."

Ward turned back into the kitchen.

"Follow me." McGarr stepped toward the *cicuta maculata* plant. "How did you know about this?"

"I've been here before. Socially. Christmas parties, after openings of library exhibitions. That sort of thing."

"Would Herrick have required your wife to . . . *administer* to him at such times?'

"Of course not—I would have—"

"When did you first think of killing him?"

"From the start. From the first. From the moment Joneux told me he had recognized her and knew who she was. A few months later he showed her that report. And *that* was the reason he had hired her, *not* because she was a trained and competent conservator. And once he had that"—again he pointed to the private investigator's report—"he had us."

"When did Herrick begin asking for money, in addition to your wife's attentions?"

Danvers-Forde lowered his head. "Sometime last year. He said he was being squeezed himself and didn't know where else to turn. 'Robbing Peter to pay Paul,' is how he put it. Through a nasty smile."

"How much?"

Danvers-Forde sighed. "Ten thousand per quarter."

Double the rate that deKuyper was charging Herrick. "And still you claim you didn't murder him?"

"I don't murder. I admit I thought of it, but I couldn't. Not even him. I'm too much of a coward."

"Then—your wife. You should understand that you may not have to spend time in prison. Have you ever been in prison?"

Suddenly, Danvers-Forde's legs seemed to give way. "Do you mind if I sit down?"

McGarr waited for him to draw a chair from the table. He sat. "I haven't, but Joneux has. Ward will come back with that, when he contacts Criminal Justice."

"For what?"

"Prostitution. She used to work some of the bars in the better hotels in Paris."

They did not allow that, McGarr knew.

"But would she have killed him?" Danvers-Forde shook his head. "Something like that? Something so arcane and devised is beyond her. She's . . . visceral and passionate. If she had killed Herrick, it would have been face-to-face with a knife or a gun. Do you know about the effects of *cicuta maculata,* the sort of death it induces?"

McGarr shook his head, even though he had watched Herrick die on the videotape.

"There's a description written by a physician in the fifteenth century, describing the death of some English children who mistook the roots of the *Oenithe* weed for early parsnips. It's the British equivalent of water hemlock, but not as lethal. Still, the details are horrific. *Cicuta maculata* poisoning is probably one of the most excruciating ways of death known to man."

"You mean Johann Jakob Wepfer's *Cicutae aquaticae historia et noxae.*" It was one of the books that was listed in the catalog of the exhibition, *Enchanted Herbs,* which had been held in Marsh's Library some years back, and which Noreen had discovered while conducting the inventory with Charlotte Bing. The book itself, however, was no longer in Marsh's Library. Noreen had checked, only that morning.

"Why—yes. You said that rather well."

"Thank you." McGarr had also studied Latin in school, and the little he had learned, he had remembered.

"Do you know the book?"

Not as well as McGarr would like, since the book was also not among those that deKuyper had attempted to steal on the night before. "You have a copy yourself?"

"No—but Herrick had. I leafed through it once during a party."

"Where? Show me?"

Danvers-Forde rose from the chair and led McGarr to the bookshelf with the "W" on the gable end, but Wepfer's volume was not on the shelf.

"When did you see it here?"

"Last September, I believe. After the opening of a fall exhibition in Marsh's. Perhaps he sold it."

Somehow McGarr did not think so, not with fifty thousand pounds of cash hidden away, not with Danvers-Forde on the hook for ten thousand per quarter, and not without a "period forgery" to slip into its place in Marsh's Library.

McGarr took a moment to think. A bell deep within the R.D.S. showground, which was beyond the alley, chimed once. "After you discovered videotapes missing just now, how did you know where to look for this?" He pointed to the private investigator's report.

"It was where Joneux said Herrick would go, after she delivered him the money. Drunk and careless. I had thought I'd come in one night, when he was busy with her upstairs, and steal the report. But Joneux reminded me that Herrick could easily get another. Her past, as Ward will find out, is a matter of record." He sighed and shook his head.

Again McGarr took a moment to reflect; Ward had joined them with a fax in his hand.

"How are you at staying put and keeping quiet?"

Danvers-Forde blinked, as though understanding something had changed but not knowing what. "As I said, I'll do anything to keep all of this quiet."

"Hughie—take our hyphenated friend up into one of the back bedrooms. Make sure it's warm, and he's comfortable." And to Danvers-Forde: "Don't dare move from that place until we come for you. Agreed?"

The man nodded and followed Ward into the dark house.

23

Ba-Bing

SEVERAL HOURS EARLIER at the Burlington Hotel, Rory O'Suilleabhain was pleased to note that Ruth Bresnahan and he were not ignored, not even in the receiving line that wound, like a serpent, into the immense ballroom.

More than a few young women left their partners to rush over and say a few words to Ruth, their eyes on her startlingly severe costume that made the most of her long, shapely legs, her narrow waist, and well, the glorious rest of her. Her head alone was . . . mountable, O'Suilleabhain thought, before rejecting the thought as not quite right. Or something. He was intelligent, but words weren't his game.

Also, she knew how to turn the conversation to him, saying to each and every one of them, "Do you know one of our newest T.D.'s? I'd like you to meet my neighbor and childhood friend, Rory O'Suilleabhain." After introductions were made, she would add, "He's also in cattle, exporting mainly," so they wouldn't get the idea that he was just another bog politician. "Libya most recently, isn't it, Rory?"

"Actually, Israel is the latest deal, Ruthie. I like to keep things balanced." And he'd get a laugh that would allow him to look away, so the women could take a long look at his dimpled chin, his thick dark eyebrows that hooded green eyes, his perfect white teeth.

When those women returned to their places in line, O'Suilleabhain also noted how the gossiping began at once, the furtive backward glances, even a bit of polite excited laughter. "Well, I was right," he whispered, lowering his face so close to her ear that it was almost like a kiss. "You're the best-looking woman in all of Ireland, so you are. How did you ever come to know all these people?"

"Through my work, of course," she replied breezily. "Felons all. They'll steal your heart in a trice, if you let them."

It was O'Suilleabhain's turn to laugh in an engaging way that again collected eyes and made him feel yet more that his plan of having her accompany him was brilliant indeed.

When they reached the taoiseach, even he knew her. "Tell me my crime, Detective Inspector. I hope it's heinous enough for a long interrogation."

"It's rather simple," Ruth answered glibly, taking O'Suilleabhain's arm. "You don't know this man well enough."

"I'd like to say I don't, just to get myself arrested, but of course I know him. You're from Kerry, aren't you? You're—"

"Rory O'Suilleabhain," she supplied smoothly, "and a great admirer of yours."

"That I am," said O'Suilleabhain, taking the proffered hand.

"From what I hear of you, Rory, you'll not be on the back bench long. The question is—where to put you? In front, sure, we'll have to issue periscopes to see around you. Maeve," the taoiseach went on, handing them over to his wife. "Have you ever seen a man so tall and broad in all your born days?"

"Or so handsome," she put in, her old eyes sparkling.

"With such a beautiful companion." To Bresnahan, she added, "I think your—"

"Uniform," Bresnahan again supplied.

"—is utterly brilliant and disarming. To the criminal element." She obviously meant her husband and men.

"Actually, I'm here to provide this man security. My job is to keep him out of harm's way."

"Then you've got your work cut out for you, my girl," said the wife. "I'll be by for a dance myself."

"I'd like that," said O'Suilleabhain, fixing her with his unlikely eyes and dark smile.

And so it went with the others in the receiving line. All Ruth's remarks seemed to strike the perfect Dublin tone, at least to O'Suilleabhain, who did not know how he would have run the gauntlet of those prominent, cosmopolitan people without her.

"Now, I'll waltz you around once or twice, just to get your pins warmed up, and you're on your own. Remember—no heavy lifting, and try to leave this place alone. You don't want to get the reputation of being 'available,' or, sure, you won't have a moment for anything else. I should imagine it's difficult to hatch deals when you're tired all the time. Do you need a drink?" She was having fun with the poor man, and it was doing her a world of good.

O'Suilleabhain glanced at the bar that was three deep in people, not one of whom he knew. "You can't just leave me, Ruthie. What will everybody say? And, Christ, who's who?"

"Well, we did agree that you only wanted me to break the ice, and we did that fine. Let me commend you for not dancing off with the taoiseach's wife right there before his eyes."

O'Suilleabhain's handsome head went back. "No—was it wrong what I said?"

"Now I really *will* get you a drink or two. You need to loosen up me boy, before the onslaught begins. Remember, it was *your* idea to come here."

Leaving O'Suilleabhain bereft in the middle of the floor, she approached the bar and enjoyed seeing how the crowd parted for her, which was something of a miracle in Ireland— drink being more vital than sex for at least twenty-three hours and fifty-five minutes of any given day.

"Been to a funeral, Red?" one man asked, meaning her black, raffish attire. His accent was American.

"Not yet, but I like to be prepared. Could you be the victim?"

"Only if I could die in your arms. I'm Frank McNabb, by the way. What are you having?" He had a fifty-pound note in his hand.

"Three gin martinis, Frank."

"For yourself?" he asked, ordering.

"I'm a big person. I prefer big drinks."

"Like Rock Hudson out there." He meant O'Suilleabhain. "And you know what happened to him."

"Not enough gin," she replied, as the drinks were set before her. "Will you save me a dance, Frank?"

"Only if you promise to be gentle."

"Don't be too long. And I despise men who try to lead." But when Bresnahan turned around, she discovered that O'Suilleabhain was already dancing with the only other woman in the large room who even approached her own height.

And where had Bresnahan seen her before? She was a tall,

older woman, nicely shaped, with a great flowing mane of ash-blond hair. Wearing a buff-colored lace evening dress with wide gaps between the patterns, she seemed almost naked beneath the weave. The dress fell to just beneath her knees and revealed much of her long, well-formed legs.

Charlotte Bing? Bresnahan asked herself, having met Bing socially at several openings in Noreen McGarr's picture gallery, to say nothing of the other day at Herrick's. No, it couldn't be. But when the music stopped, she discovered it was.

Ruth had intended two of the martinis to be for O'Suilleabhain, as a kind of bolus dose. But she offered a glass to Bing, saying, "Can I tell you something, Charlotte? You look smashing. Did this big galoot tromp on your piggies?"

"My what?" Charlotte Bing looked down at her breasts.

"Your piggies, your toes."

"Oh." Bing was embarrassed. "No. Actually, Rory's rather graceful for his size." She smiled up at O'Suilleabhain. "Big men make the best dancers, don't you agree, Ruth? What is this?"

"A cocktail. Some of this, some of that. *Nastroviya!*" Ruth raised her glass. "Let's drink like the Russians. Bottoms up."

"Agreed!" chorused O'Suilleabhain, who had never been one to pass up a free drink.

They tossed off the cocktails.

Charlotte Bing slapped her nearly bare chest. "I think that's the strongest drink I ever had in my entire life."

"I wasn't aware that you drank," said Bresnahan, as, fortunately, some other woman came up to ask Rory to dance. He excused himself, and Ruth could not help notice how Charlotte Bing's eyes followed her—was it?—date away.

"Usually, I don't. But this is a bit of a celebration for me."

Again Bing's eyes moved to O'Suilleabhain, who smiled at them as he waltzed by. "Is he *with* you?" she asked Ruth.

"Not at all. We're neighbors down in Sneem, where we were born. More like brother and sister now."

Charlotte Bing seemed pleased to hear that. "How old is he?"

"Thirty-four, I believe." Ruth turned to the bar, where the man, Frank McNabb, was still watching her. She raised three fingers and then gestured that he should join them. "Rory just won the seat from the South Kerry Mountains, and he's here for the sitting of the Dail.

"You mentioned something about a celebration."

Bing smiled almost shyly. "I can scarcely believe my luck myself. Have you heard the news?"

Bresnahan shook her head and moved closer to the woman who was nearly her own height. Were Bing's earrings diamond? From their sparkle, they seemed so, like the bracelet on her wrist.

"I was told this evening by a source, who's in a position to know—I'll be named keeper of Marsh's Library. Can you believe it?"

"Well, yes, I can. You *deserve* it, Charlotte. Congratulations."

"And also—and you must swear to keep this to yourself—"

Ruth touched her heart; she was confidence personified.

"I also received a phone call earlier from Brian's solicitor, saying, now that you people are satisfied that he died a natural death, he would like to see me tomorrow in his office. It seems"—her eyes darted around the crowded dance floor—"Brian named me—'Stella,' which is what he called me—executrix of his estate, and guess what?"

Bresnahan had no idea, but she could see McNabb

approaching with the drinks. Charlotte Bing could not speak too quickly.

"I'm the only inheritor."

"You mean—the *house*? That gorgeous house and all its furnishings?"

Bing nodded, adding rather breathlessly, "I thought for sure it was encumbered, Brian having been so"—her brow glowered—"profligate. But the solicitor assures me it's not."

"And to think, after all the years you had to put up with his . . ."

"Antics," Bing supplied. "I know it sounds cruel and disrespectful, but you've no idea of what a . . . fool and knave he was."

"I think I have some idea."

"Oh, yes—that disgusting videotape."

"Well, console yourself that at least in death he did the honorable thing. Congratulations."

But there was McNabb with the further drinks.

"What will you do with it?" Bresnahan then introduced the two and explained to McNabb that Charlotte had just inherited one of Dublin's finest houses that was furnished museum-quality antiques.

"Marry me," said McNabb. "You're rich and beautiful, and I do windows."

"Actually," Bing confided over the top of her fresh glass, "I think I'll sell it. I often thought it wasteful for Brian to live in such an enormous place, especially after he ruined the back garden with that gruesome room. As it is, my own house is rather too much for me now."

"Your mother's house in Sandymount Square?"

Charlotte nodded, as O'Suilleabhain rejoined them.

"We're not talking about *Dr.* Brian Herrick's house in

Shrewsbury Road, are we?" asked McNabb, who was a graying, ginger-haired man in his early forties. "Why, I've been
looking for a place like that myself now for a good long time.
May I give you my card, Ms.—"

"Bing," Charlotte Bing supplied, only now looking at
McNabb with interest.

Asked O'Suilleabhain, "That the house you told me about,
Ruthie?"

Ruth explained to Bing, "I really shouldn't have, Charlotte,
but, you know, we're all human."

Or too human. O'Suilleabhain now produced his own card
and asked Bing if he could see the house at the soonest possible moment. "Who knows—I might be able to save you
your auction costs and all the headache of disposing of the
bits and pieces. I've just gone through that myself with the
death of my mother."

"If you don't mind, Rock—" McNabb cut in.

"Rory," Rory corrected, holding out his hand. "And you
are?"

"Bono. You know the group?"

"U 2."

"There you have it. You two. Me one. You can ring me
anytime at this number, Charlotte. Like Rock said, we might
work something out, but probably even more to your advantage. No mortgages, no banks. Just you, me, my corporation,
and your solicitor." McNabb's card said that he was director of
European Operations of Computron Computers, Van Nuys,
California.

"What—no drink, Rock?" Everybody but O'Suilleabhain
had a glass. "If you're going that way, we could use refills."

Color had appeared in O'Suilleabhain's face.

"Or maybe you need some help with the tab?"

Bresnahan pushed O'Suilleabhain toward the bar. "Be a good man now and get us some drinks." Once he was safely away, she excused herself, ostensibly to powder her nose. Someplace private where she might make use of the telephone in her purse.

24

Cicuta Maculata,
the Effects

HAVING SETTLED THEMSELVES at either end of Brian Herrick's Shrewsbury Road house, Peter McGarr and Hugh Ward had both nodded off, when around dawn they heard the singsong warning of the infrared sensor that monitored the front door.

Ward, who was covering that portal, quickly scrambled up and concealed himself behind the door in Herrick's study. He allowed the intruder to pass. Outside, birds were chirping, and he could hear commuter buses lumbering up the Merrion Road to collect their fares in the suburbs.

McGarr did not move. He was sitting in a chair that was well shadowed in the row of "Z"s at the library end of the conservatory. He detached the earplug monitor and listened to the crisp clack of heels crossing the flagstone floor in the kitchen. The pocket doors, which he had closed after settling Alastair Danvers-Forde upstairs, rolled open. A woman stepped in.

At first he did not recognize her. She was tall and wearing a stark-white—could it be?—sable coat. On her head was a pillbox hat to match. But the hair that flowed down onto the shoulders of the coat was ash blond, and the legs—yes, it was Charlotte Bing without her spectacles and made up, having just returned from the charity ball at the Burlington. Bresnahan had been in touch with McGarr.

Bing had objects in either white-gloved hand. Passing by McGarr, she stopped at the bookshelf marked "W," then proceeded farther into the room, now carrying only one thing—a small watering can.

At the potted *cicuta maculata,* she poured off what the can contained, then turned, as though she would return to the kitchen.

McGarr was standing in her path.

"Goodness!" A hand rose to the collar of the sable coat. "You frightened me, Superintendent. What are you doing here?"

"Waiting for you."

"Why?"

"Because it's question time. You planning to water the other plants, or only your favorite? After all, it killed your mother, who was a bother to you, and Herrick, who was in your way and you resented."

Bing smirked and adjusted the fit of the hat on her tresses. "Now I've heard everything. How did your excellent wife ever get involved with you? It strikes me as passing strange how good women can be attracted to *canaille* such as you."

"And Herrick?"

"No! At the very least, Brian Herrick was intelligent."

"Was that the Johann Jakob Wepfer book you were returning?"

Her head twitched. "I don't know what you're talking about."

"The other thing you had in your hands when you walked in here. Wepfer's *Cicutae aquaticae historia et noxae.* The one that belongs in Marsh's Library. Or is it—what was that quaint phrase you used?—a 'period forgery'? Shall we check the shelf?" McGarr's hand shot out and seized Bing by a wrist, so that the watering can dropped from her hand and clattered across the floor. He pulled her toward the "W"s.

"Of course I was going to water the other plants," she complained. "You surprised me as I was returning to the kitchen to refill the can. And, incidentally, this is now *my* house, and it is you who are the intruder."

"Not quite yet," said McGarr. "We Yahoos have a curious law that says a murderer can't inherit from her victim. By that I mean your mother *and* Herrick."

"You're wild, you're insane. And let go of my wrist, you're hurting me."

McGarr glanced up at the books in the "W"s, and there it was—Wepfer's volume on water hemlock. "Do you deny you just placed that volume here?"

"Categorically. That's obviously one of the books Brian removed from Marsh's."

McGarr shook his head. "That volume was not present in this room until you walked in."

"Prove it!" Bing tried to shake her wrist free, but McGarr held her fast.

"All right, I will. All of it, starting at the top." Pulling her back to the long library table, he shoved her into a chair, then sat in another facing her.

Ward now appeared, carrying some things that he placed on the table.

"When deKuyper rang up Marsh's that Thursday afternoon

saying he had placed a packet with two bottles of Glenfinnan behind the figure on the porch of this house, you saw your opportunity. You either had a freshly prepared solution of *cicuta maculata,* or you had some left over from your murder of your mother. It seems the poison in that plant can retain its toxicity as long as it's preserved in a proper medium, such as alcohol."

Ward slid some stapled pages across the table to McGarr, who moved it in front of Bing.

"But, as we can see, the plant itself has been recently tended. And pruned." He pointed to the water hemlock in the pot near the wall. "So my guess is that you were poised, ready to strike, and you probably had a little of both."

Bing laughed. "Have you been drinking, like your subordinate the other day? Don't think I won't report all of this—chapter and verse. To the commissioner *and* my solicitor."

"You knew the scenario of Herrick's Thursday-night 'Frollicks,' " McGarr went on, "having participated in them yourself. Some years ago."

"Again—where's your proof? May I take off my hat? It's rather warm in here." She lifted the sable hat off her head and shook out her hair.

Ward slid a second item across the table to McGarr—a 16-mm film canister with *Stella, Succubus* stamped on both sides.

Bing's tight smile faded somewhat, but she said, "Brian might have referred to me as 'Stella,' in his ridiculous appropriation of the Swift persona, but I was never his—or anybody's—succubus, either on film or off." She pointed to the label. "He must have been referring to a dream-state succubus, which is the standard definition. May I see the film itself?"

McGarr opened the canister.

"There you are—I must have been Brian's dream-state succubus, since it's empty."

"It's empty because you removed the film."

"When?"

"At the time you discovered the hold Herrick had over Joneux Ariane Danvers-Forde. The report of a French private investigator about her past. It cleared things up for you. Herrick may have hired Jan deKuyper because he resembled a Brobdingnagian, and he may also have called you his Houyhnhm."

Stepping around the table, Ward added that report to the exhibits on the table.

"Teddy and Bunny Baer were without a doubt his Yahoos, and the Danvers-Forde woman may have resembled a Lilliputian, given her diminutive size. But one look at that investigator's report made you realize *why* she would engage in his 'Frollicks' Thursday night after Thursday night, when you only consented to get up on that stage once." Here McGarr was only guessing, based on the possible length of a 16-mm film in a sprocket so small.

Color had risen to Bing's face, but she said nothing.

"Knowing about the private investigator's report, understanding that the Danvers-Fordes, if anybody, had more motive to murder Herrick than you, gave you the opportunity. It all seemed so perfect. Her husband was an amateur horticulturalist. She was being exploited by Herrick. She had keys and access to the house. When she was blamed and her history came out in court—"

"—that she was a whore," Bing supplied.

"That's right. When it came out that she had been a whore—why, a conviction would be assured, and you'd be rid of them both—Herrick and his little whore.

"Also, it could be proven that Herrick had a thing for whores, like Teddy, who was the perfect fallen whore in every sense, physically as well as—"

"Morally," Bing again put in.

"In fact, he tried to make every woman he had affection for into a whore, didn't he? Much like the actual Swift, who could only have lasting relationships with women he probably never actually bedded."

Bing sighed. "This is all so *outré,* to keep things perfectly French. And ludicrous. Why, if what you say were true, did I not take that canister as well as the film that was inside?"

"Because you were afraid Mrs. Danvers-Forde might have seen the canister in the cache, and she had." Here again McGarr was bluffing, but Charlotte Bing did not even blink.

"So, as I said, when the Glenfinnan appeared on the doorstep, courtesy of deKuyper, who you knew was blackmailing Herrick, the situation could not be more perfect. You waited until the 'Frollick' that Thursday night was well under way. You had keys. You slipped into the house and went directly upstairs to the master bedroom. There you removed the flask from the false Bible."

"The *what?* I don't know what you're talking about."

"In the kitchen, you spiked the full liter bottle, which was open because of Herrick's penchant for alcoholic bravado, and you also filled the flask, thinking that if the police conducted a complete search of the house, they'd find that, too. And only a recent lover of Herrick's, who had frequented the bedroom, would have known about that. Again, Mrs. Danvers-Forde.

"The false Bible, as you doubtless knew, has no date of production on it. Nor the flask. If challenged, you could deny knowing anything about it, as you just did."

Ward now slid the folio ledger in front of Bing, the one in which Herrick had listed the date of purchase, the amount paid, and a description of most of the furnishings in the house. Ward opened the volume to the appropriate page and pointed to the entry.

"What you forgot was something that should have occurred to me, since it was you who mentioned it—that Herrick had been (what was your phrase?) a 'punctilious archivist.' And, lo, he *had* cataloged every item of furnishing that he had placed in this house, including—"

McGarr read:

Bought today with "Stella" on the Portobello Road, a fine old eighteenth century false Bible. *We'll take it back to Dublin for our bedside, nocturnal libations. "Stella" is so much more the stuff of dreams when she loosens up a bit. Grog does the trick.*

Still Bing maintained her poise, apart from a muscle that was twitching on the left side of her face.

"The poisoning done, you simply left the house to await the effects, knowing that Herrick had become such a wreck of a human being that he was virtually friendless and would be missed neither at work nor in society.

"You waited a week. The more gruesome the corpse, the less likely the police would be to investigate your crime. You had learned that with your mother's death. How many days had you waited until you made the discovery? Thirteen? Fifteen? Nobody wants to muck about in the corpse of an old woman, who by all appearances had died of natural causes after a long life."

"I was in France."

"Felicitously."

"Now you really are overstepping yourself. My solicitor—"

"In the meantime," McGarr cut her off, "you went out and bought some Glenfinnan. We'll discover how you came about it or where you bought it, don't think we won't. After you washed out the decanter, you poured in an inch or two of unadulterated Glenfinnan and placed it back on the conservatory table where you had found it, close to Herrick's corpse. I tasted it myself. It was excellent Glenfinnan.

"Closing the pocket door just enough to permit the passage of a person the size of Joneux Ariane Danvers-Forde and then pointing it out to me was your first mistake. In the video, Joneux Ariane leaves first, then the wide, soft Bunny Baer follows her out into the kitchen to get Herrick more drink. On tape we hear the doors roll open farther.

"But that was your second mistake—forgetting or not seeing the little red light on the video camera. Or perhaps you couldn't bring yourself to watch the 'Frollick,' having participated in them before yourself.

"And what a mistake! Nobody dies this hideously by natural causes. Hughie?"

Ward pointed the remote-control device at the VCR, and the television came on, showing Herrick naked, rising to let Teddy and Bunny Baer out of the conservatory on the night of his death.

"What's this? No, I *won't* sit through—" Bing attempted to stand, but McGarr pushed her back into the chair.

They could hear Herrick closing and locking the alley door. He then reappeared on the screen, his scrotum and penis swaying under his protuberant stomach.

Bing averted her head in obvious disgust.

"Don't underestimate that Gulliver," McGarr advised. "It's got one mighty shot left in it, you'll see."

Herrick was now plainly laboring under the cup that Baer had earlier poured him, but at the table he reached for the decanter and poured himself another, which he drank off at a swallow. Tugging the tall, heavy chair around, he then fell into it beside the table. At that point he was facing the camera directly.

As the seconds went by, Herrick's eyes began to close, when suddenly they opened, and his hands fell to his stomach. Rising out of his seat, Herrick opened his mouth and let out the most hideous, hair-raising, tortured cry of pain and terror that McGarr had ever heard.

Charlotte Bing clapped her hands over her ears and again tried to rise from the chair. Again McGarr shoved her down.

Arching his back with the suppleness of a contortionist, Herrick tried to scream again, but only a thin, piping sound came out. He then fell prostrate on the carpet in front of the table, and they watched his penis jerk erect, whence it issued an enormous geyser of urine that rose well above the height of the table and splashed his torso.

The release seemed to revive Herrick momentarily, and he came to screaming again, if only briefly. Convulsions, one after another, then racked him; once more his back arched like a bow, and his large body began flopping maniacally—like some great, beached fish—in front of the chair.

Now locked in anaphylactic shock, his mouth was shut tight, his teeth clamped together, as his chest heaved, and he fought for breath. His eyes were rolling, and blood began to flow from his ears. Suddenly, something like a hernia, the size of a large fist, protruded from his already distended stomach.

The pain of that was enough to flip the man over. Now facing the camera on hands and knees, he appeared to be hiccuping or attempting to vomit with his teeth still clenched tight. Vomit spilled from his nose and through the gaps in his teeth. Blood poured from his ears, and broken capillaries sprouted in his eyes, so that they, too, were blood red.

The convulsions with the arching of his back and the manic, brutal hopping or dancing on all fours continued for what seemed like the longest time but was probably no more than fifteen or twenty seconds. Then again, as suddenly, the antics ceased; Herrick opened his mouth and vomited a great mass of fluid and blood over the carpet. It was then, too, that he voided from his anus, while climbing into the chair.

Once there, he managed to pick up one of the pencils that—the Tech Squad had determined—were genuine early-eighteenth-century writing instruments.

McGarr froze the picture. "There, you see, he writes something," he said in a soft voice. "It's your third mistake, Charlotte, since, as you'll see, when he finally expires, his head will fall on what he wrote. But it's a number, or, rather, a date—'nine, five, eleven.' You couldn't bring yourself to touch him, could you? But who would have thought that a man having experienced what he had might have summoned the strength to name his killer? But he had your number. Or, rather, your date."

Bing said nothing. Pale and drawn, she looked as if she were in shock.

"Why, it's the date Gulliver arrived in Houyhnhm Land. You see, he knew it was you who killed him, because, not having the courage to face your first murder victim—your own mother—you rang up Herrick with the story that you had left your keys inside the house, and not being able to rouse her, you suspected the worst. Could he come over and help you break in? It's all here in the report Herrick gave the police at the time." McGarr slapped the table where a fax of the report lay.

Charlotte Bing jumped.

"Herrick had seen the effects of *cicuta maculata* before, but there were no purloined volumes in your mother's house, nothing missing, no sign of a crime having been committed. And then everything was so . . . putrid. But *he* knew, especially now that it was happening to him and done by his reasonable, intelligent, beautiful, and gentle Houyhnhm." McGarr reactivated his video machine.

A final convulsion then shook Herrick, and it appeared that his heart gave out. Clasping his hands over his breast, he arched back once again and fell face down into the open book in which he had just written. McGarr let the tape play on, now very much a still life of a fallen (what was the term from the eighteenth century?) rakehell. McGarr had been trying to remember it all night long.

Charlotte Bing was no longer watching; she was turning her sable hat slowly in her hands.

"Hughie—fetch Mr. Danvers-Forde."

25

Near Sight / Far Sight / Circumstantial Sight

"WHO?" Charlotte Bing asked. "Joneux Ariane's husband? What has he to do with anything?"

When Danvers-Forde arrived in his commando garb, McGarr asked, "On that Thursday night of the . . . final 'Frollick,' did you see this woman enter the house?"

Danvers-Forde shook his head. "But I believe I saw her leave. Or, at least, some tall woman who looked very much like her. I can remember saying to myself that can't be Charlotte Bing, unless Herrick had something on her, too. But it was a foul night, and I'd been dozing."

"There you have it," said Bing. "Try to summon *that* witness, and I'll make you, his wife, him, and his priceless family the laughingstock of the country. Imagine," she added directly to Danvers-Forde, "marrying a known whore."

Danvers-Forde stepped toward her, but McGarr intervened. "Why don't you go home. I'll be in touch. And not to worry—I have no interest in making your life difficult."

"May I leave now, or do you have another witness?" Bing asked.

Said Ward, entering the room, "I just found the . . . girl

reporter you had me ring up last night, waiting on the landing outside the front door, half-frozen. I warned her not to
ring the bell." Ward glanced down at the card. "Cecilia Gill,
Staff Writer, *The Irish Press.*"

"Chief, how're yeh keepin'?" She was also the young
woman who had helped McGarr up from the footpath in front
of deKuyper's "Temple of Wrath." She pulled off her coat to
reveal a lithe body.

Ward took a second look.

"Thanks for stopping by, Cecilia."

"Siss, they call me. I told you that the other night."

"Siss."

She nodded her dark head; her long, fair features were pink
from the cold. "You got it, but may I make an observation?
You don't look any better yourself. It's a hell of an occupation
you got here. Worse than mine. What time was it exactly
that this little shagger rang me up?"

Ward straightened up to his full height, which was nearly
five eleven, before realizing that she was only having him off.

Said McGarr, "Remember our conversation the other night
in the pub? You said you got onto this story because you had
a source."

Gill nodded, working her cold hands. "So I do. But I'll tell
you now, like I told you then—you have your sources, me
mine. A swap now—that's another item altogether." She
pulled a cigarette from a packet that was tucked under the
belt of her skirt and glanced over at Ward. "Got a light?"

"No smoking at a crime scene," Ward said, woodenly.

To McGarr, she said, "Do you wind him up with a key, or
does he come with batteries?"

"The deal," said McGarr, taking his lighter out of his
pocket and handing it to her.

Cecilia Gill hunched her definite shoulders and said, "I'll listen to any little thing at six of a November morning." Lighting her cigarette, she swung her eyes to Ward dramatically, as though to say, What about you?

"Your source. The one who rang you up about my being here three days ago, when the body was discovered. I need that now. More, I need you to take me to that person."

Said Charlotte Bing, "Now I insist that I'm allowed to leave. Either that or my solicitor be present."

"Who's this woman?" Gill asked.

McGarr said nothing.

"Then we have a deal," Gill went on. "I give you my source, you give me her. Exclusively. And you owe me, Chief. That story you fed me about this investigation being over? You set me up, and my editor will have me in bits, so she will."

"This woman is Charlotte Bing, deputy keeper of Marsh's Library."

"And she's your suspect."

"I am not. If anything, I'll be his accuser."

Cecilia Gill smiled. "Also, I need your home phone number—I won't abuse it, I promise—and his." She jabbed her cigarette at Ward. "No promises there."

McGarr nodded. "Agreed."

Charlotte Bing began to object again, but McGarr took her sabled arm and helped her to her feet. "We can settle this now, or I can splash my suspicions all over the pages of Miss Gill's newspaper. The choice is yours."

"I told you my choice. My solicitor should be present."

At the front door, Gill turned to Ward. "You comin', too, or do you go with the house?"

"The latter."

Gill hunched her shoulders. Fitting her arms into her winter coat, she made sure he saw all of her.

Which had possibilities, Ward imagined.

"Well, then, I'll have your number. Let me give you mine." She slipped a card into his jacket pocket. "Maybe I'll fall over you pumping iron, or wherever it is you get rigid. Notice"— she blew some smoke in his face—"I didn't say stiff."

Before leaving the house, McGarr conferred briefly with Ward, telling him about the women's garments that he had found in the upper rooms of the large house. "The coat and a scarf should do it. And roll up the legs of your trousers."

Cecilia Gill's source turned out to be a paraplegic in a wheelchair, who occupied a flat on the Merrion Road roughly two hundred yards from the front door of Herrick's house. A former British Army sergeant major, R.E.A. Smythe had been crippled during "the affair in Suez in '56," although he still competed in the Special Olympics marathon. "That's twenty-six miles, for you tyros who don't keep fit." Smythe pointed at McGarr's stomach.

McGarr wondered when he was supposed to have the time to run—or even walk—twenty-six miles. "At what age? How old did you say you were?"

"I didn't, and I won't, Paddy."

"Peter," McGarr corrected. "Do you know this woman?" He pointed to Cecilia Gill, who was standing with Charlotte Bing on the other side of the large sitting room.

"Certainly. She's the only reporter in all of southern Ireland with the proper perspective on this country. She's not responsible for her background. Nobody is." He twitched his bushy mustache, which was gray. "But she's overcome it, I'll give her that."

Which meant Cecilia Gill was a Catholic who wrote about the North as a reasonable person, at least from Smythe's perspective.

"And the other woman, do you know her?" McGarr pointed to Charlotte Bing.

Smythe squinted. "Is that a *sable* coat? Could she open it a bit?"

Bing complied, revealing a golden lace evening dress and a surplus of well-shaped bosom.

"Diana Dors?" Smythe asked. "No—Diana Dors is dead. Whoever she is, she's welcome to tea here anytime. Did you hear that, luv?"

"Ah, shit, Rick," Cecilia Gill said, reaching for another cigarette, "there goes my exclusive."

Charlotte Bing asked, "May I go now?"

"Did I say something wrong?" Smythe asked.

"Not quite yet," McGarr said to Bing. And to Smythe, "I see you have a pair of binoculars here, Sergeant Major." He pointed to the pair that were resting on the blanket that covered Smythe's lap.

"Yes. Don't think I'm a peeping Tom, Paddy, but a proper neighborhood, such as this, needs to be surveilled against the criminal element. But I don't need to tell you about that."

Coming from the element itself, thought McGarr. "German, aren't they?" McGarr could see the Gothic script on the body frame.

Smythe hefted the glasses. "Karl Zeiss lenses. Power? Twenty. Field? One hundred. I pulled 'em off a Kraut *Sturmbahnführer* in Belgium in '44."

Which made Smythe seventy at least.

"With them I could count the pustules on a prostitute's . . . well, posterior at five hundred paces."

"Really? Then who's that woman standing now at Brian Herrick's front door?"

Smythe rolled himself over to the windows and raised the binoculars. "That's neither a man nor a woman. It's Hugh Ward, your second-in-command and a hell of a potent prize-fighter in his time, wearing some strange babushka on his head and a woman's greatcoat over his body. You can tell, because his muscles are bulging, and he's got no tits at all."

Cecilia Gill began laughing.

"And what's that on his legs? Garters! I haven't seen garters on a man in a dog's age."

Smythe kept the binoculars to his eyes. "Joining him presently is another of your staff. That's 'Big Red,' I call her, with a bloke I'll call 'Big Blue.' He could do with a shave."

McGarr glanced out the window. Standing with Ward on Herrick's front porch were Ruth Bresnahan and Rory O'Suilleabhain.

Said Cecilia Gill, also looking out of the window, "Why, isn't it the girlfriend with some man-god dressed in a tuxedo. Wouldn't I like to be a flea on the poll of that cross-dresser." She meant Ward.

Smythe lowered the binoculars.

"How's your memory, Rick?"

"Like one Tommy asked of another," Smythe shot back. "How's your love life? Tip-top, but nothing's perfect."

"On the Thursday before the Thursday that Brian Herrick's body was discovered, who did you see come and go at the house?"

Smythe cocked his head. "I've been asking myself that ever since the night I saw you go in there yourself, and I rang up Cecilia. I'm a bit confused about it.

"First there was the bloody big thug, deKuyper. The

Dutchman who worked for Herrick there in Marsh's. When all is said and done, Dublin is a small town, especially for those who're notable, and Herrick didn't have many visitors. DeKuyper was unmistakable, given his size, and he visited the house, off and on. That day he came up the stairs with a large parcel. He rang and rang and stomped around some, waiting for Herrick to answer the bell, but Herrick wasn't at home."

"How do you know?"

"I'd seen him go, dressed up, like, for the library. And not come back. Invariably, he used the front door. DeKuyper left the packet he was carrying behind that shard of a Roman column that Herrick kept on his porch to show he was different from the rest of us." Smythe shook his head. "The man was an arrant scoundrel, a pompous ass, and a dirty old thing. Imagine, calling himself 'The Dean,' after the great Dean Swift. It was a dastardly affectation, if you know anything about Swift, and the shame was he got away with it."

For a time, thought McGarr.

"Thursdays were always the worst."

"What time did Herrick arrive?" McGarr prompted.

"Just as night was falling. Four-forty-five, to be exact. I know that because the streetlamp in front of his house came on as he was climbing the stairs. It illuminates the porch rather well, don't you know. He picked up the parcel and went in.

"Maybe two hours later, the others came on—the *child*, I first thought she was, until I recognized her in a photo of a horsing group out in Dunlavin. I read the papers." His eyes shot up at McGarr. "Listen to the news, sometimes even watch that bloody thing." He pointed to a television. "Also, I have contacts. We chat."

McGarr did not doubt it, given what else Smythe had to do in a day.

"Her name—the child's—is Joneux Ariane Danvers-Forde. She arrived, like always, in a cream-colored Jag with a driver, who parked across the street."

"Did he get out?"

Smythe shook his head. "He stayed behind the wheel, sort of slumped down. I never got a look at his face. Not once. Maybe ten minutes went by, when the final car that always appeared on Thursday evenings pulled down the Shrewsbury Road alley. The lights were doused behind that eyesore Herrick threw up in his back garden.

"That's when things began getting strange, because finally—and this was a *first*—Charlotte Bing, of all people, appeared maybe an hour later and used a key to get in. I say, 'of all people,' since in point of fact I know she had a fling with that tosser years ago, but she thankfully got over it. She's a goddess, you know. I'd know her anywhere." Again the old eyes met McGarr's.

"But she didn't stay long. She was in there about a half hour, before coming out"—Smythe flicked a finger at the window—"again by the front door. She went straight to her car, which was parked illegally over there." He pointed to a sharp corner. "She got in and drove away."

"What kind of car?"

"It's blue. A Ford Fiesta, I think it is. She's a librarian, you know."

"The child left not long after, walking over to the Jag that was parked across the street."

"How long after?"

"Almost immediately."

"A minute? Two?"

"Nothing like that. Twenty seconds. Thirty at the outside. The little one even opened the door and peered out, waiting until Charlotte Bing drove away. Only then did she trip down the stairs and enter the car. Quickly, you know. She's light on her feet.

"I got the impression that she didn't want Bing to see her."

Or to make Bing aware that she had seen her. "And you know Charlotte Bing by sight?" McGarr turned and regarded Bing.

"Certainly. Handsome middle-aged woman. Tall. *Built,* but, of course, a librarian, as I said."

"I'd like you to reconsider the woman sitting by the door. Do you recognize her?"

Smythe had to turn the wheelchair to see Charlotte Bing directly. He removed his reading glasses. Slowly, he moved toward her.

Bing did not change her pose. Her crossed legs were exposed to midthigh. With her sable coat open, her large breasts seemed almost naked, given the color of her lace evening dress. Her chin was high, the look on her well-formed features disdainful.

Smythe rolled closer. And closer. Finally, he said, "I've never seen this woman before in my life, although—as I mentioned earlier—we could be friends, as I said." He smiled at her. "Do you have a name?"

Bing stood and tightened the sable coat to her neck. "I hope you're satisfied, Superintendent."

"I won't be until I see you in the dock."

"Then I'm sorry to add to your frustration."

"I'm not sure you will."

But I am, her brittle smile told McGarr, as she left.

26

Big Competition

DOWN AT THE FRONT DOOR of Herrick's house a few minutes earlier, Hugh Ward had asked Ruth Bresnahan and Rory O'Suilleabhain, "What happened, you two get married?" Again he took in her black evening dress and O'Suilleabhain's splendid tux. Together they looked brilliant, he had to admit. And there he was—in drag.

O'Suilleabhain's large paw reached for Ward's shoulder. "No, little fella, but when we do, maybe you'd consider standing up for me?"

Ward's eyes flashed at Bresnahan, and the plea was pointed. He turned his head and stared down at the hand on his shoulder.

"Perhaps we'd better go in," she said, taking Suilleabhain's arm and leading him into the house before he found himself on the flat of his back. She had no doubts about the outcome of any scuffle between the two of them, big as Rory was.

Said O'Suilleabhain in passing Ward, "The garters are all wrong. They should be farther up the leg."

"I bumped into Charlotte Bing last night at the ball," Bresnahan went on blithely, speaking over her shoulder. "She inherits this place, and she told us she'd be putting it on the block. All found. Rory here—"

"Needing digs," O'Suilleabhain put in.

"—thought it sounded like just the place for him. I had the idea to show him around—you know, as a friendly gesture."

Ward believed he was getting the picture. Only three days earlier, she and he had gone over the place, front door to back, oohing and aahing over this piece of furniture or that fine detail, only to decide that it was way beyond them. Even with their two incomes, his owning the loft on the quays and she the large farm in Kerry, they would have to mortgage themselves to the grave.

But here was the Culchie cattle baron with his new banking connections—courtesy of his seat in the Dail—buying the place with no problem. For him and her.

"I take it you're in disguise," she added, closing the door on him. "Honestly, Hughie—I can't help myself. You look a sight. I wish I had a camera."

"And those fists," O'Suilleabhain went on, his head rolling as he gazed at the lovely staircase with its rosewood fretwork. "Women don't make fists like that."

"Don't take it to heart," she whispered. "He can't help it, he's just being"—she hunched her shoulders—"Rory."

"What you do after the ball—doughnuts and coffee?"

"Now, *that's* base. Actually, we did have some coffee—with the taoiseach." She closed the door.

Ward spun around and glared into the street, as McGarr opened the gate to let the reporter from the *Press* into the yard.

"Wasn't that the *girlfriend?*" Cecilia Gill asked Ward, when they reached him on the landing.

Only Ward's eyes moved to her; he was still hot, his heart pounding as if he had just gone a couple of rounds. Which was not good for him; which was not good for anybody.

"See, I know more about you than you thought. And guess what—not all of it's bad."

Still Ward said nothing.

"Looks like you got some *big* competition. Remember now, you have my card." Passing by him to step into the house, she reached out, ostensibly—he later thought—to pat the pocket where she had early placed her card. But her hand fell elsewhere, and she winked.

Said McGarr, "Maybe you better go home and get some rest. I'll clean up here and meet you at Hogan's at, say, six." Hogan's was a pub not far from the office in Dublin Castle. "We'll go over the little else we can do."

Ward pulled off the babushka and ripped off the tight woman's overcoat. He stamped down his trousers. "What about Bing?"

"We'll talk about it then." McGarr pointed toward the gate. "Knocking that big piece of baggage on his backside would do you no good, especially with Rut'ie."

Ward turned his head to McGarr. "But it's like they're taunting me, the both of them."

McGarr cocked his head. "Well, maybe *he* is, but she's *testing* you." He took the clothes from Ward and closed the door.

$\mathcal{P}art\ \mathcal{V}$

*There's none so blind
as they that won't see.*

—JONATHAN SWIFT

27

Selling Short

BEFORE A HOT, YELLOW FIRE in the back room of Hogan's early that evening, several members of the Murder Squad gathered. Each had a glass of amber-colored fluid in hand; a large bottle was on the table before them.

McKeon chucked the cork into the fire. "Just as old Heresy himself would have it. Where's he to be buried, anyhow? I'm thinking I'll wait until me bladder is full and go there and anoint the divil." He raised his glass, and the others followed his lead.

After a while, McGarr said, "We've charged the Baers with simple theft. Bernie went through the tapes, both the ones Baer lifted from Herrick's house and the others that Hughie got from Baer on his visit to the Poop Deck, and there's nothing of a criminal nature in any of them. Herrick's, I assume, were for his private use. And the ones from Baer are just a form of low humor."

McKeon shook his head. "The lowest. Some of the antics is pure tripe."

"The tax man might be interested in Baer," McGarr went on. "But that's no concern of ours."

"What about deKuyper?" Bresnahan asked.

"The same, with the difference that the value of the books he took from Herrick's is great enough to make his theft a felony. He's still in hospital and complaining of police brutality, but without witnesses—"

"He'll soon be the Flying Dutchman." McKeon's hand soared through the air, as he reached for the bottle.

McGarr nodded. "A deportation order won't be hard to arrange."

"Which leaves the Danvers-Fordes and Charlotte Bing," said Ward. "Now keeper of Marsh's Library."

"And owner of that gorgeous house on the Shrewsbury Road," Bresnahan added, "to say nothing of the sixty-thousand quid in the cache in the library."

"And Herrick's own books, the ones that were definitely his," put in McKeon. "I had a valuer take a survey late this after'. He estimates there's at least a hundred grand of rare books and manuscripts that are *not* Marsh's. Nothing like getting away with murder."

"But *has* she got away with it?" Noreen asked. "We have—how many?—three people who can place Bing at the scene around the time that the poison must have been added to the decanter and flask. We've got her returning to Herrick's house with Wepfer's book on water hemlock in one hand and a watering can for the poisonous plant in the other. We've got her mother, for Jesus' sake, and how she died. Her corpse could be dug up. Isn't it worth the effort of taking her to court?"

"And she had motive enough," Bresnahan chimed in. "Wasn't Herrick looting the collection of her precious Marsh's Library? Also, she had thrown herself away on him at an early age, only to watch him debauch at least one other employee of the place that we know about."

"Also Herrick had suspicions about how her mother died."

McKeon raised his glass. "Which should have made him more cautious."

"You being the soul of caution yourself," Ward remarked sourly.

Bresnahan went on. "You say it yourself, Chief. Murderers always try too hard—Bing washing up the decanter, glasses, and bottle, so no traces of the *cicuta maculata* remained. She wanted it to look like a death by natural causes, Herrick being an old—"

"Soak," said Ward.

"Her pointing out the way she found the pocket door. Denying she knew about the flask in the bedroom, when she was with Herrick when he bought it. All that could be brought out in court."

The others glanced at McGarr, who shook his head. "As for your three witnesses—Rick Smythe, the former sergeant major, couldn't identify Bing face-to-face, in spite of what he says he saw through his Zeiss binoculars. He's in his late seventies and in a wheelchair, and any decent barrister would make him out to be a bit of a—"

"Crank," said Ward.

"As for the Danvers-Fordes—"

Noreen sighed. "A trial is the last thing they'd want. They'd be splashed all over the papers, laughed at and shunned by society. Which is so unfair, given the conditions under which Herrick coerced the young woman into having relations with him. Regardless of her past."

"Which she was trying to escape." Bresnahan reached for the bottle, which was nearly empty. "Anybody else?"

Nobody asked for more, but she sloshed some into Ward's glass all the same. "You there, Grumpy—you drink that up. Nurse's orders. Maybe it'll improve your personality."

"What about Charlotte Bing's mother?" Ward asked.

"Cremated and cast to the winds," said McKeon.

"By Charlotte?"

"Who else? Happened almost immediately after the death. No wake, no funeral. Bing gave out the story that, because of the length of time her mother had been dead before she was found, a quick disposal of the body was necessary. The undertaker still remembered Bing's 'dispatch,' he called it, in getting rid of the remains."

Silence followed, in which they listened to the murmur of the crowd in the bar beyond the door.

"The Glenfinnan?" Ward pushed the brimming glass away from him.

Said McKeon, "I got a list of Irish retail outlets from the distiller and put every available hand on the detail, all carrying copies of the photos Herrick had in his house of Charlotte Bing. Of the eleven possible outlets, only three said they had regular customers for the stuff, given its cost. All were men. Only one said she could remember a woman purchasing a bottle from her, and the woman was foreign."

"French perhaps?" Noreen asked.

"Jamaican in accent and hue."

Again they sat in silence.

Which Bresnahan finally broke. "What bothers me most is Charlotte Bing's *transformation* last night. Not only did she look different, she acted different. It was like she was celebrating, rubbing our noses in the fact that she could get away with it. And if I hadn't been right there beside her every minute, trying to get her to open up—why, she would have snaked my date."

"Their being of the same species," Ward mumbled.

"Well, now—that's better." Bresnahan wrapped an arm over the back of the banquette where she was sitting beside Ward. "You know what Freud said about anger repressed."

All waited.

"It leads to depression. A person begins to isolate, he becomes glum and morose. Stops eating and drinking." She picked up the nearly full tumbler and placed it in his hand. "He can't manage even a smile for his friends and associates."

It was then that a knock came to the door, which opened a crack. "Sorry to disturb you, Chief, but there's a woman out here who says she must speak to you. It's urgent." It was the publican.

"No, no, she doesn't," they heard another man say.

"Do I let her in, or will you come out?"

McGarr thought he recognized the second voice. "In, of course."

The publican had trouble with the door, because Alastair Danvers-Forde had his hand on it. But the publican applied his shoulder, and Joneux Ariane walked into the small room.

"You're being stupid. I hope you know what this will mean," Danvers-Forde said, now standing in the open door. "There goes everything—Dunlavin, the country, our friends, your work, my projects. Where will we go? Where will we *live?*"

"How many times must I tell you? Everything will mean nothing, if I don't."

"What about my mother—it'll *kill* her." Danvers-Forde was plainly beside himself; his face was flushed, his blondish hair disheveled.

"Life—*real* life—is too much for some people."

"And you want to go back to real life, the real life you came from?"

The small woman turned to her husband and regarded him, her dark eyes flashing. "Is that a threat? If it is, consider me gone. Perhaps you are content to be a party to murder, but not I.

"Mr. McGarr—might I have a word with you? Alone."

Danvers-Forde's hand jumped for her wrist. "At least speak to my solicitor first. Maybe we have options."

She pulled it away. "There can be no option, and you know it."

McGarr began to get up, but McKeon stood. "No. We were on the way out, weren't we, boys and girls?"

"Really?" Noreen asked, plainly disappointed to have to leave. "But I haven't finished my drink."

"Sure, there's an entire long bar out there, pining for your glass, and the bottle is empty. Also, I've got a little present for Hughie out in me overcoat pocket."

At the bar, McKeon handed Ward a videotape.

"And that is?" Bresnahan asked.

"A trophy from the Pubic Wars."

"One of Herrick's or Baer's?"

"The latter. What Hughie does with it is his own business."

"Another sexist charade, I suppose?"

"To put it in German, you'd be surprised what sex-*ist,*" answered McKeon, but all four of them had their eyes on the door to Hogan's private backroom.

.   .   .

"Would you care for a drink?" McGarr asked the pretty and diminutive woman, after the door had closed.

Wearing some large dark winter coat that was too large for her, Joneux Ariane Danvers-Forde looked waiflike, as though she had already made her break with her husband and his millions. "No. It's better if I don't." She sat by the door, which was as far as she could get from McGarr in the small room.

"A lemon soda, then. A mineral water." McGarr reached for the buzzer; he wanted to make her as comfortable as possible. "A cigarette?"

She only shook her head, then pushed her dark wavy hair from before her eyes, which met McGarr's. "I'd like to get this over as quickly as possible, then leave. Alone. Is there another way out of here?"

McGarr pointed to the second door, which led to a storeroom and a back alley. "Herrick's house," he prompted. "That Thursday night after the 'Frollick' was over."

She nodded. "As I told your subordinate—"

"Ruth."

"—when she spoke with me in Dunlavin, I poured myself a drink from the second of the two bottles before I went upstairs to Brian's bedroom to shower and dress. When I got up there, I went into the closet off the bath, where I had hung my clothes.

"It's a large closet and quiet and dark. I wanted to be alone for a moment, before I had to go out to Alastair in the car." Again her eyes flashed up at McGarr. "After a while, there's only so much . . . guilt I can take."

Which ruled all in Ireland, McGarr thought.

"And so I sat down against the wall. I sipped from the

drink and was trying to compose myself, when I heard some-body enter the bath. Glancing out into the lighted bathroom, I saw a woman's legs. I leaned forward and was shocked to see Charlotte Bing pouring something out into the sink."

"The flask," McGarr said.

Danvers-Forde nodded. "I thought it strange, first, that she was there and, second, what she was doing. So, I decided to watch. From her coat—something like this"—she meant her own garment—"the tweed coat that Charlotte wore to the library—she took a plastic bottle and added some fluid to the flask. She shook it, replaced the top, then ran some water into the sink, and left the bathroom. After a while, I got up the courage to enter the bath and look into the bedroom, and she was gone.

"I dressed as quickly as I could, then checked the Bible at the side of the bed where the flask was kept. She had put it back, but she had not yet left the house. As I started down the stairs, I heard her footsteps in the hall. She was trying to walk on her toes, but she's a big woman, and her step alerted me. From the top of the stairs, I watched her open the door, go out, and lock it after her. She had a key.

"I waited until I thought she was away, then I let myself out. Can I tell you this? I swear I didn't know what to make of it. Not until later."

"When, after Herrick failed to appear at the library, you told your husband."

"Yes. And Brian didn't answer his phone. Then, a few days later, when I asked Charlotte where the keeper was, she said, 'You mean—you don't know?' in a way that frightened me. She was smiling, but her eyes were glittering and . . . hard. But by then it was too late."

For Herrick, McGarr thought. But not for Bernie McKeon, who had nearly died from the contents of the flask. "Why didn't you tell us this earlier?"

"Again, I was afraid. And Alastair thought perhaps Charlotte had so arranged things that I—and he—would be blamed."

McGarr waited, but the diminutive woman had nothing more to say. "What will you do now?"

"I don't know—return to France, I suppose. My mother, as you know, has a *business* in Marseilles." She attempted a smile, but it crumbled. "Or I'll go some other place."

"What about your husband?"

She shrugged. "We'll see, but he's probably had enough of me. Time will tell. It's been a debacle, hasn't it? My attempt at a new life here with him in this country. And now his life will be in a shambles as well, thanks to me." She stood, as though she would leave.

"You'll sign a statement to what you just said?"

She nodded. "It's why I'm here."

"You'll appear in court?"

"If I must."

McGarr got to his feet. "Well, may I say something? You're a rare, brave young woman, and I admire your courage and your . . . rectitude."

"Or my stupidity, as you just heard my husband say."

McGarr reached for his hat. "That's his opinion at the moment. And don't sell this country short. Dunlavin isn't the only society worth belonging to. There'll be plenty here who'll understand the reason for your . . . sacrifice, if it comes to that.

"Hang on a minute, and we'll go over to my office and

make this official." McGarr opened the door to find five pairs of eyes on him—four at the bar. Danvers-Forde was seated at a table.

McGarr waved McKeon over. "Get a court order to search Bing's residence for any sign of *cicuta maculata*. She's probably disposed of the plastic bottle she carried in to Herrick's, but not the coat. It's tweed and rather like that one—" He pointed to the coat Joneux Ariane was wearing.

"What do I do with the husband?" McKeon meant Danvers-Forde, who was now standing behind him.

"Introduce him to some of the crowd. Maybe he'll make some new friends."

28

Killing Passion

FOR DAYS Hugh Ward ignored the videotape that Bernie McKeon had given him. It lay on the large table in the kitchen section of his loft on the quays. Ward was preoccupied; Rory O'Suilleabhain was the cause.

He was everywhere Ward and Bresnahan went—for lunch, for drinks, out with friends, and always, it seemed, whenever they were alone. If either of their privately listed phones rang, Ward knew who it would be. It was as if the bastard had *radar,* and Ward could tell Bresnahan didn't mind at all.

On the least objectionable level, she was "flattered" by O'Suilleabhain's attentions, she had the honesty to admit. "He's making a show of himself, playing the lovesick fool, and I have no problem being the mistress of his malaise. If he wants to suffer, let him suffer. The longer, the better."

But Ward had a problem—O'Suilleabhain's "show" was all too convincing.

First, there was his appearance, which was impressive. The man was six-and-a-half feet tall, at least ten stone, and built with the giantism of somebody out of Swift or one of the ancient Celtic heroes. Also, he had the dark good looks of a romantic lead. Add to that his green eyes (which Ward had thought an effect of contact lenses, until Ruth disabused him of the notion), and you had what? Somebody every other young woman Bresnahan knew drooled over, and there *he* was drooling all over *her.*

It was disgusting.

Second, O'Suilleabhain seemed to have more money than any country Cuchulain should by rights possess. He had the farms in Kerry, Wexford, Wicklow, and Meath, Bresnahan had informed Ward with a note of Culchie pride. Most recently there was the cattle-exporting venture that had attracted investors the like of Fitzhugh Frenche and his crowd. Not bad for a man only a few months in town! But then O'Suilleabhain had a guide—the aptly named Ruth.

Sitting at his kitchen table in only a kimono after a long workout that had failed to calm him, Ward shook his head. How was he—a diminutive, if nicely made, rather intelligent, mere human being to compete?

Third was O'Suilleabhain's luck. Luck was hard to quantify or explain, but the Culchie prick seemed to have it. There was his seat in the Dail, perhaps Herrick's house on the Shrewsbury Road, and the Mercedes that Ward himself wouldn't mind owning (blinking blue lights removed).

Obviously, O'Suilleabhain was now lusting to add the glorious redhead, whom he was pursuing with the single-mindedness (certainly *not* the controlling organ) of a Fionn MacCool. To keep everything properly epic. And ethnic.

Ward despaired.

How was he to compete? How could she fail to choose Leading-Man-Good-Looks/Rising Political Star/Cattle Baron over poor/civil servant/diminutive him? As he had overheard said in the Poop Deck, Ward was hardly tall enough for a "decent vertical," although he had leaped that hurdle success-fully more than a few times in the past.

So—Ward now asked himself—what did women ultimately want in a man? Or, rather, woman. Strength, steadiness, and devotion? He suspected so, but perhaps all that was just the basics, and a seat in the Dail, a house like Herrick's, a blocklong Mercedes, and an emerging megabusiness were the icing on the cake.

There were other women—Ward knew from his own experience—who wanted none of that. Reaching out, he fingered the second object on the table, which was the card of Cecilia Gill, girl reporter. Ward had an idea that she was more like him (or like what he used to be), than he was now himself. And all she would want would be a few minutes of his time, when she had a few of her own to spare. He wouldn't have to run after her and worry where she was and with whom. Why? Well, because he didn't *love* her, of course, which could be a very big plus in dating a woman. Or a girl.

Ward slipped the card into his kimono pocket, picked up the tape, and walked into the "entertainment area" of his loft. With the tape in the VCR, he hit the Forward button on the remote device, and then settled himself in his high-tech read-ing chair. What appeared on the screen first shocked and then elated Ward. He leaped out of the chair.

For it was a Teddy Baer tape: one of those shot at the Poop Deck, in which she chooses a "goat" from the audience and pulls her dress over his head, while her audience of mots, bowsies, chippies, and toughs shouts "SO MUNCH!" And who was the goat who was munching? None other than the King o' the Culchies, Rory O'Suilleabhain himself. Teddy even rode him to the floor, as he struggled and heaved. And when the gobshite (literally!) came up, he was even smiling, *not* as though he was just being a good sport, but because he *enjoyed* it! Teddy buffeted his face with her huge breasts, then sat back down on his lap and began a further litany of salacious questions.

Ward hit the Eject button and checked to see if Bunny Baer had dated the performance. Yes, the Bunny was a careful man. It was just about a year ago nearly to the day, probably when O'Suilleabhain had come up from the country for a little R & R, and—get this!—*while* he had been engaged to Bresnahan.

Ward skipped a little jig. "God bless you, Bernie McKeon! I owe you a bottle of Hogan's Own!" he shouted to the rafters of his loft. Life—and luck!—did not get any better than this, he imagined. What were his options?

He could play it for Bresnahan sometime when they were together and savor her reaction. Better, he could play it for Bresnahan and O'Suilleabhain sometime when the three of them were together, and watch him squirm. No—all that would seem too pointed, too obvious, and too nakedly punitive. Or, he could mail it to her anonymously. Not that, either, since she would know it was the "gift" McKeon had given him, and he was just being mean-spirited. It might even be worse on him than on O'Suilleabhain. Women were strange. Worse, they were unpredictable.

What a dilemma! Here he had this marvelous instrument of affection destruction (in "the bloody war between the effing sexes"—Nuala Frenche; or "the Pubic Wars,"—Bernie McKeon), and, as if it were some nuclear device, he could not think of an acceptable means of employing it.

The next morning, in an act of utter selflessness worthy of Swift's early hopes for humanity, Ward mailed the tape anonymously to O'Suilleabhain in care of the Dail Eireann. Coming out of the mailing area of the post office in Wicklow Street, Ward picked up a pay phone and pulled Cecilia Gill's card from a pocket.

What Ruth Bresnahan needed was a little *live* competition, he decided, in the way that she was providing Ward with her own. What was it Swift had said?

Our passions are like convulsion fits, which, though they make us stronger for a time, make us weaker ever after.

And his present passion required some mediation, since it was killing him, he was sure.

29

Passion Arrested

RELIEF CAME QUICKLY to Ward: In fact, the next morning when he was standing with Peter and Noreen McGarr, Ruth Bresnahan, and Bernie McKeon in the lounge of a pub on Sandymount Green.

Each had a cup of coffee in his/her hand that Bresnahan, being the least senior, had obtained from a grouchy barman, who was cleaning up from the night before.

It was 8:55, a Tuesday morning. The footpaths outside were filled with people hurrying toward bus queues or the DART station, and a bright sun made the view through the smoke-smeared bar windows appear blue. Nevertheless, the front door of Charlotte Bing's neat town house could be seen plainly.

Through a yawn, McKeon said, "Imagine her being so careless not to have disposed of the tweed coat she wore on the night she did Oul Heresy in."

"Or so careful," Noreen put in, "from her own point of view. To throw out something that still had apparent value was doubtless anathema to a person who had spent most of her adult life preserving objects. And then a good case could be made for her having been repressed and anal retentive. From a Freudian perspective."

Three heads turned to Noreen and regarded her with polite resignation. It was rather early in the morning for in-depth analysis, but, of course, she was the chief's wife.

"Like Swift and Herrick?" McGarr asked, if only to demonstrate spousal solidarity.

"Yes. What was the phrase she used when describing one side of Brian Herrick's personality to you?"

McGarr had no idea.

" 'Acquisitive and materialistic,' I believe you wrote in your report. Well, it was the old pot and the kettle. She was—*is*—that way herself, as she's recently demonstrated."

"She had to know that in her haste with the plastic bottle, she would have smudged the lining of the pocket," McKeon continued concretely.

"And parking her car where she did, where she would surely get a ticket if a guard happened by—that was sheer stupidity." Bresnahan smacked a folded copy of an arrest warrant across the palm of her upper hand. Being a woman, she would make the actual arrest—her first since having returned to the squad—so Bing, who had proved herself contentious, could make no sexist accusations.

"I don't know about that," McKeon said over the rim of his cup. "You figure she only had so much time, and what was the chance of some dutiful guard coming along to write her a ticket of a cold November night." As it turned out, the guard was miffed, since he had been using the illegal space himself on Thursday nights to attend a card game up the street. "But *this* was—*is*—stupid." McKeon waved the cup at the window.

The five of them turned their heads to see a long black

Mercedes—one of the new, sporty S-class models with the rounded lines—pull up in front of Bing's house. The door to Bing's house opened, and she tripped lightly out, her bright red merino-wool coat open to reveal a short, tight-fitting suit-dress below.

"Her *transformation,* I think you called it, Rut'ie. You think she would at least have waited a decent period of time before trying to reclaim her lost youth with—"

But Bresnahan was no longer listening; she was absorbed in the scene that was unfolding beyond the lounge window. For who should pop out of the Mercedes to rush around the bonnet and open the passenger door for Bing but the—

"—the King O' the Culchies," McKeon went on, a twinkle in his eye.

Before getting in, Bing raised her head and offered her lips, which O'Suilleabhain kissed with no little ardor.

"Imagine—still hot even after a long night."

Bresnahan heard that. "What do you mean?" Her features seemed suddenly drawn.

"The Mercedes was parked round back. And has been now since Monday evening."

"No wonder the phones have been blessedly quiet," said Ward.

"I don't understand." Bresnahan could not tear herself from the scene; she even took a step toward the windows.

"What's to understand?" McKeon slid his cup onto a nearby table. "It's one of those May-September affairs, I think they're called. And here it is November. More to the point, your mahn there is quite the Lothario. Did yeh not show Rut'ie the tape, Hughie?"

Ward pumped a palm at the floor to shut McKeon up.

"What tape?"

"You better give me that, or they'll get away." McKeon tried to take the warrant from her hand, but she pulled it away.

"And it's perfectly understandable," said Noreen. "Again, from an Oedipal and Freudian point of view. In her own mind, she had turned Herrick, who had despoiled and then deceived her, into her father, who had abandoned her mother and her at an early age. Bing was nothing if not a deeply repressed woman, as I mentioned earlier. So by killing Herrick, she was also killing excrement. It was an act of . . . catharsis, which freed her—"

"For what?" Bresnahan spun around. "To sleep with her younger brother?" she snapped.

Taken aback, Noreen muttered, "Well, there's only so far you can take any academic analysis of this sort, and Rory O'Suilleabhain is not exactly the brotherly—"

But Bresnahan was out the door.

With coffee cups in hand, they watched her rush through the pedestrians on the footpath and oncoming traffic to reach O'Suilleabhain, just as he was lowering himself into the Mercedes. She said something to him, so he lifted his head, and she delivered him a stunning right cross, thrown from the shoulder, that sent him sprawling across the gleaming car and into the street.

"You teach her that?" McKeon asked of Ward.

She then rushed around to the passenger side and pulled Charlotte Bing out. Spinning her around, Bresnahan tossed the older woman against the Mercedes and patted her down. Handcuffs came next, although they were hardly necessary.

When the others got to her side, Bresnahan pointed her finger at Ward and said, "What tape?"

Ward shook his head. "It's just a tape."

"The one Bernie gave you at Hogan's? The one from Bunny Baer? What's on it?"

"I no longer have it. I gave it away."

"To him?" She pointed at O'Suilleabhain, who was now standing by the boot of the car. "Is *he* on it?"

Ward turned to McKeon. "I know it's early, but can I buy you a drink?"

McGarr stepped in. A crowd was gathering; traffic had come to a halt all around the green. "Let me give you a hand with Ms. Bing. Have you informed her of her rights?"

"I've never felt so violated in my life," said Bing. "Why she . . . *manhandled* me."

Only then did Bresnahan seem to remember that she was actually making an arrest. Straightening up, she shouted at Ward and McKeon's backs. "What were you doing—trying to keep me from knowing the truth?"

The truth sometimes hurt, which Ward found interesting. He had understood that she was possessive of O'Suilleabhain, but not by how much. They walked on.

"I'll have a copy of that tape by tonight, my man—or else."

"Or else what?" McKeon asked Ward, but they both knew what.

Over a pint in the lounge of the Sandymount Inn, McKeon said, "I'm sure the Bunny could dig up another copy. You know, for a consideration."

Ward shook his head. "Let her get her own. From him." He meant O'Suilleabhain, whom they could see being "interviewed" by her. The big goat had a bright welt on the side of his jaw. He was shaking his head, as though denying something, as he moved toward his car.

Cecilia Gill, the reporter from the *Press*, had arrived with a cameraman who was busily snapping pictures of Charlotte Bing. As O'Suilleabhain drove off, she moved in to confer with Bresnahan. About what Ward would not hazard to guess.

Swift had been right, he decided, to have conducted his relationships with women by correspondence. "I think I need a bit of a break. From women, if you know what I mean?"

"I've often thought the same," agreed McKeon, the father of a baker's dozen children.